FRACTURE

RINDA ELLIOTT
JOCELYNN DRAKE

Unbreakable Bonds Series
Shiver
Shatter
Torch
Devour
Blaze
Fracture

Unbreakable Bonds Short Story Collection
Unbreakable Stories: Lucas
Unbreakable Stories: Snow
Unbreakable Stories: Rowe
Unbreakable Stories: Ian

ALSO BY JOCELYNN DRAKE AND RINDA ELLIOTT

The Ward Security Series
Psycho Romeo

Dantès Unglued

Deadly Dorian

Jackson (a novella)

Sadistic Sherlock

King of Romance (short story collection)

Killer Bond (Coming in May)

Pineapple Grove
Something About Jace

Drew & Mr. Grumpy (a novella)

ALSO BY JOCELYNN DRAKE

The Dark Days Series
Bound to Me
The Dead, the Damned and the Forgotten
Nightwalker
Dayhunter
Dawnbreaker
Pray for Dawn
Wait for Dusk
Burn the Night

The Lost Nights Series
Stefan

The Asylum Tales
The Asylum Interviews: Bronx
The Asylum Interviews: Trixie
Angel's Ink
Dead Man's Deal
Demon's Vengeance

Ice and Snow Christmas
Walking on Thin Ice
Ice, Snow, & Mistletoe
Snowball's Chance

Exit Strategy
Deadly Lover
Lover Calling (novella)

ALSO BY RINDA ELLIOTT

Beri O'Dell Series

Dweller on the Threshold

Blood of an Ancient

The Brothers Bernaux

Raisonne Curse

Sisters of Fate

Foretold

Forecast

Foresworn

The Kithran Regenesis Series

Kithra

Replicant

Catalyst

Origin

Crux Survivors Series

After the Crux

Sole Survivors

Thick as Thieves

Remote Access

This book is a work of fiction. Names, characters, places, and incidents are products of the authors' imaginations or are used factiously and are not to be construed as real. Any resemblance to actual events, locales, or organizations, or persons, living or dead, is entirely coincidental.

FRACTURE. Copyright ©2019 Jocelynn Drake and Rinda Elliott. All rights reserved under International and Pan-American Copyright Conventions. By payment of the required fees, you have been granted the nonexclusive, nontransferable right to access and read the text of this e-book on-screen. No part of this text may be reproduced, transmitted, introduced into any information storage and retrieval system, in any form or by any means, whether electronic or mechanical, now known or hereinafter invented, without the express written permission of Jocelynn Drake and Rinda Elliott.

Cover art by Stephen Drake of Design by Drake.

Copyedited and proofed by Flat Earth Editing.

❦ Created with Vellum

Jocelynn: To the nurses, doctors, therapists, social workers, clerks, paramedics, EMTs, and more who give so much of themselves every day to save the lives of strangers.

Rinda: To Jocelynn—she knows why.

ACKNOWLEDGMENTS

Special thanks to B. Adair for his help with paramedic responses. Thanks to Hope and Jess for their sharp eyes and dealing with our deadlines.

TRIGGER WARNING

This book contains a scene that might be triggering for some: sexual assault and abuse.
If you wish to avoid that specific scene, consider skipping chapter 9.

CHAPTER 1

*H*ot water pounded down on Jude Torres's shoulders. He turned into the stream, letting it pour over his face as he thought about how he planned to spend the next week with the enigmatic Dr. Ashton Frost—or as he was better known to his friends, Snow. If Jude had his way, it would be mostly in bed.

They both had vacation time, and it had been far too long since they'd gotten in anything other than quickies with their crazy schedules.

Just the thought of more time in bed with his boyfriend had his blood pumping as hot as the water.

Normally, dual vacations meant a trip somewhere, but after surviving the hustle and bustle of the holiday season just a few weeks ago, they'd both decided on quality time at home together. The last month especially had been hard with so many out sick with the flu and Jude picking up extra shifts.

So, seven days of just the two of them, cooking and being together, sounded like heaven on Earth. God, he couldn't wait to drag Snow into their bed and keep him there. Three years hadn't dampened the explosive heat they had between them, and he couldn't see any amount of time doing that.

He wanted the man with a ferocity that still awed him.

The stall door opened, and he grinned, wiping the water off his face. "You got home earlier than you thought you would. How was little Daciana Vallois?"

Snow stepped into the shower, his naked body the best thing Jude had seen all day. "Perfect, as you can probably imagine. How could a child of Lucas and Andrei's be anything but?"

"I wish I could have joined you. My last call of the day ran longer than I'd expected. I'm dying to see her."

"She's gorgeous. Tiny and precious. Andrei's genes are strong—that baby has his dark, brown eyes already."

"Poor Lucas. He doesn't stand a chance."

Crystal blue eyes bored into his and he could see a question, one he was very familiar with, in Snow's gaze. They'd discussed having children, and though Jude knew a part of him would always long for them, he knew how Snow felt. Snow didn't want kids. The idea terrified him. And Snow came first for Jude. Always would. But those doubts he saw in Snow's eyes bothered him.

He tugged him closer under the water, loving the slide of taut muscles against him. Snow had a long, muscular body that drove him crazy, especially when it was wet. "Ready for our vacation?"

"Like you wouldn't believe." Snow's hands settled on Jude's hips.

"Oh, yeah? Because I've been fantasizing about being in your ass all day, and nothing is going to thwart my plans."

Jude turned Snow so he could nestle into that perfect ass. His hand snaked around to hold Snow's throat, his cock instantly filling as he rubbed it between Snow's cheeks. Snow moaned and leaned into him. One palm on the man's throat and he could have anything he wanted. Desire speared through Jude like lightning. It was always like this with them.

Snow turned his head to take Jude's mouth in a kiss that turned to fire fast. His general had the best mouth with a full, bottom lip and the sexiest dip in the middle of his upper one. Jude licked Snow's lips, sucked his bottom lip into his mouth, then slid his tongue along Snow's, groaning at the feel of that sexy ass cradling his dick. He reached for the soap and got his hand nice and lathered before wrapping his fingers around Snow's hard cock. Snow came up on his toes to thrust. He loved the feel of that smooth length in his hand, the crinkle of pubic hair against his knuckles.

Jude marveled over the connection they still had, over how powerful his desire seemed to grow for Snow. The man could break him down until all he felt was need. *Raw, basic need*. He wanted to bask in Snow for the rest of his life.

He tightened his grip, knowing Snow liked things on the edge of rough, knowing he could add that extra bit of pressure to make the man beg. There was nothing like reducing his general down to monosyllables. Snow was in charge in every aspect of his career and quite often in their life—until it came to the bedroom. There, he beautifully gave up control often to Jude in a way that made Jude feel like the most blessed man on the planet. He lived for turning Snow into a sweating, heaving mess. There was nothing like it.

He couldn't imagine a more perfect man for him.

As Jude stroked Snow's dick, his mouth opened over Snow's, their tongues sliding against each other. He bit and nipped at Snow's sexy lips, then slid his tongue in deep again to search out Snow's unique flavor. Snow groaned into his mouth, his hand coming up to cradle Jude's head. "Want you," he whispered into Jude's mouth. "Now."

Snow's hands hit the tile, the veiny muscles in his forearms braced, water pouring down the strong muscles of his back, his silvery hair wet from the shower. Glittering blues looked at Jude over Snow's shoulder. The long, lean lines of his form and his round, tight ass beckoned Jude.

He was so fucking sexy, Jude growled and reached for the lube they kept in there. He kissed Snow's neck, opening his lips to suck warm, wet skin. He slowly rubbed his fingers around and around, then worked the lube into Snow's hole, reveling in the way he spread his legs to give Jude more room to work.

The grip around his fingers made him moan. *Slick, wet heat*. Snow rolled his hips back, spreading his legs even more. Fuck, he was so hot, he made Jude's toes curl on the tile. He had an innate sensuality that burned bright at all times and turned Jude to putty.

When he pressed his dick up inside him, Jude's eyes rolled back into his head at the unbelievable pleasure of that tight clasp around him. He could barely breathe past the sensations rolling through him, powerful as always. *Mind-bending.* He fucked deep into Snow's body, and the man's head tilted to rest on his shoulder. Jude wrapped arms around Snow, stroking his palms everywhere he could reach, loving the taut muscles and silky, smooth skin. He bit down on Snow's ear, and the man cried out and clenched around him. Snow's ears were big erogenous zones, and Jude loved his uncontrollable response to any stimulation there.

Jude gasped and picked up his pace, sawing in and out of Snow's body and reaching down to grasp his cock again. He jacked him in time with his thrusts, feeling the tension building in the muscles against him. When Snow let out a rumbling moan and came all over his hand, Jude pumped into him a few more times before his own orgasm rushed through him and his vision whited out. He bit down on Snow's neck, and Snow's hand came up to cradle the back of his head again. Jude braced his hand on the wall, his legs feeling like jelly as he panted and rested against Snow.

God. This man was his whole world.

When he got his legs steady again, he pulled back to find Snow's eyes at half-mast and his breaths starting to slow. He gave Jude a lazy grin. "Now this is how to start our vacation."

"There will be plenty more. I have nothing on my plate for seven days. Just you. And I plan to feast over…" Jude kissed his ear. "And over." Jude nuzzled into the side of his neck, noting that the water was starting to cool. He sighed and grabbed the soap and began washing Snow's backside, his fingers slipping in to rub slowly over Snow's hole.

"Didn't get enough, did you?"

"I never will," Jude murmured, leaning in to kiss Snow's shoulder.

Snow's eyes locked with his and something passed between them —something that made his belly flutter with an excitement he'd thought for sure would have waned by now. But no, everything about this man thrilled him. Snow leaned over and kissed him just as the water went cold.

Jude yelped and shut it off, causing Snow to chuckle and snag a couple of towels, handing one to Jude. "I picked up enough groceries to keep us going for a week. We don't have to even leave the bed tomorrow." Snow dried off, dropped the towel, and grabbed his toothbrush.

"I hope it's easy food, because I don't plan to let you out of bed for days."

Jude was admiring the strong, lean lines of Snow's back again when his cell phone rang. He picked it up and saw it was his *mana*. Shaking his head, he showed the screen to Snow, who snorted and started brushing his teeth.

Anna didn't usually call this late at night, but his mother did keep her own weird hours. She'd undoubtedly marked her calendar when she heard they were taking a week off work and lined up some things she'd like them to help with around her house.

"Hello, *Mana*," he said into the phone as he ran his hand over Snow's lower back.

"Jude!"

Her choked cry instantly made his blood run cold. "What's wrong?"

Snow stopped brushing to watch him in the mirror.

She was breathing hard into the phone, and he could barely understand her through her sobs. "Jordan is in the hospital. Oh Jude, it's bad. Somebody beat him and shot him. *Shot him, Jude!*"

"Shot him? Someone shot Jordan?" He met Snow's startled eyes, his brain utterly locking up at the thought of someone shooting his little brother. It didn't make an ounce of sense. He nearly asked his mother if she was sure the hospital had the right person, but he tossed the thought aside. Of course they did.

Years of training as a paramedic finally shoved his brain past its shock. He'd worked through plenty of traumatic experiences and this was no different. He ran into the bedroom and grabbed a pair of jeans from his drawer, moving more on instinct than clear thought. "Which hospital?"

"UC." She continued to cry.

Snow hurried into the room and handed him a sweater before rummaging for his own clothes.

"I'm on my way."

"Hurry!"

He clicked off his phone and jerked the sweater over his head. His gut was in knots, his mind scrambled because he couldn't think of one situation that would put his baby brother in front of a gun. Jordan worked construction for their uncle. He was a good kid. Different scenarios ran through Jude's head as he tugged on his socks and shoes.

"Your brother was shot?" Snow asked as he tugged a sweatshirt over his head and slipped on his shoes.

"That's what she said." He ran for the stairs, Snow at his heels.

The whole drive, his hands remained tight on the steering wheel. He barely noticed the lights of the city passing as he made the familiar drive to the hospital where both he and Snow worked. All he could think about was his little brother.

CHAPTER 2

Snow rushed through the emergency room with Jude. His heart was pounding so hard it was like he could feel it in his throat, threatening to choke off his airway. A sinister nagging voice in the back of his head kept repeating, *Three years, three years, three years.*

Roughly three years ago, he'd run into this same hospital to find one of his best friends on the floor, his entire world falling apart because his wife had been killed in what had appeared to be a car accident. And he hadn't been there to operate on her. To save her life.

Melissa Ward had been light and laughter and happiness. She'd brought joy to all who knew her.

And Rowe Ward had been devastated to lose her. They all had been.

They'd nearly lost Rowe to his grief.

Now Snow was running through the hospital where he and Jude worked nearly every day. He was vaguely aware of familiar faces registering surprise and flashes of sadness as they passed by, but it didn't matter. They stopped only long enough to find out that Jordan was in surgery and that Jude's family was already in the surgical ICU waiting room.

"Snow," Jude said in a low, shaky breath as they waited for the elevator to ascend to the correct floor. That broken sound gutted him.

He reached over and wrapped his hand around the back of Jude's neck, pulling him tight against his taller frame. "We'll figure this out," he replied, forcing the words past the lump in his throat while telling himself that this was not going to be like Mel.

Jordan was a strong young man. Not even twenty-one yet. A good guy who loved to laugh. Definitely not the sort to seek out trouble. This had to be nothing more than him being in the wrong damn place at the wrong damn time. The doctors on call would be able to fix him up and get him safely on the mend.

But he couldn't give Jude promises that he couldn't keep or offer fake platitudes. Jude had worked as a paramedic for several years now. He'd been the paramedic first on the scene for Mel. He knew how quickly things could turn bad with nothing anyone could do to stop them.

"My brain won't accept it. Not Jordan."

"I know," Snow said. "But he's young and he's strong. That works in his favor."

The elevator doors parted, and they were quickly moving again to the large, quiet waiting room. There were three different groups spread across the waiting area, huddled together, talking only in whispers. A few stared dully up at the TV that had some game show turned on, but the sound was muted.

At the far end of the room, Anna Torres stood up from where she'd been sitting next to Jude's other brother, Carrick. Her face was splotchy and smeared with tears. Her normally neatly styled hair had been pulled back into a messy bun, and she wore a pair of older jeans and an oversized T-shirt. She looked like she'd already been settled in for the night when she'd gotten the call. Just grabbed some shoes and a coat before running out the door.

But that was Anna. Jude's *mana* had swept into his life much the same way her son had, claiming him as one of her own without so much as asking if Snow wanted her to. Anna took one look at him and loved him, dark shadows and all. He didn't know what she saw when she gazed up at him, but it must have been enough to convince her that he was worthy of her son, because she accepted him the first time she met him.

And right now, seeing her cling to Jude as she wept into his shoulder, Snow's heart broke for her. This good woman didn't deserve this kind of pain and suffering. Snow slowed his steps a little, giving Jude a moment with his mother.

Carrick rose from his seat. A year younger than Jude, he was the quietest of the three Torres sons, though he could throw teasing barbs across the dinner table just as easily as Jude and Jordan when the moment presented itself. He now looked drawn and shaky. His face was paler than normal, his dark eyes rimmed with red.

"What's going on? Have you heard anything from the doctor yet?" Snow asked when Anna's crying grew quiet.

Jude's *mana* released him, and she stepped over to tightly hug Snow. "We just know that he's in surgery now and that his condition is critical, but he's been in surgery for four hours already. Why won't they tell us anything?"

Snow looked over Anna's head at Jude, who gave a little shake of his head. The attending nurses wouldn't come out to provide updates if things looked bad. All their concentration would be on saving Jordan's life.

"Sit with Jude and Carrick. I'll go see what I can learn."

He felt Anna nod against his chest before she returned to the seat. Jude looked up at him, eyes filled with both fear and gratitude. He wasn't quite sure which would be worse at that moment: sitting in the waiting room and not knowing what was wrong or knowing and potentially having all hope stolen away that his brother would make a full recovery.

Brushing a quick kiss across Jude's temple, Snow turned and jogged out of the waiting room. He pulled his key card out of his coat pocket and swiped it in front of the reader. The doors started to automatically open and he darted through as soon as he could fit. He was immediately hit with the muted sounds of various beeping and machines that normally filled the background cacophony of his life, but tonight was an uncomfortable reminder that he knew someone who was dependent on those machines.

A pair of nurses looked up and blinked a couple of times at him in surprise from the nurses' station.

"Dr. Frost? I thought you were on vacation for the next week. We have all your patients covered," Caroline Conway said as he drew close.

"Jordan Torres was brought in today. He's in surgery now. My mother-in-law would like an update on his condition."

His demand for patient information was technically bending, if not breaking, the rules, but neither nurse said anything as he came behind the counter and sat down at an open workstation. He had to try three times to enter his password correctly, his fingers refusing to obey his commands as his anxiety mounted. It took only a minute to locate Jordan's chart, and Snow's heart nearly stopped in his chest.

Sitting next to his mother, Jude lowered his head and rubbed his sore eyes as they all waited for Snow to return. It had been a damn long time since he'd been on this end of things. He wracked his brain, trying to remember the last time he'd been to the hospital when he wasn't on shift. A little more than a year ago, his friend Shane Stephens had a bullet graze the back of his thigh. Jude had popped in to check on him at the end of his shift and tease him a bit. Two years ago, Lucas had been shot at his own engagement party/holiday charity ball. The injury had been life-threatening, but Snow had gotten it under control quickly.

Before that? Both he and Snow had spent a short period in the hospital after tangling with Dwight Gratton.

But not his family. Not his brothers. Hospitals and gunshot wounds were the territory of Snow's unique family and their crazy lives. Not his.

Lifting his head again, Jude stared at the blue-and-white pattern of the carpet in the waiting room. All the family rooms were painted and decorated to give a feeling of calm and peace, but he was sure that the people stuck in those rooms rarely noticed. They were completely lost to their own pain and uncertainty.

When was the last time he saw Jordan? Two weeks ago? No… longer…a month. He and Snow had missed the last two family dinners at his *mana's*. Too many long hours at work. When he'd been off, he simply hadn't had the energy to drag himself over to her house. She'd left more than one meal in his fridge recently for him and Snow.

But Jordan had been Jordan when he last saw him. He looked tired and maybe a little thinner than normal, but Jordan said that he'd also been working a lot of long hours at the construction site. The weather had been a little warmer than usual through most of December, and he'd been pulling some long hours outside while the temperature was on their side. At least, that was what Jordan had said.

Of course, Jordan had missed some dinners too. Jude hadn't thought too much of it. He was young and always a bit of a social butterfly. He'd moved out on his own a year ago. Jordan had probably been burning the candle at both ends, working hard and partying just as hard. There was nothing unusual about that. God knows, he'd partied plenty before he met Snow.

Then what?

"How long have you been here?" Jude asked, looking from his mother to Carrick.

"We arrived about fifteen, twenty minutes before you," Anna said.

"And you said that he's been in surgery for at least four hours already?" That just didn't add up. Anna whimpered and Carrick put his arm around his mother's shoulders, drawing her close to him.

"The cops found him in a field up in Sharonville," Carrick said softly. His voice was low and raspy as if his throat had been scraped raw. "He was naked and beaten. No ID on him. He was brought here immediately, and the docs started working on him. I think it was one of the nurses from Snow's team that sort of recognized him. Thought he looked like you." Carrick paused and looked down at his mother for a moment before directing his eyes back up to Jude. "They didn't want to call you in since they figured it was a long shot, so the nurse got ahold of Rebecca, who was on shift."

"Dammit," Jude mumbled under his breath and squeezed his eyes shut. Rebecca was a paramedic and had been his partner for several years now. She had also been dating his brother Carrick. A regular at the Torres dinner table even before she started dating Carrick, she would have been able to easily identify Jordan even if he was badly beaten.

"Yeah, I guess they were afraid he might have a preexisting condition or at least wanted to get in touch with his family. They had her come to the OR."

Poor Rebecca. She adored Jordan like a little brother. To have to see him like that in surgery, to see him hurt like that, had to have upset her greatly.

"Where's Rebecca now?"

"She called just before we arrived. There was a major accident on I-71 and she had to go. She'll be up as soon as her shift is over."

"That poor girl. She's got to be exhausted," Anna murmured.

"I won't let her stay long," Carrick said. "But I know there's no talking her out of being here."

A small smile tried to form on Jude's lips. There was no convincing Rebecca to do anything she didn't want to do. If she wanted to stay with Carrick as they waited for news after putting in a ten-hour shift, then that was what she was going to do. She was sarcastic, mouthy, stubborn, opinionated, and Jude absolutely loved her. He was pretty sure that she was exactly what his too-serious brother deserved in his life. Carrick just needed to finally get around to proposing to her.

Shoving to his feet, Jude walked a short distance away from his brother and mother. He pushed both of his hands through his hair, trying not to look at the time on his watch. How long had Snow been gone? Just a few minutes. He could wait. These things took time. Let the doctors do their work.

In the distance, the sound of automatic doors opening jerked him back toward the entrance to the waiting room. At the same time, he saw the other occupants of the room look up expectantly as footsteps thudded down the hall, drawing closer. Everyone was desperate for a crumb of news, even bad news at this point. Something that moved their lives past this moment of painful waiting and into planning and doing. Feeling useful again.

Snow appeared around the corner at last and Jude took a step forward, then stopped, his knees threatening to give out on him at his lover's grim and drawn expression.

"What? What is it?" Jude demanded when Snow was only a few feet away.

Snow gently gripped his arm and steered him back toward his mother, who had also jumped to her feet. He got them to all sit again, while Jude just wanted to shake him, get him to finally spit all the words out.

"I didn't get to speak to anyone working on him. I just read his chart and what's being added to it by the nurse as they work," he hedged. Snow paused and licked his lips. "I think…I think you should prepare yourself for the worst."

"No!" Anna gasped, her voice cracking. Carrick gathered her close while blinking back his own tears.

Jude swallowed hard against the lump trying to cut off his airflow and grasped one of Snow's shaking hands. He didn't want to hear any more, just wanted to rewind the day to when his little brother was safe and healthy, but he needed to hear it, needed to plan for the worst and help his mother.

"The bullet went through his chest, and it looks like one of his lungs collapsed because of it. They got it re-inflated, but I think either it collapsed again during surgery or possibly the other one collapsed, because he's now on a ventilator to help him breathe. There was other internal bleeding, and one of his kidneys has been removed."

Snow paused again and waited, watching them. Jude could tell there was more, but he felt sure he couldn't handle what Snow was holding back. Didn't want to hear the words, but he still found himself nodding for Snow to continue.

"The real concern right now is both spinal damage and brain damage. There was swelling and pressure on his brain. To relieve it, they've had to cut a small hole in his skull. There's also a great deal of swelling on his spinal cord right now. They will have to get the swelling down before they can determine if there's any permanent damage."

"Are...are you saying that Jordan could have brain damage? Or even be paralyzed?" Carrick asked. His voice shook as he spoke, and the words came out choked, like he couldn't imagine any of them being used to describe his brother.

"I'm afraid so, yes."

But that was also assuming that Jordan made it out of surgery.

Jude closed his eyes, trying to force his brain away from the dark, shadowy things he suspected, like the fact that Snow was possibly sugarcoating even this news.

A nurse would be in the room recording every piece of equipment and drug used. Snow would be able to read that information and know what was happening, almost step by step, as if he were in the room performing the operation. Ashton Frost was one of the best trauma surgeons in the country. He'd undoubtedly been in situations just like the one the doctors found themselves in now. He knew what was happening in that room without being there; Jude was sure of it.

"Who's in there with my brother?" Jude asked.

"Sanders has the lead. Diaz is on anesthesia while Carter is pulmonary. I saw Broderick has already started entering orders for scans on Jordan's brain as soon as they get him stabilized out of surgery. They're all good, Jude. I can vouch for all of them. They're damn good and will fight to save Jordan's life."

It was on the tip of his tongue to say that none of them were Frost. The irrational part of him wanted Snow in that room, taking care of his brother. The irrational part of him screamed that while the others would fight hard, Snow would work miracles to save Jordan. But he knew it wasn't true. There were limits to what even Snow could accomplish.

"Thank you, Ashton, for finding out for us," Anna said. Reaching across, Anna wrapped her hand around one of Jude's and clung to

Carrick with her other hand. "We've got some good doctors working on Jordan. Let's ask God to lend a hand as well."

Jude stared down at his mother's soft, trembling hand. He wanted to say that he didn't want to trust his brother's life to the whims of God. But he knew too well the limitations of man. And he'd take any help they could get to save Jordan's life.

Oh God, please let my baby brother make it through this.

CHAPTER 3

*J*ude stared at the doctor as he rattled off all the things Snow had already told them. The man's face was drawn with exhaustion from the hours-long surgery and Jude didn't miss the slight, bleak look in his eyes. His list didn't deviate from Snow's, nor were there any hopeful notes.

"He's out of surgery," Dr. Sanders said. "He's being moved now to a room. The nurses will need at least another hour to get him settled."

"Will you need to go back in?" Snow asked.

Dr. Sanders sighed and shook his head. "I don't think so, but we don't know the full extent of the potential damage to his brain and spine. Dr. Broderick has ordered some scans, but we won't know much until the swelling starts to go down and Jordan starts coming out of his coma."

"Thanks, John."

"How long do you think it will take for him to wake up?" Anna asked.

"The average is a couple of weeks. His injuries are severe, but he is young and healthy, which may help to speed up his recovery, as long as he doesn't suffer any setbacks. We should know more over the next few days."

"Thank you," Anna whispered.

"You should also know that we've had to file a report with the police because of the gunshot wound. Some basic information will be provided for the police report. I imagine that a detective will be in contact shortly with more questions."

Anna let out a fractured cry, pressing her face into Carrick's shoulder at the mention of the police. It wasn't enough that his brother was lying in a hospital bed, fighting for his life, but now he was also wrapped up in a police investigation.

"A nurse will tell you when you can see him. For now, he's limited to one person at a time and only immediate family, please."

With each word the surgeon spoke, Jude's anger rose in his chest like a black, hungry thing at the thought of someone taking fists to his brother. He stood in front of the doctor, heart pounding hard against his ribs, and felt helpless. He hated the feeling.

Rebecca had joined them. Standing next to Carrick and Anna with Carrick's hand on her shoulder, she looked utterly drained from her long shift and the news of Jordan's condition. Carrick looked as if he alternated between trying to comfort his mother and girlfriend and trying to digest the news the doctor had dumped on them.

He met his brother's eyes, seeing the same anger and confusion muddied there.

God, Jude needed to do something. Anything. He looked at his mother. "I'm going to run to his apartment and get him a few things, and I'll be right back. You can sit with him."

Anna grabbed his arm before he could get more than a step away from the group. "Wait. You need to see him before you go. The doctor said we could go back in about an hour. Just wait and see him first."

Jude could easily read between the lines. She wanted him to see Jordan in case something happened while he was at the apartment. Sanders had made it very clear that Jordan's condition was going to be incredibly delicate for the next few days. Anna wanted to make sure Jude had a chance to see Jordan in case he died.

His rage threatened to boil over at the very idea. Clenching his teeth, Jude nodded and dropped down in his seat rather than risk shouting at his *mana*. Emotions bounced wildly about in his chest, leaving him wanting to scream at everyone around them that they weren't doing enough to save Jordan or that his brother shouldn't be there in the first place. But instead, he sat silently, his skin crawling and his leg bouncing as his anxiety mounted.

He wasn't sure how much time passed until the nurse finally came back to usher one of them to see Jordan. Anna placed her hand over the fist resting on his leg and nodded for him to go first. He wanted to argue with his mother that she should go, but he couldn't get the words out. When he got to his feet, Snow slid into his chair, placing his arm around Anna's shoulders. Snow would watch over his mother while he was gone.

Following the nurse to Jordan's room, he was vaguely aware of her telling him things like visiting hours and other restrictions, but he couldn't really pay attention. Her words were just garbled noise as he looked around. He'd seen this part of the hospital a couple of times in the past, but not often. His days usually had him limited to the emergency room and the meeting rooms for the paramedics.

But even having been there before, it all looked so foreign to him. There were fewer than a dozen rooms, and the walls were mostly glass. They were only big enough for the beds and all the equipment that surrounded the patients. The usual mind-numbing noise of constantly beeping machines was mostly missing. There was still some beeping and the hum of machines working, but it was all muted so as to not disturb the patients as they healed.

The nurse directed him to Room 6, but Jude got no farther than the open doorway. He gripped the metal frame, keeping himself upright as his knees tried to buckle. A choked sound jumped from his lips that was half moan and half sob. *Jordan...*

This couldn't be his brother.

He looked so thin and frail in the large bed. His usually tan skin was papery and nearly as white as the sheets he lay on. A tube snaked out from under his arm, drawing the air and moisture from his chest to help preserve the vacuum and keep his lungs inflated. There were bandages across his chest and wrapped around his fingers as if they'd been broken. But most disturbing was his face and head. There was a thick bandage around his head like a turban and a brace around his neck to protect it from movement. Ugly bruises covered his face while both eyes were swollen shut. Jude couldn't begin to imagine how Rebecca had been able to recognize him, looking as he did.

"Here we go," the nurse gently said. A firm hand grabbed his elbow and she expertly maneuvered him into the chair just inside the door before he could no longer hold himself up.

"How?" he whispered, his voice fracturing around that one word. "How is he going to get better from this?"

That same firm hand moved from his arm to his shoulder and squeezed. "Look at that monitor there."

Jude's gaze followed as she pointed to the monitor that clearly displayed Jordan's heart rate and blood pressure.

"His heartbeat is good and strong. We start from there, and that's more than a lot of people who come in here have going for them. We'll be right here to help him fight."

Blinking back a fresh rush of tears, Jude looked up at the woman beside him. Her skin was a rich brown, and her eyes were a warm amber with a fierce look in them. He believed her. She'd be there to help Jordan fight, and she'd fight for him when he needed her.

"Thank you."

She cocked her head to the side a little. "You're the Jude I've heard about. The one who taught Dr. Frost how to smile."

"Yes."

"Well, if you can work that miracle, then I'd say your brother probably has the same fighting spirit in him."

"Thank you." It was all he could think to say, but the nurse didn't seem to expect much more from him. Giving his shoulder one last squeeze, she left him alone with Jordan.

Jude lingered only another few minutes. He knew his mother was anxious to see her youngest son, and he didn't want to talk to his brother. If Jordan could hear him, he didn't want to disturb him. After surgery, he needed his rest more than anything else.

Slowly standing, Jude took a couple of tentative steps to the bed and placed his hand carefully on his brother's leg. "I don't know what happened, but I will find out who did this to you," he vowed in a whisper and then returned to the waiting room, wiping away the tears as he walked.

Anna was back on her feet the moment she spotted Jude striding across the waiting room. "How does he look?"

"He looks bad, but his heartbeat is good," he said, clinging to the one thing the nurse had pointed out. "You should go and spend some time with him. I'm going to his apartment to get a few things for him." She nodded, her tear-streaked face ashy in the hospital lighting.

He turned away and strode out of the waiting room. He ignored all the looks of sympathy from coworkers as he hurried through the hospital with Snow right beside him.

"Get him a few things?" Snow asked when they stepped back out into the cold. "Or look around his apartment?"

Snow wasn't fooled for a second. Jordan was in a coma in surgical ICU. He wasn't going to need anything the hospital wasn't already supplying for a while. But Jude had to get out of there and do something. Anything. He couldn't just sit there and pray that everything was going to be all right and that the cops were going to locate the fucking bastard who hurt his brother.

"Both. I have a key to his place, and I need answers. Jordan isn't going to provide any for a while."

"My gut is screaming that this is more than a random beating. It was too harsh—too personal."

"It seems that way to me too. I keep going over it in my head, unable to come up with one reason why he would have been beaten and shot. Shot, General!" His voice broke as he was once again filled with the image of his brother, naked and bloody, in a damn field. His hands curled into fists. "He lost a damn kidney, and there's the possibility of brain damage! What if he's fucking paralyzed after this?"

"Hey," Snow said softly, stopping them in the parking lot to pull Jude into his arms. He wrapped strong arms around Jude. "He's strong. He's going to fight this."

But Jude didn't want to be held. He wanted to hit something. Rage at the stars. His fear for his brother threatened to choke him, so he pulled away from Snow. "Let's just go to his apartment and see what we can find."

※

What they found was nothing. Literally nothing.

Jude looked around at the tiny, bare living area and frowned. There was a threadbare brown couch, a small coffee table, and an empty table under where the television used to be. That was it.

"His television, game system, and everything is gone."

He strode through the bedroom and bathroom, unable to even find his brother's laptop. It looked like the place had been picked over, but it was all too neat.

"Do you think he was robbed?" Snow asked when he came back into the living room.

Jude shook his head. "It doesn't look messy—it just looks like he got rid of things."

He walked into the tiny kitchenette and opened the refrigerator and the cabinets. "He hardly has any food or dishes. It looks like he's living in poverty, and I happen to know his construction job pays well." He stopped in front of the empty wall in the living room where the television had been the last time he was there. "This doesn't make any sense. If I had to guess, I'd say he's been hocking all his things. I know our uncle pays him well."

"He's young—maybe he got into bad credit card debt?"

"I don't know. Possibly. But this doesn't feel like Jordan. I know he's still basically a kid, but he was brought up to be cautious, and getting into debt doesn't seem like something he'd do—not when he's got a decent salary."

A year ago, Jude had helped him move into the apartment. They'd borrowed a truck from their uncle and loaded it with Jordan's bed, dresser, and a couple of shelves he put his DVDs and video games on. The whole process had taken less than two hours and only one trip with the truck and Jordan's car. It was just a tiny one-bedroom place, but Jordan had been over the moon. The apartment building was in Oakley and five minutes from the expressway. Jordan figured that it was only fifteen minutes from where he played intermural basketball in the winter and ten minutes from where he played softball in the summer. A movie theater was another ten minutes away. To him, it was the perfect location.

Jordan's joy had been a palpable thing in that apartment that day. He was taking the first steps into adult life—his own life—and he couldn't wait. How could Jude have missed things going so wrong for him?

Jude cursed and ran his hands through his hair. "But I haven't been paying attention. I noticed he'd missed a few dinners but didn't think anything of it. I haven't really seen him much for months, so I have no idea what's going on in his life." The guilt felt like a lead weight in his gut.

"Hey," Snow said, coming close. "He's twenty years old and has a social life, and you've been working a lot of long hours. This isn't your fault."

"But I should know what's going on in his life." He waived at the empty wall. "I should know why he can't seem to afford even a television. Fuck!"

Snow grabbed him and pulled him into another hug. Jude frowned and pushed him away. "Sorry. Just not now, okay?"

He ignored Snow's frown and turned to go back into his brother's bedroom. There wasn't even a bedside table to snoop in. He grabbed a backpack out of the closet and threw it on the bed. The dresser held only clothes, so he tossed soft sweat pants and T-shirts onto the comforter next to the backpack. He went into the tiny bathroom and opened the medicine cabinet, but there was nothing in it other than the toothbrush and deodorant he snatched up to add to the items he was taking to the hospital. His brother didn't even have ibuprofen—nothing to tell him anything about what was going on in his life.

Frustrated beyond all reason, Jude packed up the few things, adding socks and not feeling bad about digging around in that drawer.

Still nothing. His brother had absolutely nothing in his small apartment that could clue him in to what was going on.

He angrily snatched up the backpack and walked back into the living room where Snow still stood, a thunderous frown on his face. He didn't care if he'd angered the man—his skin was crawling with a mix of worry, fury, and confusion, and he felt like clawing at it.

Someone had beaten and shot Jordan, and he could only picture what that must have been like for Jordan. His terror. His pain. Nausea slammed into his stomach, and Jude stopped moving and closed his eyes. This was bad. He opened his eyes and looked around the barren room before meeting Snow's eyes. "There is something really wrong going on in my brother's life. I can feel it."

"I feel it, too," Snow said quietly. "Either he's spending more time living somewhere else, or he's sold all his belongings. Either way, we'll get to the bottom of it."

"If I hadn't been so wrapped up in my own life, I would have sensed something."

"You can't blame yourself for this, Jude."

"I sure as hell can. I've spent most of my life caring for that boy, and just look at this." He pointed to the empty table. "Even his games are gone. Every one of them and he loved those stupid things." A sick, bleak feeling joined the nausea. "We have to keep this from my mother. I'm going to find out what's going on in my brother's life."

"We're on vacation, so we have the time."

He couldn't even feel bad that their plans had been destroyed. All he could think about was Jordan and why his home looked like this.

"Jude…" Snow started.

The hair on his arms stood up at that tone. He knew that tone. The clever surgeon's mind had pinged on something. He looked back to find Snow slowly walking to the center of the living room, his eyes sweeping over everything quickly.

"Where is Jordan's cell?"

"Fuck! It would probably be with his clothes…and the bastard who beat him." His mind was racing as he pulled out his own phone.

"Does he have an iPhone or an Android?" Snow asked, coming to stand right next to Jude.

Tightening his fingers around his own phone, Jude closed his eyes and tried to get his frantic brain to slow down and pull up the memory of the last time he saw Jordan's phone in his hands. Did it have that little apple on the back or was it…

"Samsung!" he shouted as the memory cleared. "He's got an Android phone. He switched about a year ago to a Samsung because he liked that damn little stylus thing that came with it." He was typing in his phone, pulling up the "Find My Device" option for Android-based phones.

But he only got as far as entering Jordan's email address. The blank password box glared at him. He had some viable guesses based on what he knew of his brother and the fact that he'd shared a password with him once a few years ago, but he wasn't one hundred percent certain. If he made too many wrong guesses, would the system block him? Would it lock everything down so they could never access it or its location?

"I'm not certain my guess is right," Jude admitted.

"Try one. It won't block you with one wrong guess."

Taking a deep breath, Jude very carefully typed in his first guess, making sure to get the spelling right. His thumb was shaking when he pressed the submit button, but it immediately came back that the password was wrong.

He snarled, wanting to throw his phone against the wall. He was sure that this could lead them to where Jordan had been or possibly even to the location of his attacker—if only he knew what Jordan's damn password was.

"It's okay. We can try again. Or we can even reach out to Rowe. He might have a few ideas."

Jude forced himself to nod, hating the calm tone that Snow was using, like he was some kind of wild animal that needed to be talked down from attack. He didn't want to be the irrational, emotional one. That was always Snow's job.

But it didn't matter. Snow was right. Rowe Ward always had a few tricks up his sleeve and for once, Jude didn't give a shit if all of them were illegal. He just wanted the truth.

Snow drove them back to the hospital, and Jude watched the city lights go past the window, too upset to focus on any one thing. There was no new information when they reached Carrick and Rebecca still in the family waiting room.

"*Mana* is still in with him," Carrick said as he shoved his hands into his pockets. Rebecca had her arm around him, but she looked at Jude with worry.

"Have you seen him at all lately?" Jude asked his brother.

Carrick shook his head. "Just at one family dinner. He's missed the last several."

"Have you been to his apartment?"

"No. In fact, the last time I was there, he wouldn't let me in. Said it was a mess."

"Has he talked about money or anything like that?"

"What's going on?" Carrick asked.

"Don't tell *Mana*, but it looks like he's sold all his things—the apartment was basically empty."

"He hasn't said anything about needing money." Carrick frowned. "And I know he's been going to work. I saw our uncle just the other day and he bragged about what a good employee Jordan is." Carrick's voice lowered. "What do you mean he sold his things?"

"I'm just guessing on that, but even his games were gone. Has he talked about any of his friends recently?"

"No, nothing. I'm sorry to say that I've been preoccupied with my own job and just haven't been paying attention. I figured if he needed something, he'd reach out."

"We've all been busy," Rebecca said. "What about the girlfriend?"

Jude perked up. "What girlfriend?"

"I thought he had one, and that was why he'd missed some of the dinners. We were teasing him about not wanting to bring her to meet the family."

"I don't think there's a girlfriend, but we can ask around." Jude thought of Jordan's best friend. "What about Brian Perkins? Do you have his number?"

"No, but our *mana* does. I'll get it from her. Last I heard, he was working at that baseball hat shop out at the Florence Mall."

Once again the image of his brother naked in a goddamn field filled Jude's imagination, and he dropped the backpack on a chair and scrubbed both hands over his face.

Just what the hell had his brother gotten into?

CHAPTER 4

Jude wandered through the Florence Mall, his body feeling like a heavy weight around him. He'd gotten little sleep the night before. His brain replayed over and over again the image of Jordan lying helpless and hurting in the hospital bed. Frustration built in his chest as he tried to find some reason behind why it happened, how Jordan could have found himself in such a situation. But there were no answers to be learned by staring at the bedroom ceiling.

After some coffee, he and Snow returned to the hospital, where he checked on his mother and Carrick while Snow sneaked a peek at Jordan's chart. There had been no changes overnight, which at this stage was to be taken as a good sign.

But Jude couldn't sit around the hospital and simply wait. Something had to be done.

So, they tracked down the last close friend of Jordan's that Jude did know about at the mall.

The place was largely a ghost town for the middle of the day just a couple of weeks into the new year. Most of the time he enjoyed strolling through the mall with Snow, window-shopping and people-watching as a way to spend a couple of relaxing hours out of the house and away from work.

But today, the people annoyed him. They seemed painfully oblivious to the world around them and the dangers that lurked, waiting to steal their lives away. Jordan was lying in a hospital bed right that second, hooked up to machines and tubes to keep him alive. He was lost to a coma, and they didn't know if or when he would wake up.

"Do you know where the hat store is in here?" Snow asked. "I can't remember the last time we came to this mall."

"It's down by the Macy's, but I can't recall if it's on the first or second floor."

Snow grunted and they started off past the food court that smelled of cinnamon, sugar, and fried rice. Jude glanced inside to see a handful of people scattered across a number of tables, eating fast food with their heads down, eyes locked on their phones. They passed a few shoppers with kids, but most of the stores were empty. The overhead skylights revealed gray, overcast skies as the temperatures lingered near freezing. After a mild December, winter had finally moved into the area, though they had yet to see any snow accumulation.

They paused at the center of the mall where there was a huge opening to the first floor. In that space was a children's play area and a few kiosks set up selling candles, sunglasses, and other random knickknacks. But standing at that railing, Jude remembered another time.

The mall had been decorated for Christmas, and a long line snaked out of a North Pole setting. Parents and children patiently waited for a chance to talk to the big man in the red coat and white beard and get their picture taken.

Jordan had been three that year, and he was so excited to see Santa. The screams of little children echoed through his mind, and Jude remembered dreading the moment that Jordan was placed on Santa's lap. He'd cried the year before and regardless of his excitement, Jude was sure that Jordan was going to cry again.

That following January, Jude was turning sixteen. He had so many other places he wanted to be other than in that line with all the little kids.

Carrick hadn't been much better, terrified that anyone from school might spot him. But they were there because their *mana* demanded that they be there for a family picture. As soon as they were done with Santa, he and Carrick would be allowed to prowl the mall on their own for a couple of hours while *Mana* shopped with Jordan.

When they finally reached the front of the line after what felt like an eternity, Jordan was lifted up and carefully placed on Santa's knee. For a moment, Jordan's chin quavered and his breathing became short little pants as he stared up at the strange man in red and white. Jude had sighed and shifted from one foot to the other, preparing for his little brother to break out in an eardrum-shattering scream. Santa asked in a low, gentle voice if Jordan had been a good boy. Jude was surprised when Jordan managed a small nod.

Santa then asked what Jordan wanted for Christmas and leaned closer to hear what Jordan whispered into his ear. Anna grabbed Jude's arm for a second and then started snapping a bunch of pictures. It was a damn cute image. Carrick loudly sighed beside him, and Jude gave him a nudge to pull his shit together.

"You want a car?" Santa asked suddenly.

Jude's eyes snapped back to the scene to find that Jordan was now pointing at him. Jordan had asked Santa to bring him a car. The little guy had heard him talking about it to his *mana* and just about anyone who would listen. He planned to get his license as soon as he could the next year. He'd been working odd jobs for years and giving their mother part of his earnings to help support them, but now he wanted to keep it all so he could buy a car. *Mana* had said no. Another car in the family was an extra expense they couldn't afford.

Jude had argued and tried to come up with solutions, but reluctantly he'd had to agree. They didn't have more coming in, and another car would need money for gas, insurance, and inevitable upkeep. It killed him, but he wouldn't be getting his own car until he was out of school and could work more hours.

But Jordan saw a solution for him. Ask Santa.

His heart ached at the sweet gesture, and it felt like the first time he truly noticed Jordan as a real person. Sure, he loved Jordan when he was born because he was his brother. But until that moment, he was just noise around the house and another mouth to feed. Someone to keep from getting underfoot.

The little kid had to feel like an only child. There were thirteen years between himself and Jude, while twelve years separated Jordan and Carrick. Neither one of them spent much time playing with him. He almost always played alone or maybe with some cousins closer to his age when they were over for a visit.

He missed or couldn't remember the rest of what Jordan and Santa talked about. The three kids got into position with Santa for the picture, and then they were free. But Jude couldn't walk away.

"Hey, *Mana*...I'll take Jordan," Jude found himself offering that afternoon.

Anna blinked at him in surprise. "Really?"

"Yeah, we'll go hang out at the toy store for a while," he said. He extended his open hand to Jordan and the little boy ran to him, his face lighting up. Carrick was already gone to troll the food court to look for his friends.

He couldn't remember the time they spent in that toy store other than to know that Jordan had been happy. They'd both been happy. He'd almost missed that moment with his brother. To treat him like a brother. To be there for him and to laugh with him. So their baby brother wouldn't feel like an only child. So he knew that he had two older brothers he could always turn to.

What the fuck had happened to him?

Jude knew the attack could have been entirely random. Jordan could have been in the wrong neighborhood, grabbed, beaten, stripped, and shot for no reason, but Jude's mind rebelled against that idea. It was too extreme not to be personal. If that was the case, he didn't know where to begin searching for Jordan's attacker. He didn't feel sure that he could ever locate that motherfucker. That was why he had to be sure that there was nothing going on in Jordan's life that could have led him down this dangerous road.

In truth, neither option was good or let him sleep at night, but he had to try something, do something, while they waited for Jordan to wake up from his coma.

"Jude?" Snow's deep voice pulled him from his swirling, destructive thoughts and the warm memories of his little brother.

"Yeah, let's go," he murmured, leading the way around the center railing to continue across the mall.

Snow was largely a silent shadow following him at all times, like he expected Jude to suddenly fracture into a million pieces. He could hold it together. He would hold it together for Jordan, for his mother, for his family.

The store they were looking for was a narrow little place with ball caps lined up along three walls from floor to ceiling. The area was empty except for a young man sitting on a high stool behind the counter. He was playing on his phone like most of the mall occupants, but his head popped up quickly when their footsteps echoed across the fake hardwood floor of the shop.

"Jude!" the guy cried out. He immediately jumped to his feet and shoved his phone into the back pocket of his dark jeans.

Brian Perkins had been one of Jordan's closest friends all through middle and high school. He'd been a somewhat regular at their dinner table over the years, though Jude had started seeing far less of him after Jordan moved out of his mother's house. Last he heard, Brian was taking computer science classes over at Northern Kentucky University.

He could never understand why Jordan hadn't wanted to go to college. Jude hadn't been fond of school, but he'd seen it as a necessity to achieving his dream of becoming a paramedic. Carrick had always been more into learning and only recently completed his MBA at Xavier University.

But when Jordan graduated, there was no talk of going to college or even a trade school. He just wanted to work for their uncle's construction company. Jude knew that some people weren't made for college, but a part of him hoped that Jordan would at least go to a trade school at some point. Maybe he should have pushed harder. Talked to him about it more.

"Long time, no see," Brian said as he walked around the counter. He extended his hand to Jude and pulled him in for a quick hug. When he stepped back, he gave a quick little nod to Snow. "Are you and the mister enjoying a day off?"

"Actually, I was looking for you," Jude said. He paused and cleared his throat. "When was the last time you and Jordan hung out?"

Brian made a noise and shook his head. "I haven't seen Jordan in person in probably six months. Maybe even longer."

"What? I don't get it. You were always close."

Brian gave an awkward shrug and moved from one foot to the next. He stared at the ground, his hands shoved in his pockets. "Yeah, well…things change, I guess."

"Don't give me that shit, Bri."

Brian's expression hardened when he looked up at Jude again. "Man, I don't mean no disrespect, Jude. I've always liked you, but Jordan's gotten to be kind of a dick. Ever since he started working that construction job, he just kind of blew me off like he was too good to hang out with me. He stopped answering my text messages, and he says he doesn't have any interest in just kicking back with some video games or movies."

"And you said you last saw him six months ago?" Snow said.

"Yeah…he stopped in one evening. Bought a new hat. We talked for a while. He was acting cool and said we should get together at his place to watch a movie. I even offered to bring the pizza. When I texted the next day to work out some plans, he never answered." Brian shrugged again. "I got the fucking picture, so I stopped trying."

"Did he ever mention to you who he was hanging out with? Or did he come in here with anyone?"

Brian shook his head. "He was alone that last time I saw him. What's going on?"

Jude turned and walked toward the entrance of the store, shoving both hands through his hair. This didn't make any sense. Who the hell was Jordan hanging out with? Why would he stop talking to the guy who had been his best friend for years?

"Jordan was found shot and beaten the other night," Snow said in a low voice.

"Oh, fuck!" Brian cried. There was a soft scrape of shoes on the floor like the man had stumbled back a step.

"He's in a coma now, but we're trying to determine how this happened to him," Snow continued.

"I'm so sorry. I have no idea how this could have happened to him. He and I...we just don't talk anymore. I always kind of wondered if it was because I was going to college and didn't do construction like him, but he's always known I wanted to work in computers and coding," Brian babbled. Jude turned to see the younger man shake his head. "What hospital is he in? Can I go see him?"

"He's at UC, but they aren't letting visitors back. Just immediate family."

"Well, if there's anything I can do to help you or your mom. You guys always treated me like family when we were growing up."

Jude walked over to the counter and grabbed a pen and the first piece of paper he could find. After quickly scribbling down two sets of numbers, he handed it over to Brian. "This is my cell number and Snow's cell. If you can think of anything that might help, anyone that you know Jordan was hanging out with, please contact me or Snow."

"Oh yeah, of course!"

Jude led the way out of the store and through the mall. When he reached a quiet section, he dropped down onto an empty bench while Snow sat down beside him. A large hand settled on the back of his neck and started to rub in slow circles, easing some of the tension that was tightening all the muscles in his neck and shoulders.

"I just don't get it," Jude muttered under his breath. "Jordan has known Brian forever. They were inseparable for years. Why would he suddenly stop hanging out with him?"

"Do you think they might have had an argument about a girl?" Snow suggested.

Jude shook his head. "Brian would have mentioned it. The kid has always been a straight shooter. He reminds me of you—no filter between his brain and his mouth. If he and Jordan fought over a girl, Brian would have said that Jordan was being a douchebag about some girl."

"Then it sounds like Jordan made a new set of friends who might have gotten him into some dangerous shit."

"Like what?" Jude snapped. "Drugs? Gangs?" Jude shook his head again and then pushed to his feet as renewed nervous energy filled him. "He knows better than that crap. I pounded that idea into his head so many times as he was growing up. He's too smart for it. I know Jordan. He wouldn't do that."

Snow stared at him and Jude couldn't hold his gaze. Fuck, he knew how he sounded. It wasn't Snow he was trying to convince with his little temper tantrum. It was himself.

Brian hadn't been an honor student, but he had been driven. The kid didn't do more than a little underage drinking when they were younger. He didn't want to mess up his chances later in life.

Was that why Jordan walked away from their long friendship? Because he was getting involved in shit that he knew his best friend wouldn't approve of?

Despite what he said to Snow, he didn't know his brother any longer. He'd gotten so damn wrapped up in his own life, in spending time with Snow, that he hadn't made his family the priority it should have been. If he'd been around more, he could have spotted the change in Jordan. Maybe he could have intervened before things got to this point.

But now all he was left with was trying to unravel the truth behind the attack and getting his brother some justice. He knew it was going to be the only way he could ever look himself in the mirror again.

CHAPTER 5

A bitter wind blew through the city, causing Snow to lift his shoulders and lower this head, trying to better protect his face and ears with the collar of his coat. Rare sunlight was shining down from a pale blue sky, seeming to make the air even colder rather than warmer. The sun wouldn't last. Winter in Cincinnati was largely months of gray skies and alternating blasts of rain and ice with just a little accumulation of snow. But the one thing they could always count on was a heavy overcast of dark clouds.

By February, he'd usually had enough of it and escaped somewhere south for a long weekend just so he could see the sun again. It had been a tempting suggestion for their week-long vacation, but as it turned out, it was better that he and Jude hadn't left town.

He followed on Jude's heels. His lover appeared to be unmoved or possibly just unaware of the cold weather. His gaze was locked on the tan trailer to the left of the construction site.

Snow had woken that morning to find Jude sitting at the kitchen island, nursing a cup of coffee. He wasn't sure whether it was his first or second cup. It was no surprise that Jude wasn't sleeping, and for now, he would leave him be. It had only been two days since they'd been called to the hospital. There was no pushing Jude to eat or sleep yet; his focus was solely on unraveling the mystery behind Jordan's injuries.

The whole thing had Snow baffled. He might not know Jordan as well as Jude, but the young man didn't strike Snow as someone who would get involved in something dangerous. Sure, he had the same mischievous streak as his older brother, but it was harmless. What had he gotten involved in that would put his life on the line?

His fingers practically itched to dial up Rowe and ask the former Army Ranger to use his in-house hackers to do a little digging. The first morning, Snow called and asked his advice about the cell phone. Without the password, there wasn't much they could do. Gidget, Rowe's IT specialist, discovered that the last cell tower Jordan's phone used was the one closest to his apartment, which wasn't any help at all.

For now, they were letting the police do their job as they dug into the assault and shooting. This was how the rest of the world dealt with things, right? Let the cops do their job. And Jude asking a few questions helped to keep his mind off his brother's precarious health.

That morning, Anna had called them to report that there had been no change in Jordan's condition yet again. They'd showered and were preparing to head back to the hospital to continue their vigil when Jude's aunt called to tell him where his uncle was working. It was the same construction site that Jordan had last worked before he was attacked. The new apartment complex was in the opposite direction of the hospital, but Jude wanted to check it out before going to see Jordan.

Jude rapped on the door to the trailer a few times and stepped back. Their sneakers partially squished in the mud that wasn't quite frozen yet. Some gravel had been thrown down, but it looked like the constant foot traffic and rain had caused it to be largely swallowed up, requiring more to be spread.

The door was opened by a large man with a heavy beard on his face that helped to protect him from the bitter cold. The dark hair was liberally sprinkled with gray, while the hair on the top of his head was almost completely salt-and-pepper. He had the same dark eyes and easy smile as Jude.

"Jude! Snow! This is a surprise!"

"Hey, Uncle Gary," Jude said, his voice lacking his usual enthusiasm.

"Come in! Come in! Get out of this damn cold wind." He stepped out of the doorway, letting them into the narrow building. As soon as the door was closed, Gary wrapped Jude in a tight hug. The man was a brute with huge shoulders and chest. It looked as if he bench-pressed tractors in his spare time. And when he hugged Jude, it was as if he completely enveloped the man, even though Jude wasn't particularly small.

Snow glanced around the little trailer that smelled of old, burned coffee and dust. There was a desk at the far end of the open room with a large walkie-talkie, old paper coffee cups, and piles of papers. Another table was shoved against the wall, with more papers and rolls of what appeared to be blueprints. Dusty old plastic blinds covered the windows but were open enough to let in the bright sunlight while revealing the worn and shabby appearance of the trailer. But at least it was warmer in the trailer than outside, thanks to the large heater he'd spotted at the other end of the long room. Snow was willing to guess that Gary had been working out of this space for a number of years and was as much at home here as he was in his own house with his family.

"I'm so sorry about Jordan. That kid didn't deserve what he got," Gary murmured against Jude's head.

"Thank you, Uncle Gary," Jude said. He stepped backward, his jaw hard like he was clenching his teeth.

"It's good to see you, Snow."

"Gary," Snow answered, shaking his extended hand.

He'd seen Jude's uncle several times over the years at various family functions and dinners. The man was a jovial, big-hearted guy with four kids and a wife who absolutely doted on him. But Gary was full of love. He'd been thrilled when Jordan asked to come work for him. From what Snow had gathered, none of his own kids were interested in construction, and Gary was looking to make his company into a family business that could be handed down over the generations.

"I was wondering…Jordan worked this site, right?" Jude asked.

"Yeah. He's made some great progress since he started with me. Last week, I had him up on the second floor doing some framing."

"Do you know if Jordan made any friends with people who worked the site? Did he hang out with anyone after work?"

Gary frowned as he scratched his bearded chin. "I don't really know. Lot of the regular guys on my crew are late twenties to thirties. Got wives and kids to go home to. Not much for hanging out after hours." He paused, his face scrunching in thought. "But there are a few framers who are young like Jordan. Maybe. You don't think Jordan got hurt because of something here?"

Jude shook his head. "No. I just want to make sure Jordan didn't get into something that got him hurt. He's not hanging out with his old friends, and I was wondering if someone he worked with knew who he was hanging out with."

Gary released a long sigh, plopping his fists down on his hips. "I don't know what's going on with that boy. I didn't see him much on the site recently. I've had inspection delays and other issues keeping me off the site. But Jordan wasn't at the last family dinner. Your aunt thinks it's girl troubles. He stopped dating that Emily girl with all that…stuff," he said, waving his hand in front of his face, "about six months ago."

Snow had to look away to keep from laughing. He'd met Emily once at a family dinner. The young lady had lip and eyebrow piercings. Apparently, that combined with her rather dramatic eye makeup, had left an impression on some of Jude's family.

"Do you mind if I talk to some of his coworkers? Ask if they knew who Jordan was hanging around?" Jude inquired.

"No, just let me grab my coat—"

"I meant without you. I'm worried if they see you, they might be afraid to talk."

Gary stared at his nephew for a couple of seconds before he finally nodded with another sigh. It was breaking safety regulations without a doubt, but he at least realized that his workers were less likely to talk with the boss hanging around. Turning back to a worktable shoved against one wall, he grabbed a pair of bright-yellow hard hats and handed them to Snow and Jude.

"Wear these. Don't stay long."

"This shouldn't take long," Snow said, accepting a hat.

"Jordan's crew was working the second floor of the second building, but they should be up on the third today. Look for a thin, young guy. Blond hair with freckles. Kind of squirrely. That's Austin Finch. I've seen him and Jordan talking on several occasions. He's your best bet on the crew."

"Thanks, Uncle."

Jude started for the door, but Gary grabbed his arm, pulling him in for another bear hug that tried to swallow him up. Snow smiled. Jude was fighting to suppress all his emotions, but his family kept pulling him close. Whether Jude wanted to admit it or not, it was exactly what he needed.

"You or your *mana* need anything, you tell us, okay? Your Aunt Maria is making up a couple of special casseroles, and she's planning to leave them in your *mana's* fridge so she doesn't have to worry about food for a bit. I think Shelly is going to cover this weekend."

Jude gave a muffled thanks and finally got free again. Snow tried to follow Jude, but Gary pulled him for a quick hug as well.

"You watch over our boy there. He's gonna need you," Gary murmured low enough that Jude couldn't hear it.

Yeah, Gary couldn't be more right. Even if Jordan did survive these next few critical days and weeks, the long-term recovery was going to be just as difficult.

※

With hard hat in place, Jude walked across the construction zone with Snow. At a quick glance, it looked like one of the buildings was close to being completed while the one they were walking toward was probably about a month behind. Windows were still being installed and as they got closer, it looked like some of the apartments needed to be drywalled. The development was just outside a large subdivision in Northern Kentucky and not too far from a busy shopping center. It was going to be a hit with the new residents when it was finished.

Their heavy footsteps echoed off the concrete stairs as they climbed. The sharp smell of sawdust assailed his nose as they moved deeper into the building. There were some people working on the first floor, but they didn't hear the loud banging and sawing sounds of construction until they reached the third floor.

Stepping out onto the third floor, they found that they were still setting the wooden beams that would form the skeleton of the walls for the various apartments. There were four men working on the floor, but they all came to a stop when they noticed Snow and Jude.

"Hey, can we help you?" asked the oldest of the four men.

"Hey guys," Jude said, giving a little wave. "I heard Jordan Torres works with you."

A young man matching Gary's description stepped forward. He lifted his hard hat and ran his gloved hand through his sweaty blond hair, leaving it standing straight up. "Yeah, Gary said that he was in the hospital. That he was in some kind of accident. He gonna be okay?"

"We don't know," Jude replied, his voice growing a little tighter.

"Are you Austin?" Snow asked.

"Yeah. Austin Finch."

"Can we talk to you for a minute?"

The young man hesitated and looked back at his companions before he finally took a couple of steps toward Snow and Jude. "Are you guys cops or something?"

"No, family," Snow said.

The guy's entire demeanor relaxed with Snow's answer, and he willingly walked across the hall to the other side of the building. Austin took off the thick construction gloves he'd been wearing and wrapped his hands around both of them tightly.

"What's up with Jordan? Is it bad?" Austin immediately asked in a low voice.

"Yes, it's very bad," Jude said between clenched teeth.

"We're trying to track down where Jordan might have been recently or who he's hanging out with," Snow said.

Austin immediately backpedaled, holding up both hands with his gloves clasped in his left. "Whoa now…Jordan and I just bullshit and talk while on the job. He's a funny guy, and we joke around a little bit. I don't know what he's up to when he's not on the job."

"We're not accusing you of anything," Jude grumbled. "We just know that Jordan isn't hanging out with his old friends. We don't know what he's up to when he's not at work."

Rocking from one foot to the other, Austin stared for several seconds at Jude. "You're Jordan's brother, aren't you? You kind of look like him…in the eyes and nose."

"Yeah, I'm his older brother Jude."

Austin nodded. "The paramedic. He's told me some of the stories you've told him, about some of your crazy calls. He cracks everyone up with those stories."

Jude grunted. He and Rebecca had received more than their fair share of insane calls over the years. God help him, he'd take some Viagra antics or even a head stuck in a staircase railing at the moment, but that reality seemed so very far away. Felt like he'd never get back to that normal again.

"Shit…I don't want him to get pissed at me, but you're his family," Austin mumbled under his breath. He took a deep breath and dropped his hands noisily to his sides. "I know he's got this friend. Anthony. Don't know his last name. He meets up with him at a bar called Dana's up in Norwood. I went with him once, but the place is kind of a gun-and-knife club. Not really my scene so I never went back."

"Jordan isn't twenty-one. How the fuck did he get in?" Jude snarled.

Austin snorted and rolled his eyes. "This isn't the kind of place that's carding people and even if it was, I'm pretty sure Jordan's got a fake ID."

Jude paced away from Snow and Austin, roughly scrubbing a hand over his face to try to clear away the equal mix of disgust at his own thinking and his disappointment in Jordan. Of course his little brother had a fake ID! Jude had a damn fake ID at his age and sneaked into more than his fair share of bars. But the places Jude had been sneaking into were gay bars where he could dance and look for a quick hookup. It hadn't been about getting wasted or risking his life. What the fuck was Jordan doing in a bar like Austin was describing? It didn't make any sense.

How had he gotten so far out of touch with his brother? He and Carrick didn't talk often, but he didn't feel like he was out of touch with Carrick's life. But then, he spent most of his days with Rebecca, who had been dating his brother for close to three years. He knew far more about his brother's sex life than he ever could have dreamed. He could do with knowing a little less about Carrick.

But Jordan was proving to be a complete enigma to him. The little kid who had tagged along after him and regularly popped by his first apartment just to eat his cereal in the mornings was fucking gone.

"Thanks for talking to us, Austin," Snow said, dragging Jude from his thoughts. He turned to watch Snow hand over the business card that had both their cell numbers on the back.

"No problem. I don't want to see Jordan hurt."

Too late for that. Jude pushed down the thought and nodded his good-bye to Austin. He appreciated the information, but he didn't have any more energy to focus on being nice or personable. It was a topsy-turvy world when Snow was the people person between the two of them.

Walking to the car, they paused one last time to return the hard hats to Gary and thank him again for allowing them onto the site. Back on the sidewalk and away from the other workers, Snow put a hand on Jude's shoulder and squeezed.

"It's a start," he murmured. "We'll head to the hospital and spend some time with your mom. She needs you. Then tonight, we can pop by this Dana's. Scout around and see if we can find this Anthony."

"What the fuck was he doing going to a place that Austin would call a gun-and-knife club?"

"No idea, but we also don't know what kind of place Austin is into. The guy could have a thing for piano bars and country line dancing."

Jude slowed up a step and looked over at his lover. He let the small smile tease up one corner of his mouth. "Really? Is that the kind of vibe you were getting off Austin? Line dancing?"

"I don't know. Maybe it was the guy's name."

Taking a deep breath, Jude slowly released it, pushing out some of the anger that was constantly bubbling right below the surface, "Thanks, General," Jude murmured.

Snow grabbed the back of his head and pulled him closer, placing a kiss against his temple. "Anything for you."

It was on the tip of his tongue to give Snow one of his patented flirty comments, even though he wasn't really feeling it. Snow's concern for him was written all over his body, and Jude felt bad for making him worry. But the flirty comment was forgotten when his cell started ringing and vibrating from his pocket. Snow released him, and he immediately missed his touch. Jude grabbed his phone, his stomach clenching to see Carrick's name flash across the screen.

"What's up?" Jude said.

"Where are you?"

Jude stopped walking to his car, willing his heart to slow down from the panic it was already racing toward. This could be nothing. He could be asking them to pick up some food on the way to the hospital. "Kentucky. I stopped by Jordan's work."

"You need to get here. Now."

"What's wrong? What happened?"

"Jordan flatlined. Something about his breathing and oxygen levels. I don't know what they're doing. They kicked us out of the room, and everyone is running around."

"Fuck!" Jude shouted. "We're on our way."

Snow was already hurrying toward the driver's side, keys in his hand. When they moved in together, they gave each other spare keys to their cars just in case. In that second, Jude couldn't be more grateful that they had. He couldn't drive. He couldn't even think. He just put one foot in front of the other as quickly as he could until he found himself seated in his car.

"He's not going to die," Jude whispered to himself. "He's not. He's not going to die." Every day felt like two steps forward and one step back, but he had to tell himself that Jordan was making progress. Every day that Jordan was alive was another day he was becoming stronger. He wasn't going to lose this fight.

The lump was back in his throat. The same lump that had been with him since he first learned of his brother's injuries. It was tearing his throat raw so that it hurt to speak or even swallow. He wanted to breathe free again with the knowledge that Jordan was through the danger zone, but he'd seen enough injuries in his career to realize that Jordan was far from in the clear. The odds were not in his brother's favor, and if Jordan didn't recover, he wasn't sure if tracking down the bastard that hurt Jordan was going to be enough. Handing the fucker over to the cops and putting him behind bars wasn't going to be enough.

And if that wasn't enough, would Snow still be able to look at him, love him, when he finally reached what was enough?

CHAPTER 6

Snow kept glancing at Jude as he pulled out the ingredients for sandwiches. Sergeant, who always seemed to know if one of them was upset, wove around Jude's shins and purred loudly in the silent kitchen. Jude slumped into a chair, and their cat jumped onto his lap. He gave him a tired smile and stroked his back. Even in his exhaustion, Jude showed the cat love, and Snow was determined to not let the man push him aside tonight. Jude needed him and that was all there was to it.

They'd put off the trip to the bar for the next night after spending this one in the hospital. Jordan's brother had flatlined. Fucking flatlined. The fear Snow held in his chest had to be nothing compared to what his partner was feeling. They hadn't left the hospital until his brother was stable again, so here they were hours later, both hurting more than Snow could bear.

Lines of fatigue pulled at Jude's features, his mouth turned down into a fierce frown. Not knowing what had gotten Jordan into this situation was killing him.

Snow set the food down in front of Jude, who got up to wash his hands. Snow sat across from him and forced himself to eat, though the food tasted like nothing and sat in a heavy lump in his belly. He watched Jude pick at the sandwich, wishing he had the right words to help him.

"Jordan is strong, Jude. He'll pull through."

Jude sighed and closed his eyes before burying his face in his hands. "Seeing him like that…" His voice trailed off and he leaned back in his chair to stare at Snow. "I hate this. Hate that he's barely holding on. Hate that we have no idea how he got beaten and shot. Everything in my gut is screaming that he got into trouble somehow, and here I've been going about my life like nothing's been wrong."

"If he hadn't shared what was going on, how could you have known? How could any of his family have known?"

"He's never been so secretive, and I'm so damn scared." He pushed his plate away. "My stomach is too messed up for food. Sorry."

"Don't apologize—it's just sandwiches. I wish you'd eat, though. I remember a time in the not-too-distant past that you were dealing with me. Who made sure I ate then?"

He was referring to the time he'd returned home after his trip to Oklahoma right before Lucas's wedding. The trip back to his hometown to rescue Lucas's niece had also put Snow face-to-face with some of his relatives. Seeing them after so many years had awoken a lot of old anger, and he'd been a mess for a few months.

"You worked through all that on your own."

"Because I had your support."

Jude had stood by him the whole time, quietly supportive and so damn strong. Snow had finally come to the conclusion that he had a wonderful new life and the best lover and friends a man could wish for—that his past was just that. The past. He'd finally buried it all where it belonged. "I'm here for you now. Lean on me."

Jude's smile was soft. "I will. But right now, I just want a shower."

"Then go take one while I clean this up and feed Sergeant."

Jude tried to give him another smile, but it wavered and disappeared. "Thanks, General."

At one time Snow had hated the nickname because it came from coworkers in the hospital calling him surgeon general behind his back. But the moniker had stuck, and now it came as a sign of affection from Jude, so he loved it. It was a good sign—him using the nickname. A part of him was still here and functioning despite his overwhelming worry.

Snow cleaned up the dishes and took care of their cat, then made his way up the stairs to the master bath. He watched Jude stand in the shower, his shoulders slumped, and decided it was time for some one-on-one time.

When Snow stepped into the shower stall, he didn't expect to have sex. Right then, Jude needed tending and he was only too happy to do it. He reached for the shampoo and started on Jude's hair. Glittering brown eyes stared up at him and he smiled. "Let me take care of you tonight."

"I'm sorry I've been pushing you away. My head has been a mess."

"It's understandable," Snow said, though he had to secretly admit that he was a little rattled. Jude was the steady one of them. The rock. Strong and unshakable. In the years they'd been together, he'd never seen his lover like this, and he was worried whether or not he could be enough to hold Jude together.

"Some vacation, huh?" Jude muttered.

"I wouldn't know what a normal vacation looked like these days anyway. But I hate the way this one has gone. The worry over your brother."

"Do you really think he'll pull through? As a doctor. Not as my sweet lover trying to protect my heart."

"I do," Snow whispered as he soaped Jude's hair slowly. "I hope."

"That's all we can do right now. God, I just feel so helpless." His hands came to rest on Snow's hips. "I had all sorts of wicked things planned for us this week."

"Your family comes first."

"Our family," Jude corrected.

Snow paused and leaned down to kiss Jude's mouth softly. "Yeah, our family."

That was something Snow was still getting accustomed to when it came to being with Jude. After leaving Oklahoma with Lucas, Snow had clung to the small family he and Lucas had built with Rowe and Ian Pierce. He'd never expected to have more than that.

But all that changed when he met Jude. The bossy paramedic had essentially forced his way into Snow's life, and Snow had never been happier that he had. Jude had also come with a loving mother, two younger brothers, and a massive extended family that loved to be a part of their lives. Add in the partners that Lucas, Rowe, and Ian had found, and Snow now had an enormous, loving family. He couldn't imagine wanting more.

"I want to get married."

Snow's arms froze while his heart slammed painfully in his chest. "Is this a proposal?" he asked when he could get his brain working again.

A weak chuckle left Jude. "If it is, it's a shitty one. I know we've said we don't need the ceremony, that we're basically married already, thanks to mounds of financial and legal documents, but I do want to marry you, Ashton. I love you."

"I love you, too. If you want to be married, then we'll get married."

"Don't you want that, too?"

He made sure all the suds were out of Jude's hair and pulled him close. "I still don't feel a ceremony is needed, but a part of me is ready to actually be married. License, rings, and all that. So if we do this, we're eloping."

Jude's laugh bounced off the walls of the shower stall. It was the first real laugh he'd heard from Jude in over two days, and it lifted Snow's spirits like nothing else could. "And risk the wrath of Ian? Not to mention my *mana*?"

"This is about you and me and nobody else. Yes, I want to marry you." Snow stopped and smirked at Jude. "I never thought those words would pass my lips."

"Yeah, me neither." Jude wrapped his arms tight around Snow. "Let's finish washing and go have sex. I need you in me tonight, General."

Something deep inside of Snow centered and felt at peace with Jude's words. This was back to a world he knew and understood well.

Leaning forward, he brushed his mouth across Jude's and breathed, "Then you'll have me."

They finished washing and dried off slowly, Snow watching the towel swipe over Jude's muscular body with relish. God, he loved the man's form. Jude was built thick and powerful—broader than Snow while he wasn't as tall.

By the time they moved to their bed, Snow was breathing heavy, his cock hard and leaking. He loved Jude's wide, hairy chest and his flat, hard stomach. Loved the dark hair that shadowed powerful thighs. He marveled over the desire that never seemed to dull when it came to this man, and he knew Jude felt the same about him.

Jude had been pushing him away the last few days, and Snow understood why. But now heat brewed between them, and Jude was looking at him with lust in his dark eyes.

They needed this.

When their lips met, that heat boiled over, and Snow took Jude down to the bed and flattened out on top of him. God, Jude felt good underneath him, and he rubbed himself on the raspy hair on Jude's chest, his breaths already becoming choppy and ragged. Jude's hands splayed over his back and he spread his legs, so their cocks were nestled beside each other. Snow opened Jude's mouth wide for his tongue.

Jude groaned and thrust up against him, his hand clasping Snow's ass to hold him tighter to his body. They rubbed on each other as the lust built in Snow's chest. The need to take Jude, to dominate him came over Snow, and he brought up one of Jude's legs, his fingers on the sensitive skin of Jude's inner thigh.

"Yeah," Jude breathed, still thrusting against Snow, his breath hot in Snow's mouth. He tasted so damn good, Snow couldn't get enough. He took possession of Jude's mouth, showing with his tongue what he planned to do to Jude's body. He fucked into his mouth and gripped his thigh. Blood roared in his ears. Pleasure coiled, dark and deep, in his gut.

Jude made a strangled sound in his throat, his fingers digging into Snow's ass cheek hard. Even when he submitted, Jude kept his toppy vibe. In the past, Snow had never been with men like Jude—he'd always been the one in charge—but Jude had blown all his knowledge of himself out of the water. The man fucking owned him.

Always would.

He kissed down Jude's neck to his collarbone, opened his lips to taste flesh warm from the shower. He moved to take a nipple into his mouth, nuzzling Jude's chest hair with his nose and cheek. Jude's hands mapped his body, touching everywhere he could reach. Snow kissed his belly, then the head of Jude's cock. He licked at the beads of ejaculate gathered there, before running his tongue down Jude's length.

Snow spread Jude's legs and licked his sac, taking one ball into his mouth. Jude's thighs tensed around him, and a groan rumbled over his head. He came up and took Jude's cock into his mouth, the urge to deep throat him drumming throughout Snow's body, the urge to pleasure Jude consuming him. He ran the flat of his tongue over the veins and pulled him in as deep as he could, his lips touching the crinkly hair at the base of Jude's cock.

"Want you in me," Jude rasped. "Need it tonight."

He pulled away to reach for the lube they kept in the bedside drawer. He coated his fingers and brought them to Jude's hole, groaning when Jude spread his legs wide. "You want to be on your stomach?" He knew that was Jude's favorite position when he bottomed.

"No. Wanna see your face. Wanna look into those pretty eyes."

God, the intimacy just shredded Snow. Jude never let him back down from anything. Never let him hide. And he hid nothing from Snow. The man's need was stamped on his face in living color, so goddamn sexy, Snow held his breath. He breached Jude with two fingers, pressing up inside him with strong, sure strokes. God, the heat of his body pulled Snow in, and he couldn't wait to sink into Jude.

"Want you to fuck me through the mattress," Jude murmured, his voice thick with lust. "Push up inside me and make me feel it for days. Take everything away."

Snow added a third finger, moaning at the warmth and tight clasp of Jude's body. He pulled his fingers out and stroked once over that tender flesh, then got up on his knees to guide himself into Jude. He pressed his palms on Jude's inner thighs, then stroked his hands over the soft hair to his knees. Muscles clenched. "So damn gorgeous," he moaned. "So mine."

"All yours. Fuck me, General."

He pushed inside Jude as far as he could go, his teeth clenched hard at the heady pleasure. Jude grimaced and he slowed as he pulled out, then pushed back in. He watched for the pain to change over to pleasure and was rewarded when he nailed Jude's prostate and the man yelled out. "That's it," Snow said. "Feel me."

He continued to fuck into Jude in that spot, watching as his eyes closed and his mouth fell open. Gasps spilled from his lips, and his hands came up to touch Snow's chest. He clenched his fingers in the muscle there, a long rumbling moan coming from his throat.

Snow couldn't take his eyes off Jude, marveling over the absolute delight it was to watch him as much as it was to feel him. The grip of his body, the way he panted, the glazed look of passion on his features. He wanted to crawl all the way inside him and just live there.

Jude punched his hips up and clenched around Snow's dick. Snow cried out and moved faster inside him.

"Yeah, fuck me! Make me forget everything but this." Jude's words were slurred and sexy as hell. Snow stared down at him, their eyes locking, and the love this man held for him showed bright in his brown eyes.

"I love you so goddamn much," Snow growled, pushing into his body over and over. His cock felt like it was gripped in a vise, and he loved it. Loved everything about Jude. The man had come into his life and turned it inside out in the best possible way. Snow hadn't wanted another man since the moment he'd first crawled into bed with Jude, and he didn't see him ever wanting anyone the way he did Jude. The man was his everything.

Jude reached down to grab his cock, and Snow's eyes half-shut at the eroticism of watching Jude touch himself. "That's it," he breathed. "Touch yourself."

Jude clenched his ass and Snow let out a cry and fell forward, bracing his hands on either side of Jude. "Do that again."

"Agh," Jude breathed as he tightened around Snow again and again.

Snow couldn't stop the hoarse cries spilling from his throat. "I'm going to come," he warned.

"Do it. I want to feel you come inside me."

Snow came so hard and fast, he grew dizzy. He threw his head back, every muscle in his body going taut as he spilled into Jude, the flood of pleasure overwhelming. Jude's hand sped up, his knuckles bumping into Snow's stomach and Snow abruptly pulled out of him and hurried down to suck Jude into his mouth. The soft head of Jude's dick hit the back of his throat, and he tightened his suction, bobbing his head slowly, then quickly. He sucked hard, three years of experience letting him know it would send Jude over.

Jude roared and came, spilling on his tongue. Snow swallowed and licked him clean, then fell to the side, sprawled on his back, one leg thrown over Jude's. "Fuck," he whispered, his heart racing wildly in his chest.

"Yeah," Jude whispered, his voice raspy. "Holy hell, General."

"Feel better?"

"I don't feel anything right now." His chuckle was warm and low. "You blew my mind."

"Good. That was the plan."

Jude rolled over and pulled him close, slinging his arm and leg over Snow. "How did I get so lucky?"

"I don't know about that." For some reason, the one major issue they had came to Snow's mind. The one about kids. But he kept it to himself because he didn't want to ruin the mood. Instead he wrapped his arm around Jude and looked him over. He looked a little better. Worn out, but that was to be expected.

"We're going to figure out what's going on with your brother. I know it."

"We have to. I can't lose him."

It wasn't long before Jude went heavy with sleep, and Snow was glad he'd been able to give Jude some modicum of relief. The man needed to sleep. He was bottling up so many heavy emotions lately, he'd felt ready to collapse earlier. So, the sound of his heavy breaths and the weight of his arm lulled Snow into sleep with him.

CHAPTER 7

Jude stumbled through the hospital, feeling like his brain was trapped in a fog. It had started early, barely even five in the morning, when he got a call from Carrick that Jordan's temperature had spiked during the night. He'd rushed to the hospital with Snow to find that the doctors thought Jordan might have developed an infection, and they were starting him on a new course of antibiotics. They mentioned that they might have to go back in, that maybe something had been missed during his first surgery, though nothing was showing up on any of his X-rays or scans.

Hours passed with no news, even with Snow sneaking into the ICU to access his chart. Jordan's temperature didn't start to creep down until late afternoon, showing that the antibiotics were finally doing their job. Jude felt drained. There was no trying to talk his mother into going home for some real sleep. Carrick had left an hour ago, but only because Rebecca had threatened to drug him and stash him in a supply closet so he could get some sleep. She was still in the family room with his mother. Currently she had her tablet out, and she was going through a bunch of silly BuzzFeed quizzes to determine which princess his *mana* was and which Hollywood hunk was her perfect match. It was all nonsense, but for at least a few minutes his *mana* was giggling and not thinking about her youngest son clinging to life.

Fuck…he didn't know what he'd do without Rebecca. If he'd been even a little straight and not crazy in love, he would have made a pass at her. Carrick was damn lucky.

Rubbing his eyes as he walked, Jude was shuffling off to the cafeteria for more coffee and something with a little protein. He'd not eaten yet. He needed to grab something for his mother as well. She'd eat if Rebecca needled her into it.

Snow had been swept off to the ER to consult on a case that had just come in. He hated the guilty look in his lover's eyes, but the surgeon could at least do more good for the poor injured person than he could sitting around in the family room waiting for news like the rest of them.

The normal sounds of the hospital barely permeated his consciousness any longer. People rushed around him, moving patients and equipment from one place to another. Every once in a while, he'd encounter a familiar face who would offer their sympathy, but for the most part, the hospital was so big that he was just another weary person waiting for good news while preparing for the worst.

As he got close to the large bank of elevators, he slowed his steps and yawned, when someone small crashed right into him. His yawn turned into a gasp, and he stumbled back a step as he focused on a surprised young woman with bright blue hair.

"Oh, gosh! I'm so sorry. I didn't even see you there," she said, covering her mouth with both hands. "Oh! Wait! You're Carrick. No, you're Jude."

Jude blinked against the rush of words, trying to get his exhausted brain to catch up to what he was hearing while taking in the person's appearance. She looked familiar, but it wasn't until she dropped her hands to reveal a lip ring that he realized that he was looking at Jordan's ex-girlfriend Emily. Of course, now she had a couple more piercings in her ears. Her long black hair had also been chopped into a pixie cut and dyed blue to nearly match her wide eyes.

"Emily, right?" he said slowly.

"Yes. We met at a dinner over at Jordan's mother's. Well...I guess your mother's too," she said with a blush. "I...I heard about Jordan. I'm so sorry."

"Thank you. How did you hear?" It wasn't like they were advertising it on social media that Jordan had been beaten and shot. The news was kept to immediate family for the most part.

"I ran into Brian Perkins at NKU between classes. He told me. How's Jordan doing?"

"He's still in critical condition, but he's fighting it." Jude paused and swallowed back the lump that was forming in his throat again. He had to cling to positive thoughts, especially after the rough start to the day. "It's going to be a very long recovery for him."

Emily nodded and stopped to wipe her eyes. "Jordan has always been a fighter. For as long as I've known him."

Her comment pinged something in his brain, and for a moment Jude was able to push aside his worries and focus on another issue. "Can I ask how long you've known my brother?"

"Oh...ah...I think we met back in our sophomore or junior year."

"You went to the same high school?"

Emily shook her head. "No, I was out at Dixie, but we met through some mutual friends. We all used to hang out on weekends and just kind of goof off. Then we tried the dating thing for a while. But...you know..."

No, Jude didn't know, and that was what he was trying desperately to get to the bottom of. He flashed her a smile that he didn't feel in the least just to keep her from getting scared. "How long did you and Jordan date?"

Emily's eyes dropped to the ground instantly, and she shoved her hands into the pockets of her puffy pale blue coat. "Not long. Six months, maybe." Her voice became softer and she sniffed.

"I'm sorry, Emily. I don't mean to bring up something painful. It's just...this whole thing doesn't make sense to me. Why would anyone attack Jordan? I'm trying to talk to his friends, find out what was happening in his life prior to the attack."

The young woman looked back up at him and held his gaze for

several seconds. He could see the pity there in those blue depths before she shook her head again.

"I don't know how much help I can be. Jordan and I haven't talked for months. He...well, it just didn't work out, and we went our separate ways. It's not like we had a big fight or anything."

"Can I ask why?"

She stared at him again and he was starting to get afraid that she'd blow off the question, but to his surprise she said, "Have you ever been sitting with someone, but knew that they weren't even aware you were in the room?" Jude gave a small nod and she continued. "It didn't start out like that, but in the last couple of months, it was like he didn't care if I was around or not. And I wanted to date someone who wanted to spend time with me. I thought we'd be able to stay friends, but I never heard from him again. After talking to Brian, I get that he stopped talking to a lot of people, but I really don't know why."

"Thank you, Emily. I really appreciate your honesty."

"I'm sorry I can't help more." He nodded and pointed her in the direction of the family room, where she'd be able to pass along her sympathy to his mother. She liked Emily. He remembered her remarking after that dinner that she liked the girl's spunk.

Turning toward the elevators, Jude punched the call button and sighed heavily. While interesting, Emily's information didn't really help him out a damn bit. When the doors opened, Jude stepped inside and was instantly grateful that it was empty. He selected the button for the floor he needed and leaned against the wall. Closing his eyes, he tried to sift through all the information he had, but it did no good. There were too many missing chunks to fit anything useful together.

The doors of the elevator slid open, and he was stunned to find himself looking into the face of someone he knew very intimately. Shane freaking Stephens. A very old friend from school and before Snow, the occasional fuck buddy.

"Shane?"

The private detective smirked at him. "Just the person I was coming to find."

Jude quickly stepped through the doors before they could close and threw his arms around Shane. His friend hugged him back tightly and whispered his sympathy in his ear. But while the warm affection was welcome, Jude could feel it breaking down the wall he'd built to hold all his emotions back.

Pushing out of Shane's arms, Jude stepped away and shoved a stiff smile on his lips. "How did you find out?"

"Rowe. I stopped by Ward Security this morning to drop off lunch for Quinn, and Rowe caught me. He told me since he knows we're close." The lighter expression that appeared on Shane's face every time he spoke of his boyfriend disappeared almost as quickly as it formed, and he glared at Jude. "But I figured with something like this, you would have called me personally. We are still friends. I care about you and your family."

"Yeah, sorry about that," Jude countered, his tone growing sharp. "I've been a little busy with Jordan in ICU and my *mana* falling apart and trying to find out what fucking bastard shot Jordan in the first place."

Shane didn't back down an inch in the face of Jude's rising anger. In fact, he reached out and gave the tip of Jude's nose a little flick. "Don't give me your self-righteous attitude. There are a few hundred other people who are dealing with ugly shit same as you. You're just a dumbass for trying to carry it all on your own."

Jude's mouth dropped open to fire another shot of rage at Shane when it hit him that he was being a dickbag to one of his best friends. A friend who had come to check on him and his family.

"Holy fuck, you're right," Jude breathed. "I'm sorry."

"Feel better?" Shane asked with a grin.

"Not really."

"Yeah, I'm too easy of a target." Shane stepped closer and dropped his arm across Jude's shoulders, directing him toward the cafeteria. "After you're done here, we can stop by Ward Security, see which bodyguards Rowe's got lying around. You can shout at them. That'll be more fun because they'll take a swing at you."

"You're such an asshole," Jude muttered, but he was so damn glad Shane was there. He loved Snow more than anything in the world, but

Shane knew him in a different way. Shane wasn't going to watch him like he was a ticking time bomb. Shane was going to poke at him and prod him until he finally exploded, then help clean up the mess.

As they entered the cafeteria, Shane made idle chitchat, filling him in on some recent cases he'd worked on and what he'd been doing with Quinn now that they were living together. Shane was also excited to share the news that his father was dating someone and that they were moving in together.

But as soon as they had their coffee and a slice of pie, Shane's tone became serious.

"Talk to me."

Jude sat with his hands wrapped around his cup of coffee as if its warmth could reach all the way down to the part of his soul that grew cold when he thought of what happened to Jordan. He could relay all the same things that Snow had told Brian, but that wasn't what Shane was asking.

"Someone beat my brother, shot him, and then left him naked in a field in Sharonville. My little brother. Why? Why would someone do this to Jordan? It doesn't make any sense." Jude shook his head. "There's no reason for anyone to hurt my brother."

Shane stared at him, a frown on his face like Jude had said something wrong.

Groaning, Jude waved for Shane to hit him with it.

"Really? You ready for tough love?"

"As long as you know I reserve the right to punch you."

Shane didn't look impressed. After a deep breath, he said, "You talk about Jordan like he's still five. He's nineteen—"

"Twenty," Jude corrected.

"God, you're old."

"Fuck off. You're just as old as I am," Jude snapped, but he got the point Shane was trying to make. He couldn't help but think of Jordan as a little kid. Yes, he'd watched him grow up into a young man, but the person lying in the hospital bed weak and clinging to life reminded Jude more of the vulnerable little kid he'd tried so hard to protect.

"Jordan is twenty. He's got a job, a car, and his own apartment. That means he's got his own damn life that he's living. And he's making his own damn mistakes."

"But he was raised better than this. He can't be involved in gangs or drugs or other illegal shit. He's smarter than that."

Shane stared at Jude like he was a freaking idiot, and he hated to admit that he was starting to feel that way. "How many things did you and I get into that would horrify you if Jordan did them now? Things that we were so-called 'smarter than'?" Shane even lifted his hands to make the fucking air quotes.

His friend was right. Jude had done more than his fair share of stupid things when he was Jordan's age. And yeah, he'd definitely known better, but he'd done them anyway for a number of equally stupid reasons that had seemed sensible at the time. He'd just been lucky enough not to land in the hospital.

"What am I supposed to do, Shane?" Jude whispered. "He stopped hanging out with his old friends. His place looks like it's been cleaned out. I don't know my own brother anymore."

Shane clamped a hand down on Jude's wrist. "First, you stop prepping Jordan for sainthood. I love Jordan too, but he's a dumbass just like the rest of us. He's done dumb things in the past, and he's going to do more when he gets through this. Exactly like his older brother."

"Okay," Jude said, trying to let Shane's words ease some of the worry still nagging at him.

"If you start thinking of Jordan as a twenty-year-old guy, and not some five-year-old kid, you might have more luck figuring this out." Shane paused and picked up his fork. He cut a bite off his apple pie and motioned with it toward Jude. "Of course, it doesn't hurt that you've got a private eye for a friend. I can dig into things if you want."

"Thanks for the offer. Snow and I are good on our own at the moment."

Shane shrugged and continued to eat his pie while Jude sipped his coffee. Shane made an excellent point. The changes in Jordan's life didn't make sense to him because he was determined to see Jordan as this unchanging figure in his life. But people changed, grew, found other interests, and inevitably...fell in with the wrong people at times. Jordan was no different.

"I'd personally like to hear more about this younger guy your dad is dating. Think he's enjoying the new sex life?"

Shane stopped with the fork midway to his mouth, closed his eyes, and shuddered. "It's good to see you haven't completely lost your ability to be an asshole." But there was still a hint of a smile when Shane opened his eyes again.

Jude snickered. Yeah, he still knew how to get under Shane's skin when he wanted. They'd been friends too long to ever lose that.

CHAPTER 8

"I don't think even Rowe would like this place," Snow grumbled as he climbed out of Jude's Jeep.

A single light towered over the small parking lot to the left of the bar, but it wasn't doing much to push back the shadows that filled the area. There were a few other cars in the lot, and they were all showing off a collection of dents, dings, and rust spots. Silver duct tape and plastic covered a few windows. There was a sharp stench of piss and rotten garbage in the air that assaulted Snow's nose.

It was definitely a good decision to bring Jude's Jeep rather than Snow's Mercedes. The Jeep was still in great shape, but it didn't stand out as much as the Mercedes would have.

Frigid January wind swept over him and Snow pulled his coat tighter around his throat. "Maybe we should have brought a gun."

"We're definitely overdressed for this place," Jude said.

Snow glanced down at his jeans and thick navy-blue sweater. Jude was similarly dressed. Their clothing was relatively nondescript, but it was obviously of high quality. But the dead giveaway was Snow's Tom Ford coat. With a sigh, he peeled it off and tossed it into the front seat before shutting the door. They didn't need to stand out more than they already did. At least it was a short distance to the bar.

Walking back to the sidewalk with his hands jammed in his pockets, Snow glanced up and down the street. It was quiet despite being barely after eight on a Thursday night, with no one out and only a few cars on the road. A quick glance around revealed some crumbling apartment buildings, a liquor store, a pawn shop, and a dingy gas station. This part of town had seen better days. Though it looked like those "better days" were about forty years ago, judging by the architecture and signs in the store windows.

It had taken them a couple of days to get around to checking out Dana's since meeting with Austin. Jordan had suffered more setbacks, and Jude had decided to stick close to the hospital. The cops had popped by as well, asking all of Jordan's family members more questions about who he hung out with and where he might have been the night he got shot, but so far not one of them had any answers for the cops. And it was increasingly obvious that the police didn't know much at this point either.

Snow was all too accustomed to working around the police when it came to tracking down the right people behind bad things, but he'd never wanted that for Jude. It was bad enough Jude had gotten dragged into his messes in the past—he didn't want his lover to see this hands-on approach as the best way to handle bad shit. Why pay fucking taxes to support the police if they weren't going to rely on them to do their jobs?

The streetlights were brighter than the interior of the bar as he and Jude stepped inside. He waited for his vision to adjust. His shoes stuck to the floor, and he grimaced as he looked around. The scent of beer and at least a couple of unwashed bodies filled the room. A few of the round tables held people, and five men sat on barstools at the bar. The only noise came from the television hanging over the bar, which was tuned to a twenty-four-hour news station. And not one of the decent ones either. *Great.*

"You remember that one time in Newport?" Jude said in a low voice as he surveyed the room before them.

"You mean our first date?" Snow teased.

Jude looked over at Snow, his eyes narrowed and not an ounce of amusement on his face. That "first date" had been them sneaking into a highly illegal sex club and praying they got out alive again.

"Yeah, I remember," Snow admitted, barely keeping the laughter from his voice.

It wasn't a thing he was at all likely to forget, but then Jude had surprised him that night in a big way. And it was the first step to falling so completely in love with him. After three years, Jude was still finding ways to surprise him.

"I'm thinking this feels worse than that place," Jude muttered.

Snow winced. "I don't know about worse, but it definitely gives it a run for its money."

"Then let's make this quick."

They settled in at the far end of the bar on wobbly stools. The bartender was a grizzled man with thinning gray hair and a beefy build that was probably a good mix of muscle wrapped in fat. The guy was most likely accustomed to tossing out drunks when necessary, but Snow was also guessing that he probably had a gun within easy reach as well.

Snow ordered two beers and when the man set them down in front of them, Jude held up an image of Jordan on his phone. The picture was solely of the young man. It had been taken two months ago at Thanksgiving. He'd been smiling and laughing and cutting up with the entire family just as he always had.

"Have you seen him in here before?" Jude asked.

"You cops?" the bartender demanded right back.

Snow inwardly cringed as it felt like all the eyes in the bar suddenly snapped over to them. "Nope," he replied louder than necessary. This didn't feel like the kind of place where police would have been welcome. He then slapped a hundred-dollar bill on the bar and smiled tightly at the bartender. "Keep the change."

The bartender snatched up the bill and stuffed it into his pocket with a sniff. "Yeah. He was in here about a week, maybe two weeks ago."

Well, that was a start at least.

"Was he with anyone?"

"Don't recall."

Snow rolled his eyes, but he dug into his pocket and pulled out another hundred that he slapped on the bar. The bartender grabbed it up just as quickly, adding it to its brother in his pocket.

"Yeah, tends to come in with the same guy two or three times a week. They sit and drink, maybe play some cards for a bit."

"And do you know the guy's name?" Jude pressed, lowering his voice a bit so they couldn't be overheard by the other bar patrons. "Is he in the bar now?"

The bartender crossed his arms over his chest and looked over at Snow. He stared right back. The bartender cleared his throat and made a little waving motion with his fingers.

"The bank is closed after this," Snow snarled. He reached into his pocket one last time and pulled out one more hundred. He slapped it on the bar but kept his fingers on it even as the bartender tried to slide it away. "Just tell me this is going to a kid's college fund."

"Braces for my granddaughter," the older man said without hesitation.

And the scary thing was that Snow actually believed him. That reason he could live with. So, he released the bill.

"Don't know his name, but he's at the other end of the bar. Skinny blond."

The bartender tucked the final hundred in his pocket and moseyed to the middle of the bar and started cleaning some glasses and stacking them with the others as if they'd never spoken.

Snow grabbed his beer and took a long drink, ignoring the revolt of his taste buds. It was cheap domestic, and he wasn't in the mood for a beer. He missed Lucas's stupidly expensive whiskey. When this was all finally over and life settled back into its normal routine, he was looking forward to lounging on Lucas's couch and sipping that whiskey with his old friend while they reminisced over old adventures.

Jude took a few sips of his own beer, but Snow could see him eyeing the guy at the end of the bar. The young guy looked lost in his own world. He had a beer in front of him, but his eyes were locked on the phone in his hand.

They waited only a few moments before grabbing their beers and walking to the other end of the bar. Their footsteps on the old floor seemed louder than the damn TV, and Snow could feel the eyes of a few of the big bruisers already giving them looks.

Neither he nor Jude fit into this seedy atmosphere. He curled his hand into a fist, ready for anything. A gay bashing would be just the kind of thing he'd expect in this place.

"Are you Anthony?" Jude asked the guy, who turned to look them up and down.

He was scrawny in a way that Snow was sure he'd never once had enough to eat in his life. There was something hungry and a little desperate in his blood-shot brown eyes. His hair was bleached blond, but it wasn't a good dye job. It was like he had a sister in beauty school who did it, but she wasn't the top of the class. It stood straight up in these weird chunks like pale yellow nails sticking out of his skull.

"Who wants to know?" His beady eyes shifted from Jude and locked on to Snow. A slow grin stretched his thin lips, and Snow nearly groaned. Not everyone in this bar was straight. He just had a knack for attracting the strange ones. Though Geoffrey Ralse, a man who'd been somewhat relentless in the past, was looking far more appealing than this punk, not that he'd ever dream of touching Geoffrey when he had Jude in his bed every night. "I may be Anthony for you."

"Not interested," Snow sneered.

The guy's mouth snapped closed and he shrugged, his gaze going to Jude. "What do you want?"

"My name's Jude. I heard you're friends with my brother."

The guy made a scoffing noise and started to turn back on his stool to face the bar. "And who the fuck is your brother?"

"Jordan Torres."

Anthony's expression went instantly blank as he paled enough to see even in the low light. "I-I don't know no Jordan. You got the wrong guy."

"I don't think so. You've been seen with Jordan by several people. We're just trying to find out information about where my brother has been hanging out. Was it here with you?"

"Like I said, I don't know no Jordan." He turned his back to them and lifted up his phone again, dismissing them. Snow almost wanted to laugh at the balls on this punk. Like they were going to walk away so easily.

"Look," Jude said as he put a hand on the guy's shoulder. "Nobody is accusing you of anything, we just need to—"

Jude broke off when the guy suddenly jumped out of his seat and shoved between them, knocking them back a step to catch their balance. Anthony took off for the door, weaving between tables and patrons who stood, wondering what the sudden noise was about.

"Son of a bitch," Snow snarled, his spine slamming into the edge of the bar. Pushing back to his feet, Snow took off after the little fucker, dodging people who were now shouting at him and Jude. Jude's heavy footsteps echoed behind him, only a bit off his own heels.

They busted out the front door and paused for a second to find Anthony running down the sidewalk, his arms and legs pumping as fast as they would carry him. With a growl, Snow took off after him with Jude right beside him.

Anthony was young, small, and fast, allowing him to more easily dart sharply around corners and hop over fences.

But Snow and Jude didn't slow. Thank God they regularly worked out and ran. He hadn't expected that they'd need the endurance for a chase through a shadowy part of Cincinnati, but life brought strange surprises around every fucking corner.

Anthony cut through an empty church parking lot and over a sagging chain link fence before cutting through someone's backyard. Snow swore under his breath as he went over the fence. He didn't want to be seen running through someone's yard late at night and risk some homeowner shooting at him and Jude. It would be just their luck that they get shot while chasing after Anthony when they just wanted a little fucking information.

His slick-soled shoes slipped on the damp grass and he exhaled a breath of relief when they hit the pavement again. He'd worn the wrong damn shoes for a pursuit, but then he'd not been expecting to run after anyone tonight.

His breath fogged in the cold, his lungs complaining against the frigid air. His feet pounded on the sidewalk, sending little shocks of pain up his legs and into his knees. Definitely the wrong footwear for a run. He imagined that Jude couldn't be doing much better, but they were keeping pace with Anthony so far.

The younger man bobbed behind a truck and crossed the street. Snow and Jude followed, Jude's desperation for answers making him run just a bit faster.

As Anthony hit the next sidewalk, he left behind the last of the residential buildings and crossed into the industrial side of Norwood. The sound of cars rushing by was a little bit louder as people raced along the Norwood Lateral Expressway, cutting east and west across the city as they likely headed home or to their job on the night shift. This wasn't a part of town that Snow was extremely familiar with. He was pretty sure there was a chemical plant nearby and a recycling facility. As long as most of those places had high fences around their property, Anthony was going to start running out of places to hide.

Unless, of course, the fucker was also part monkey and he could out-scale them on the damn fences.

Fuck, why didn't he bring his gun? He could have just clipped him in the thigh and stopped all this running much sooner.

Anthony hit a high fence surrounding a warehouse of some sort and bounced off. He paused, looked up at the fence and then over his shoulder at Jude and Snow before starting to run again. Apparently, he didn't think he had enough time to climb the fence before they reached him.

Frustrated with running, Snow slowed his step as they crossed through the business parking lot of what appeared to be a recycling center and scooped up a rock. He took a few running steps and chucked it at Anthony. The rock cut through the lamplight just before it thumped against the back of his head. Anthony stumbled, holding his head, and fell to the ground.

"What the fuck!" Jude yelled as they closed in on Anthony.

"What?" Snow shrugged. "I was tired of chasing him."

"Yeah, but we need answers from him. Can't get them if you knock him out."

Before Snow could answer, Anthony was shoving gracelessly to his feet. Snow and Jude were already grabbing him. Anthony swung wildly, clipping Jude hard enough to snap his head back. With a snarl, Snow fisted Anthony's shirt and slammed him up against the wall.

Anthony grabbed at Snow's hands, pushing them off. Chest heaving and eyes wide, he lifted his fists, ready to fight off both of them. "What the hell! Why are you chasing me?"

"Why'd you run?" Jude strode to him and pushed him into the brick wall behind him when Anthony tried to take a step away. "You know my brother."

"Fine! Fuck! I know Jordan. We hung out. Drank. Bullshitted. Played some cards. Who gives a fuck?"

"Then what? He beat you at cards, so you shot him?"

"Shot him?" Genuine surprise filled his expression. "Jordan was shot?"

Even Snow believed the guy was truly shocked. He was too stupid to fake that emotion. "He was found beaten and shot four nights ago. What do you know about it?" Snow demanded.

"Nothing. I didn't have nothing to do with that. I haven't talked to Jordan in a week at least, I swear."

"Where did you meet Jordan?"

"What? I don't know. At a bar or through friends or something. Who gives a shit? We just hang out. I didn't fucking shoot him!"

Jude swore under his breath as he paced away from Anthony. It looked as if the chase through the streets of Norwood had only made Jude's temper worse. They certainly weren't getting much useful information out of Anthony, and they didn't have any other leads to follow.

The wind picked up, sweeping down the empty street and cutting through Snow's sweater. The run had helped to hold the cold at bay, but the longer they stood there, the more it was starting to slash through his clothing. They needed to move this along.

"Why the fuck is Jordan hanging out with you in the first place?" Jude snarled as he swung back to face Anthony. He grabbed two handfuls of the smaller man's shirt, pulled him forward, and then slammed him into the wall again. "My brother has a good job, a family that loves him. A good life. And you…you look like some junkie that's just wasting his life and pulling down everyone around him. Did my brother get shot because of something you did?" Releasing his hold on Anthony's shirt, Jude backhanded the man.

"Hey!" Snow grabbed Jude's shoulders, pulling him back. Jude's desperation was rising; he could feel it in the tension vibrating in his muscles from head to toe. This was not the man he loved. He'd been pushed too far, passed too many days mired in ever-worsening fear and worry. He was doing things he'd later regret.

"Fuck you, Torres!" Anthony shouted. "You think your brother is so sweet and better than everyone else, then maybe you don't know your brother. You want to really know what he's gotten himself into, go to Moneyshot.us and you see for yourself."

Snow and Jude stood perfectly still for several heartbeats. Snow couldn't even drag a breath into his lungs at Anthony's angry words. While they were both in shock, Anthony darted past them and started running down the street. Jude reacted first, pulling free of Snow to make a grab for the smaller man. But he was too quick. He dodged Jude's hand and disappeared into the darkness.

"Let him go," Snow said, weariness creeping into his voice. Anthony had too big of a lead on them, and Snow didn't want to throw another rock at the asshole. "I think we got what we came for."

"You believe him?" Jude cried. He swung around, staring at Snow with incredulous and pain-filled eyes.

"I do."

They were easily two of the hardest words Snow had ever had to say to Jude, because he would see both the desperate denial and crushing pain warring in his expression. But Anthony had only given up the information when pushed to an angry and hurt outburst. His words had felt true.

"Let's go home and check it out," he continued. He placed a hand firmly on Jude's shoulder and directed him back the way they'd come. "Judging by the URL, it's one of two things. And if we don't see anything that points to Jordan, then we know where to find Anthony again. We'll think of a more interesting way to lean on him for info."

They walked a few blocks in silence. The cold wind cut through their clothes and bit at their exposed skin, but Snow was more worried about Jude. He could see him drawing into himself with each step.

"I think he's right," Jude said softly when they were nearly to the car.

"Anthony?"

Jude nodded. "I don't know Jordan anymore. Not like I used to. I'm beginning to wonder if I ever really did. Maybe I just told myself I did so I wouldn't feel guilty about being so wrapped up in work and my own life."

Snow stopped and pulled Jude into his arms, not caring that they were standing in the middle of the sidewalk in the freezing cold. "You know Jordan. And he knows that you love him. It's just that somewhere along the way he got into some shit and made some bad decisions. We all do that. We'll figure this out together."

Jude sighed, pressing his face into Snow's shoulder. "I don't know, Snow. I just don't know."

CHAPTER 9

Snow and Jude stood around the island in the kitchen, a bottle of Jack between them. Snow had splashed a couple of shots into a pair of tumblers when they got in and Jude had followed him. Now they stood there in an uncomfortable silence. He'd expected Jude to head straight to the computer in the office they'd set up in one of the bedrooms, but his lover had dragged his feet into the house and showed no problem with joining Snow in the kitchen.

They were afraid to pull up the website and face what they might find there.

Snow was pretty sure they wouldn't just stumble across a video of Jordan being shot and beaten, instantly answering all their questions. Instead, it was going to be something that led them deeper into the rabbit hole, into a world they'd been sure couldn't have possibly touched Jordan's life.

Looking across the counter, his heart broke at Jude's pale face and glassy eyes. He appeared to be worn down to his very core. Jude was running on empty from days of worry and frustration. But their first potential break, the first glimmer of truth, was likely to be something darker than either of them wanted to contemplate.

Throwing back the last of his whiskey, Snow set his glass down with a loud thunk. "Let's just mentally prepare before we go in there. What do you think the site is?"

"Porn," Jude said without hesitation.

"Gambling," Snow shot back.

Jude lifted disbelieving eyes to Snow and shook his head.

"I'm not saying that it can't be porn. Just that it could also be a gambling website."

Jude sighed, his broad shoulders slumping. "Yeah, it could be a gambling site too. I know he likes to play poker. I guess he could have gotten in over his head." Jude might have been saying the words, but Snow could tell by his tone that he wasn't convinced at all.

"And if it's porn, that's not the end of the world. We have both met a number of people in the industry who are kind, intelligent, wonderful people. There's nothing wrong with porn."

Nodding, Jude took a deep, steadying breath. "No, you're right. Porn and gambling aren't the end of the world. Porn isn't exactly something I expected Jordan to do if it's that, but that's okay if it is. We just want to get to the bottom of why he was hurt."

"If you want, I can go check it out. I'll report what I see," Snow offered.

Jude slammed back the remaining shot of whiskey and set his glass on the island counter. "No. This is my brother. I need to see this for myself."

Snow walked around the island and pulled Jude into his arms for a tight hug. There was no missing the fine trembling in his frame despite his brave words. He didn't want this for Jude, wished he'd just let Snow look at this site and report back, but it wasn't going to happen.

In the office, Snow quickly claimed the swivel chair behind the keyboard. Jude might have decided to be right there to view the website, but Snow was going to be the one in the driver's seat. He needed that control, if only to protect Jude.

Waking the computer from its slumber, he opened an incognito browser window so that cookies and the site wouldn't be saved to his history. Rowe's hacker Gidget popped by once, about a year ago, to make sure they had top-of-the-line security on their computer to prevent viruses and hackers from getting access. Still, even with all that, he was a little anxious about visiting this unknown site.

They pulled up the website, and the computer screen was instantly filled with bare ass and tits. Yep, it was a porn site.

"Fuck, thank God I'm gay," Jude muttered. He stood behind Snow's shoulder and rubbed his eyes.

The first page was splashed full of videos for different fetishes and categories. There were flashing ads, offering the chance to talk to popular stars and meet up with singles who want to fuck. Everything about it looked like a normal porn site, though there wasn't nearly enough cock on it compared to the sites that Snow had visited in the past.

With a grunt, Jude grabbed another chair from across the room and dragged it over so that he could sit beside Snow. "I'm guessing we can't just search the site for him," he muttered.

"I'd like to think that Jordan has enough brains in his head to not use his real name, so searching the site is likely out."

"Do you think maybe Jordan isn't in the porn? Maybe he runs the site? Anthony didn't state exactly what Jordan had to do with this site," Jude suggested.

Snow just narrowed his eyes at Jude. Unless Jordan had been secretly taking classes at night and running a business after hours, Snow couldn't imagine how he learned to build the website and set it all up. Plus, there was good money in porn. If Jordan was running the site, his apartment wouldn't look like he was living on the edge of poverty.

"I think it's a stretch, babe."

Jude flopped back in his chair and glared at the screen. "Yeah, I know. I really don't want to sift through pages of porn searching for my brother. I'm beginning to feel like Anthony sent us on a wild goose chase so that he could escape."

Neither did Snow. Even if it was wall-to-wall gay porn, he really didn't want to sift through it all in search of the guy he viewed as his brother-in-law.

Frowning, he spotted a black box boasting access to the premium videos. He had a feeling that if they were going to start their search anywhere, it needed to be there. Clicking on the link, it immediately took them to a sales splash page. For two hundred dollars, the subscriber would have unlimited access.

Snow leaned forward and dug his wallet out of his back pocket.

"If we're going to pay for this, then it needs to be on my card. This is potentially my brother," Jude said, getting up to get his wallet as well.

"Nope. I don't want this traced to either of us if this does have something to do with Jordan." Snow pulled a folded piece of paper from a hidden pocket of his wallet. On it was written John Smith along with a credit card number and all the necessary information.

"You have a card linked to a fake ID?"

Snow started typing in the information, frowning at the screen. "Years ago, back when we were dealing with Jagger and trying to protect Ian, the three of us created a fake identity and got him a credit card. That way we could use the card for various online things if we needed to track or torment Jagger without it being traced back to us. We all pooled some money and jointly paid off the card whenever it was used. Since Jagger's death...I never thought I'd use the card again. I'm not sure any of us have."

"Won't they see the charge on the account?"

He looked over at Jude and gave him a small, encouraging smile. "Yeah, but they're family. You really think Lucas or Rowe is going to judge you or Jordan because of this?"

Jude rubbed his face again before he nodded. "I know. You're right."

Snow finished putting in the credit card information and the site instantly changed to something much darker. The background went from red to black and the thumbnail images for the videos took on a more sinister feel. There was now more of a mix of heterosexual and homosexual images. But now, many of the people didn't even look legal. The categories changed from typical BDSM and playful fetish to kidnapped and non-con. And judging by the expressions of pain and terror, Snow was willing to bet that these people were not acting.

Jude covered his mouth with his hand and swallowed hard as if he was struggling to keep his dinner down. Dread ran like ice through Snow's veins, and he hesitated to continue. But Snow slowly scrolled lower on the page. Jude's harsh gasp drew Snow's eyes down to a thumbnail that clearly displayed Jordan's face, his mouth stretched in what looked to be a scream while a large man in a mask was positioned behind him.

"My brother's not gay," Jude said on a noisy gulp of air. "He's-he's-he's not into anal sex."

Snow knew that too, which meant this video was of only one thing.

It took two tries to get the mouse click to register and the video to start to load. Bile rose in his throat and Snow was sure he was going to be sick. He'd lived through all kinds of painful and gory moments in his life, but it all seemed to pale as they waited for the screen to change from black to a bare white-walled room. There was a large, sturdy framed bed in the center of the screen and a dingy mattress with no sheets.

Jordan lay in the center, his hands and legs tied. And he was absolutely terrified. There was no faking it. No acting. Jordan feared for his life, and he had not chosen to be there.

A huge, bare-chested man straddled him. He wore a mask that hid his hair and face completely, but he'd not been smart enough to cover the tattoos that were liberally spread across his arms and chest. The man wielded his fists and there was nothing consensual about any of it. Jordan's head whipped to the sides over and over as huge, meaty fists pounded his face. Blood spattered the walls and the bed. The guy wasn't holding back; there were no safe words being voiced. Jordan's whimpers and cries jumped from the computer speakers and filled the room so that there was no escaping what was playing before them.

Jordan took a beating unlike any BDSM scene Snow had ever witnessed. It was more akin to the types of things that he'd been into before he'd met Jude. But while the pain he sought in those dark sex clubs had been brutal and vicious, every bit of it had been consensual. Jordan begged for the man to stop, but the fucker never slowed.

When Jordan lay there quietly sobbing, no longer even trying to protect his face and body with his hands, the man climbed off Jordan. Snow inwardly pleaded for this whole incident to finally be over. The man grabbed Jordan by the shoulders and tossed him on his stomach toward the end of the bed so that he was facing the camera. He then lined up behind Jordan. Thick, blunt fingers grabbed Jordan's hips and spread his cheeks.

New life burst forth into Jordan and he started struggling again. He twisted and grabbed at the bed frame, desperate to break free of the man's hold all while pleading for him to stop. The cries were choked and high pitched as he screamed for help.

"No!" Jude howled. Snow looked over to find tears streaming down Jude's face. He held the edge of the desk with both hands, his knuckles white. Jude cried out again, but this time it was perfectly timed with a new scream of pain from Jordan.

Jude turned and fell to his knees, grabbing the trash can next to the desk. Violent heaves wracked Jude's body, forcing the contents from his stomach. Snow whipped around, stopped the video, and turned off the computer screen so they no longer had to look at the vision of Jordan being raped.

The room fell deathly silent except for the fractured sobs and painful heaves coming from Jude on the floor. Snow closed his eyes and took his own steadying breath, needing a moment to push aside those images before he could even reach out to Jude.

Very slowly, he laid his hand on Jude's back, hating to see how he initially flinched at the contact. He didn't know what to say. There was nothing he could say that would ever make this better. Jude had watched his baby brother get beaten and violated. There was no taking back that moment, no going back to the life he and his brother had before.

"They fucking filmed him…being beaten and raped," Jude said. He spit into the trash can. His voice was ragged with a mix of horror and rage. "That wasn't porn. That wasn't consent."

"The guy beating him didn't hide his tattoos. We can get Rowe's people on this," he offered.

"I want the man who touched my brother. I want the person who fucking filmed it and put it on a website," Jude said, enunciating each word.

"I'm so sorry, Jude."

"There is no sorry, Ash. My brother was fucking beaten and raped. I want those fucks who did this to him," he replied, his voice growing louder with each word.

"We need to call the police," Snow said calmly when he was feeling anything but calm.

"I want Rowe on this."

Those words slithered cold and hard between them. He didn't like this turn for his lover. Jude was always the voice of reason. He believed in allowing the cops to do their job. He believed in working within the system, not outside of it.

Snow and his friends were definitely not the poster boys for working within the system. And he knew if that video had been of any of his family, there would be no calling the police. He'd only be happy when he killed that tattooed fuck with his bare hands.

And right now, Jude felt the same way.

Picking up his cell phone from where he'd placed it on the desk, Snow dialed Rowe.

"Hey, old man! What are you up to?" Rowe laughed when he answered the phone.

"I need you here."

"Twenty minutes," was all Rowe said in a hard, even tone and the line went dead.

Snow had twenty minutes to help Jude into the bathroom to clean up and then hold him. He needed to hold Jude and tell himself that they'd get through this. That they'd find a way to help Jordan through this when he finally woke up again. That they'd be able to close their eyes and not see those images flashing through their brains.

And then, when those twenty minutes were up, they'd plan to set the world on fire.

CHAPTER 10

Snow had just gotten Jude back down to the living room when Rowe showed up on his doorstep. He was surprised his friend didn't just use his key to enter the house, but he figured Rowe had given him a minute to answer the door before he walked in on his own. A scowl drew his features taut as sharp eyes swept over him from head to toe. Rowe didn't say anything. He just grabbed Snow and pulled him into a tight bear hug that brought tears to his eyes before Rowe released him again.

He could easily imagine that he looked like shit. Jude looked worse. His partner was seated on the couch, pale and drawn. His hair was a mess, sticking up in every direction after the number of times Jude had run his fingers through it.

Noah Keegan silently followed Rowe into the house and hugged Snow as well, his expression matching his lover's. Snow wasn't surprised to see Rowe's shadow following close behind. After getting a second chance at love, those two were rarely apart now and they both seemed perfectly happy with that arrangement.

And that was fine with Snow. Noah and Rowe might both be crazy, but they also had double the Army Ranger experience between them.

Snow joined them in the living room, where Rowe was watching Jude with a curious and cautious look, while Jude had yet to look up or even acknowledge them. Both Rowe and Noah were aware of the attack on Jude's brother. Snow had talked to each of his friends once since they got that initial call, and he was sure they'd all shared information and concerns between them.

"Rowe..." Snow paused and cleared his throat. "We need your advice on something."

"Anything," Rowe immediately said, and Snow's heart swelled. When Rowe said that, he meant it completely. If it was in his power to do something, he would do it.

"I need you to go up to my office and watch the video that's up on my computer. You...you won't need to watch it all, but you may want to start from the beginning."

Rowe nodded before he and Noah wordlessly jogged up the stairs.

"You might want to pour them some drinks," Jude whispered. It was the first time he'd spoken since he stopped sobbing in the bathroom.

Snow grunted. Rowe and Noah were definitely going to need drinks. Stepping into the kitchen, he pulled down two clean tumblers and poured two fingers of whiskey into each. He then got another glass that he filled with ice water and put down in front of Jude in the living room.

Jude picked it up and shook his head, but he still took a couple of tentative sips before putting it down again. Yeah, Snow got it. He'd much rather have the alcohol, to drown in fucking alcohol until he couldn't remember his own name. Snow would much rather have that. But after puking his guts up for ten minutes and then dry heaving on top of sobbing, Jude was dehydrated. Alcohol wouldn't help him.

And if Jude was about to make some point-of-no-return decisions, Snow wanted him to be stone-cold sober for it.

The video was less than fifteen minutes long, but it was more than twenty minutes before Rowe and Noah descended the stairs again at a much slower pace. He wasn't sure if they'd watched the entire video, or if they'd simply stopped it and made some notes and plans between the two of them.

Snow placed a reassuring hand on Jude's back as his friends stepped into the living room. They both looked a bit paler than they had when they went up the stairs. Rowe's hair was a little mussed now as if he'd run his hands through it a few times.

"I made you drinks. On the island," Snow directed with a jerk of his head toward the kitchen.

"Thanks," Noah murmured. He walked into the kitchen and grabbed both while Rowe dropped into the chair opposite the couch. Rowe accepted the drink and downed both shots in a single swallow.

Leaning forward, Rowe placed the empty glass on the table and rested his elbows on his knees. He wrung his hands together over and over again, his brow furrowed in thought. In some ways, they'd been down this road before with Ian. Snow felt a little bad about dragging Rowe into this, but he knew Rowe had zero regrets about getting involved to save Ian's life. And he knew in the long run, Rowe would have no regrets about helping Jordan.

"What can we do?" Snow asked when neither Rowe nor Noah was offering anything up.

"Call the police," Rowe simply said.

"No!" Jude said with a burst of fire. His head snapped up and he glared at Rowe. "There's got to be something we can do. I am not just handing this over to the police so they can potentially fuck this up. Jordan deserves justice after what happened. My brother deserves justice!"

Rowe didn't even blink at Jude's outburst, while Noah sipped his whiskey as he continued to stand just behind Rowe's shoulder.

"And I'm suggesting that you call the police," he repeated calmly. "Let them do the digging. It's their job. They can track all the fuckers down related to this and put them behind bars for a very long time."

"And drag my brother through a horrific court trial, assuming that he wakes up, forcing him to relive it all over again. No!"

"Jude—" Rowe started, but Jude jumped to his feet and cut Rowe off.

"No! Don't put me off. You had no problem breaking all the rules to save Ian from a fucking drug lord and sex trafficker. My brother was beaten and raped, and you are just going to abandon him. Abandon me!"

"You're ready to break the law? To kill a man to get your justice?"

Jude looked over at Snow, his pain-filled eyes briefly meeting Snow's gaze.

Rowe jumped up faster than Snow thought the man was capable of. Taking a step around the table, he roughly snagged Jude's arm. He started dragging him around the table when Snow lurched to his feet, but Noah was right there, placing a restraining hand on his shoulder. He didn't honestly think Rowe would hurt Jude, but he knew his lover wasn't thinking clearly. His emotional state was fragile, and Snow didn't want Rowe making things worse with his usual heavy touch.

"It's okay," Noah murmured in his ear and Snow willed himself to relax.

With one hand on Jude's bicep and another wrapped around the back of his neck, Rowe dragged Jude across the room to a decorative mirror hanging on the wall, forcing him to stand in front of it. Jude tried to look away, but Rowe released his arm and roughly grabbed him by the jaw. He held his head up, forcing him to look at his own reflection.

"Don't look at Snow for your answer," Rowe snarled. "This is who you need to worry about. You do this, you go after this bastard personally, and this is who you've got to be able to face again." Rowe paused and shook his head before he lifted his own eyes in the mirror to Snow's reflection. "Snow, Lucas, me? We made the choice to go outside the law a long time ago, and we've had to make peace with those demons. Ian didn't have a choice, and he still found a way to make peace."

Rowe released him and Jude continued to look in the mirror, his eyes filling with tears while his breathing grew more ragged.

"But you...you're straight and narrow," Rowe softly continued. "Yeah, you've helped us in the past, but you did that for Snow. You do this now…it's not for Jordan. You're doing this for you. And you've got to be able to live with that."

The tears slipped down Jude's cheeks, but he stayed staring into the mirror. "Every time I look in the mirror, I see that video, I see him lying in the hospital…and I think of how I failed him. How I should have been there…should have—" Jude's voice broke. His shoulder slumped and Jude started to fold in on himself.

Snow instantly pulled free of Noah's loose hold and crossed the room to Jude. He wrapped his arms around from behind and he pressed his face into Jude's neck.

"But if I do this my way…no cops…" he continued softly a moment later, "then maybe I won't feel like a failure. Won't feel like this is all my fault. I'll be able to take back a little bit of what they stole from my brother."

"I'm with you," Snow whispered against his neck. "I'm with you no matter what you decide. You know that. No regrets. Whatever you need."

"We're with you on this, Jude," Rowe said. His voice had lost its hard edge, becoming more understanding and compassionate. "I needed to be sure that you made your peace with this. I don't want you to have the regrets that we have."

"Regrets are inevitable," Jude said. "But handling this might mean that I'll be able to sleep at night."

Snow continued to hold Jude for a few more minutes, trying to let his warmth and support soak into Jude. This man was his entire world now. Jude had been there when his world was falling apart, and his mistakes had come back to haunt his family. Jude had never wavered when things got ugly, and Snow was desperate to show that he'd be there for Jude the same way.

When Jude was breathing a little easier, Snow guided him over to the couch while Rowe returned to the chair. With a little smirk and nod to Noah, his boyfriend placed a small pad of paper and a pen on the table in front of Jude before sitting down on the arm of Rowe's chair.

"Jude, I need you to write down your brother's cell number, his address, email address, and his cell service provider," Rowe said. He sat back and flinched when Sergeant jumped into his lap. Noah instantly scooped up the cat and snuggled him against his chest. Rowe wasn't much of a cat person, where Noah had proved that he just loved animals. "Snow told me that you tried to use the 'Find My Device' app with no luck. It's unlikely we'll be able to hack the phone's location, but we might be able to see which towers the phone frequently accessed. Could give us an idea of his habits."

Picking up the pen, Jude nodded and started filling out the information that Rowe had requested. "The website…"

Rowe sighed heavily. "Normally I'd give this to Gidget, but after the Boris Jagger thing…" The former Ranger paused and shook his head. Snow watched his friend, hating to see the grim look fill his usually happy eyes. Even more than a year after his death, that bastard Jagger still had the power to cast a dark pall across their lives with his memory. "I'm going to pull in Cole McCord. He's damn good, and he'll keep this private from everyone. No one else at Ward Security beyond us will know about this."

"I appreciate your discretion, Rowe," Jude said. He cleared his throat and continued. "But my priority is finding out who this bastard is and getting justice for Jordan. I trust you and Noah. If you have to involve more people, then do it."

"We'll stick with just Cole for now. He will examine the video and the website. See what he can pull out about the person who set it up."

"I used the Smith credit card to get the premium access," Snow said.

Rowe flashed Snow a wicked grin. "Lucas and I were just talking a couple of weeks ago about finally shutting down that entire account. Guess we should hold on to it a little while longer."

"Hopefully this will be the last time we have to use it."

"Cole will also see if he can track the money."

"What about the man…the tattooed man?" Jude asked, his voice cutting out slightly at the mention of Jordan's attacker.

"The tattoos give him away," Noah replied. He gently placed Sergeant on the floor so he could wander under the table toward

Snow and Jude. "The ink is clear and distinct. Cole will be able to pull the images and run them through our database and the local cop database. It'll give us a good start."

Jude grunted. He didn't seem to be reassured, and Snow couldn't blame him. There was a chance the man had never been arrested, at least not locally, and that would mean that he wasn't in their databases. But Snow clung to the idea that his attack of Jordan hadn't been his first. They would find this bastard.

"It would be helpful if you could also write down the color, year, and make of Jordan's car," Noah suggested. "That we can give over to Quinn or Gidget. They have made a fine art of accessing the city's traffic cameras."

Jude's head suddenly popped up from where he was writing. "We don't know where his car is. I don't think the police even told us where he was found. Just that it was a field in Sharonville."

Rowe grunted and even Noah frowned at that bit of information before he said, "The police should have mentioned it, at least to find out from the family what Jordan might have been doing in the area."

"Unless, they think it might tie into another bigger investigation," Rowe added. He lifted his eyes and met Snow's gaze. "We'll try to sneak a peek at the police report."

"Is there anything else we can do to help?" Jude asked.

Noah rose and tore the piece of paper Jude had written on away from the rest of the pad. Rowe stood as well, shoving his hands into his pockets. "Honestly, just be there for your brother and wait for us to get back to you. Don't go looking for these people or any other vigilante shit." Jude glared at Rowe, but the security specialist just glared back at him. "I don't want you to tip our hand to these assholes by you and Snow mucking around in places that you shouldn't be. You want help? Let us do our job."

"Fine. Thanks."

Rowe gave a little shake of his head before he started for the front door with Noah. Snow rose and followed them out, rubbing the side of his neck as he walked. Jude wasn't the type to be rude, but he knew that his lover was preoccupied with finding the people who hurt Jordan.

"Rowe—"

"Don't," Rowe said, holding up his hand and stopping his apology. "Just be there for your boy. He needs you."

Snow hugged Rowe tightly. He couldn't fathom what he'd do without Rowe, Lucas, or Ian. Those three men had become an integral part of his existence, saving him from his own self-destructive tendencies more than once. And now he was the one who was the pulled-together, level-headed one. The world had truly become a fucked-up place.

After Rowe and Noah left, Snow returned to the living room to find Jude slowly pacing the room, both fists tightly grasping his hair.

"What do you need?" Snow asked. He wanted to pull Jude back into his arms and hold him until the pain went away, but he knew from his own experiences that Jude might feel trapped instead of comforted.

"I…I want that fucker dead. I want the person who owns that website dead. I want everyone who has hurt my brother dead," Jude listed in a voice that seemed to crack with every word he spoke. "But I'm afraid. Afraid of what you will think of me. Afraid…"

Snow closed the last few steps between them and roughly pulled Jude into his arms. He blinked back his own tears as he buried his face into Jude's warm neck. "Don't. You know every inch of my past and that includes all the stupid and horrible things I've done. Yeah, some of them have been justified, but a lot of them weren't. And you have never judged me. Never stopped loving me."

Jude's strong arms suddenly wrapped around Snow, holding him so damn tight. "I will never stop loving you, General. Never. No matter what happens."

"And I will never stop loving you, Jude. Whatever you need to be at peace again, then I support it."

"Even if it means…?"

"Yes." Taking a deep breath, Snow lifted his head and brushed his lips across Jude's temple. "For now, one step at a time. We let Rowe and his team work. And when we find the culprits, you'll make your decisions then. We can hand it over to the cops. Or we can put a couple of slugs in their heads and walk away. I can live with either."

Snow would stand by Jude no matter what. He didn't know where this dark turn in their lives was going to take them, but he wouldn't leave Jude's side. He protected his family. And if he was honest with himself, he was still sorely tempted to put two bullets in each of the culprits even if Jude decided to hand them over to the police.

But for now, they waited for Rowe to work his magic and for Jordan to heal.

CHAPTER 11

*J*ude couldn't sleep that night, his fury and pain a living thing in his chest. He stared at Snow, passed out beside him. Moonlight filtered through the open blinds of their second-floor bedroom, glowing on the man's silver hair. Strong, naked shoulders made him want to touch, but he looked peaceful in his slumber, which was the only reason Jude didn't reach for him. He needed him, but he needed answers more right then. And tonight with Rowe...well, that had left him all out of sorts.

Instead of burying himself inside his boyfriend, he quietly got up and gathered his clothes. Snow had been trying so hard to be supportive, but all Jude could think about was his brother. He dressed downstairs, his movements jerky and unsteady, then let himself out of the house.

When he got to the hospital, it was to find his mother asleep in the waiting room. She had one of her colorful, pink sweatshirts on and her dark hair pulled up into a ponytail. He reined in his anger and worked to flatten his expression as he softly kissed her forehead. Her eyes opened, alarmed at first, then softening when she focused on him.

God, the thought of her knowing what had really happened to her son gutted him.

"You need to go home and rest," he said, keeping his voice low. "I'll sneak back and sit with him awhile."

Anna's lips quivered. "I'm afraid he'll wake when I'm gone."

"He's not going to wake anytime soon. Please go home. Do you need me to call you a ride?"

"No, I'm okay to drive." She stood. "The police still have no information. One of them came by earlier to see if he'd awakened to question him. They know nothing, Jude."

"I know," he said quietly. "But they will. We just have to be patient."

"I'll go, but I'll be back early. You don't stay too long either, okay?" She cupped his cheeks and came up on her toes to look him in the eyes. "Promise me, *yie mou*."

"I promise." He kissed her forehead again and she smiled tiredly as she picked up her purse and left the room.

The hushed atmosphere of the hospital at night washed over him and he walked back to his brother's small room. His gaze skimmed over the monitors, noting there was still no change but that his heartbeat was steady and strong. He stared down at his brother, at the livid bruises mottling his pale face and the bandage around his head. They still had his neck immobilized. Now that Jude had seen the actual beating, he knew how they'd come to be, and his gut twisted.

A meaty fist snapped into his face and he cried out, his blood splattering the wall behind the bed.

Jordan trying to twist away from the man coming over him.

For the life of him, he couldn't get those images out of his head and he knew that when Jordan woke, he'd be in for a world of emotional pain as well as physical.

Anger curled his hands into fists in his lap.

"I wish you could talk," he whispered. "Wish you could tell me why you didn't come to me for help when you needed it. When have I ever made you feel you couldn't?" His voice broke and he cleared his throat. "What did you get yourself into, Jordan?"

His brother just lay there, breathing thankfully, but still.

Jude buried his face in his hands. He thought of the years after the Santa incident and how close they'd been after that. How he and Carrick had stepped in and done everything they could to help their single mother raise her youngest. Babysitting and driving him back and forth to practices. Jude had even paid for his brother's braces. Jordan had been such a good kid, even later when he'd developed the usual teenage attitude. It had never gotten as bad as Jude knew it had with some of his friends.

His mind skipped into a memory.

It was right after Jordan's sixteenth birthday, and Jude waited in the driveway of his mother's house, hoping Jordan would be bringing the car back. He still lived at home, their place on a quiet street across from train storage buildings that were mostly hidden due to overgrown bushes. Moonlight shone down on the street, the only other light from the few streetlamps and glowing windows. He glanced up at the window of the house where his mother sat waiting for Jordan to come home, and he tried not to imagine him in an accident, but his paramedic job kept nightmare images in his mind.

Jordan pulled into the driveway and spotted him, a grimace twisting his features in the streetlamps. He sat in the car after turning it off, then released a visible sigh as he got out. He stood next to the car, hands in his pockets.

Jude stalked toward him. "You took Mana's *car. What were you thinking?"*

"I was thinking that I need wheels," Jordan snapped. "I'm working and she won't let me buy one, so I borrowed hers."

"Without asking?"

"I asked. She was just...doing something and didn't hear." Jordan shoved his hands deeper into his pockets.

"Do you have any idea how worried she's been? I got home, and it was the first thing out of her mouth. You just turned sixteen, and you think you're ready to just take the car whenever you want?"

"There was a party—"

"Was there booze at this party?"

"Yeah, but I didn't have any. Promise." Jordan came close, dressed in a gray pullover and jeans. Since his usual outfit consisted of T-shirts, he'd obviously dressed up for a party. His hair was also neatly combed, so more

than likely a girl had something to do with this. "Smell my breath, if you don't believe me."

"I don't want to smell your breath. As far as I know, you haven't lied to me before, so I'd hate to think you're starting now."

Jordan's lips tightened. "All my friends have cars, Jude."

"I happen to know that's not true. Brian doesn't have one. You just turned sixteen! It hasn't been that long since I was sixteen—"

"It's been forever." An engine revved as it came up the street.

He couldn't help but smile at that as he watched a car pass their driveway. Other than that, the night was quiet with only the sounds of the occasional birdcall. They'd all grown up on this peaceful street, and it hadn't changed much. "Thirteen years may seem like forever to you, but it feels like I was sixteen yesterday. I didn't have a car then either."

"Bullshit. I remember Uncle Craig gave you a car."

"The one I'm driving now? Yeah, it was Craig's, but he didn't give it to me. I bought it. And I was almost eighteen. We couldn't afford the expense of another car then any more than we can now."

"Your friend Shane had a car."

Jude rolled his eyes. "Shane borrowed his father's car."

"And we don't have a damn father—"

"Really?" Anger made Jude take another step closer to Jordan. "You're going to pull that card right now? Do you know how hard our mother works to take care of us? Do you?"

Jordan's face fell. He lowered his head, throwing his features into shadow.

"That car is her only way to work. What if you'd wrecked it, Jordan?"

"I was really careful, and I got my license."

"Do you feel that excuses you taking the car without permission?"

He shuffled his sneakers on the pavement. "I just really wanted to go to the party and couldn't find a ride."

Thirteen years might have passed, but Jude could remember what it was like to be his brother's age and excited for a party. He wrapped his arms around his brother. "You'll be grounded, but you deserve it."

"I know," Jordan mumbled into his neck. "It was still worth it."

"Let me guess. There's a girl."

"Of course there's a girl." Jordan pulled back and grinned at him. "I'm not like you. I don't go for the dick."

Jude smacked his head lightly. "Watch your mouth."

"What? I'm just saying I like girls."

"We all know how much you like them." He slung his arm around his brother's shoulders to walk him to the house and their very angry mother. "Tell me about this girl while you can still talk."

Jude looked at his brother now, four years older and still seeming as young as he had then. But outside of a few mishaps, he'd been a great kid. He'd never gotten involved with any gangs when several of his friends had, and he'd worked part-time for their uncle Gary as soon as he was old enough. He'd always wanted to work in construction.

"You have what you wanted. An apartment and a job—what happened?" Silence met his question.

He brushed the back of his hand lightly over Jordan's cheek.

"I'm trying to find out who did this to you. Went to my friend, Rowe, for help. If anyone can dig for answers, it's him. I promise I'll get justice for what they've done to you. If you needed help, why didn't you come to me?"

But Jordan had no answers for him, and frustration beat at Jude's mind. It didn't ease during the two hours he spent next to his bed. When he finally left, all he could think about was who had done this to Jordan.

❋

Snow woke sometime in the middle of the night. The heater kicked on and he turned toward Jude to find his side of the bed empty. He blinked at the clock beside the bed and saw it was after three in the morning. His worry for Jude had kept him from falling asleep until close to midnight, but Jude had still been there. He knew what they'd seen had to be eating Jude from the inside out. His concern sent him from the bed. Still naked from his earlier shower, Snow grabbed a pair of pajama pants and quickly slid them on.

He padded downstairs just as Jude walked through the front door.

"Did you go to the hospital?" Snow took in his drawn features and slumped shoulders.

"Yeah. There's no change." Jude pulled off his coat and hung it in the closet next to the front door. He unwound his scarf from his neck and draped it over a hanger. He wore jeans and a thick black sweater that matched his hair, eyes, and close beard. "I finally talked my *mana* into going home. She was there when I arrived."

"Good. She needs the sleep. You've got to get some, too. You start work soon."

"I know." He scrubbed his hands over his face. "I just keep seeing that video. I can't get it out of my head, and it's killing me. Any word from Rowe?"

"Not yet, but it hasn't been long. Give him time."

"I don't have time!" Jude yelled.

"Whoa." Snow held up his hands. "Of course you do. What the hell, Jude?"

Jude turned and slammed his fist into the wall. "Jordan's just lying there and he can't tell me anything and I wish I knew who shot that video."

"Hey, hey," Snow whispered, moving toward Jude. "We're going to get to the bottom of this. Let me see your hand."

"No. It's fine."

"Let me see your goddamn hand. Shit, that stucco is tough." Snow grabbed his wrist and winced at the scrapes on his knuckles. "You could have broken your fingers."

"I didn't hit it hard enough." He yanked his hand away. "It's fine. I don't need to be coddled."

"Then what do you need?"

"Fucking answers!"

"Well, you're not going to get them tonight! So let's go to bed and try to sleep."

"I don't want to sleep."

Snow blinked at his boyfriend, feeling at a complete loss as to how to help him in this volatile mood. This was such a role reversal, he wanted to smile, but he was too worried about his man. "If you don't want to sleep, then I'll make you something to eat."

"I don't want anything to eat either."

Snow threw up his hands. "Then what do you want?"

"Fuck, General! Will you stop? I don't need you taking care of me. I'm a grown man. Stop coddling me. Stop acting like I'm about to fall apart with every damn breath I take. I don't need to be wrapped in fucking cotton and protected by you or anyone else!"

"Then what the fuck am I supposed to do when you're not taking care of yourself and walking around like your world is ending!" Snow shouted back. As soon as the words were out of his mouth, he regretted them. The week of ceaseless worry, horrifying revelations, and never knowing if Jordan was going to have another setback had left his nerves frayed, but he should never have lashed out at Jude. His lover had it so much worse.

"There! I can see it. You feel guilty about what you said."

"Of course I feel guilty."

"*My* general wouldn't feel guilty about losing his temper or telling me the truth." Jude stepped close, getting right in Snow's face. "*My* general would just say what he's thinking and not treat me like I can't handle shit. Since when have you ever censored anything when talking to me?"

"Fuck you! I'm not always a total asshole." Snow placed his hands on Jude's chest and gave him a shove back. This almost felt like they were about to come to blows. If that was what Jude needed to let off a little steam, that was fine, but Snow wanted to have enough room to maneuver.

"No, but you at least treat me like I'm a capable human being. Not someone who needs to be taken care of at all times."

"Fine. Then you take care of this." Snow grabbed the back of Jude's neck, holding him in place as he slammed his mouth down on his. There was nothing pretty about the kiss. Lips crushed, teeth scraping, and tongues fighting for control. It was angry and hungry.

But Jude didn't melt into him like he usually did. He pushed against Snow's chest and Snow immediately released him.

Backpedaling, Snow stopped when his spine touched the hall wall, his breathing short and fast. A wicked grin flashed across Jude's mouth before he crashed back into Snow, his mouth covering Snow's.

A laugh nearly bubbled up Snow's throat. Jude hadn't wanted to stop. He just wanted to be in control. Jude's hand slid up his chest and snaked around his throat, sending blood surging straight to Snow's cock. This was his Jude.

Almost as quickly, Jude was pulling away, his worried gaze going to the hand around his neck. Snow knew he was thinking of the video, wondering if what they were doing was right.

"Don't!" Snow snapped when he started to move his hand away. Jude's gaze instantly jumped up to his face. "Don't compare what we do to that fucking video. You and me—what we have blows my mind. I never felt like this with anyone before you, and I'll never be with anyone after. It's you and me, Jude." He grabbed Jude's hand and brought it to his throat. "And I like it when you hold me down. When you push me into walls. I like your force and your passion. There is nothing about you I don't love."

Jude snarled and turned him around and pressed him into the wall. "Like this, do you?"

"You know I do. Now fuck me."

Jude latched on to Snow's neck and bit down. He scraped his fingers over Snow's skin, his raw passion flaring through his touch. He kissed down Snow's back, then shocked him when he dropped to his knees and yanked Snow's pants down to his ankles and off. He split Snow's ass wide with his hands. His tongue came out to flick and Snow's asshole clenched.

"Just jumping right into it, eh?" Snow breathed on a gasp.

"Take those horrible images out of my mind, Snow. Give me something better."

Jude stabbed his tongue into Snow and he widened his legs, his dick becoming full and achingly hard so fast, he felt dizzy. It felt so decadent, being naked while Jude was still fully clothed. He pushed his ass back into that hot mouth. Jude's tongue stabbed into him again and it was so good, his knees wobbled. When Jude turned him and took his dick into his mouth, Snow yelled.

Wet heat enveloped him and he closed his eyes, his head hitting the wall. Jude wrapped his hand around the root of his cock and used strong suction, moaning around Snow's length in a way that had lust screaming through Snow. He watched him bobbing up and down and tried to fuck his face. But Jude had one hand wrapped around him and the other holding his hip hard to the wall, keeping him immobile.

"Fuck, Jude," he rasped, his hands opening and closing as pleasure swamped him. He loved this forceful side of Jude more than he loved air.

Jude sucked him down deep and swallowed around the head of his cock. Then he pulled off and turned Snow back around. "Don't move," he growled.

He disappeared and returned with lube in his hand. His dark brown eyes stared hard at Snow as he dropped the lube and pulled his sweater over his head. That possessive stare did what it always did to Snow—made his belly flip, his body flood with fire. Jude moved to his pants, opening them and pulling them off, leaving him in only his socks. His dick stood, stiff and proud, the tip already shiny with excitement.

Snow couldn't look away, couldn't take his eyes off the man who thrilled him like no other.

Jude swiped up the lube and coated his hand. He came back to Snow and put his mouth on Snow's shoulder. "So damn sexy, you take my breath away."

"Good." Jude needed to think about this—about them and not his brother—in that moment.

Jude pushed his lubed fingers up into Snow and Snow hissed and came up on his toes. Jude licked into his ear and a shudder rolled down Snow's back. He bit down on the lobe, then kissed that sensitive spot right below. When he pulled his fingers free and replaced them with his dick, Snow curled his hands into the wall. That first bite of pain hit, and he gritted his teeth, knowing that pleasure would soon follow.

Banding his arm around Snow's chest, Jude thrust up into him hard. It was like being held in a vise, and he gloried in the strength of Jude's muscles, his powerful body moving in and out of Snow's.

Their skin was soon slick with sweat, their breaths erratic.

"So good. You feel so goddamn good," Jude breathed into his neck. "I want to live inside your ass." But he pulled out and manhandled Snow into the living room, bending him over the couch. Snow loved every second of it. When Jude slid back in, Snow groaned long and loud as he impaled himself to the hilt.

Joy speared through Snow. He loved being fucked by Jude. Loved the power coursing through him, the pleasure of being filled—loved listening to the hoarse cries of pleasure coming from Jude's mouth.

He felt so connected to him in these moments, it felt like his heart could burst from the love that swelled within it.

Jude stroked inside his body, hands tight on his hips as he pounded deep. Pleasure built, drawing Snow's balls tight. He reached down to grab his cock, the couch arm in the way. Moaning with frustration, he pushed back harder onto Jude. "Yes!" he yelled when Jude reached around and wrapped strong fingers around his dick. His fingers were still slick with lube, and the slide made Snow clench his teeth. He rocked his ass into Jude over and over as Jude hit that spot in him that felt so damn good, he actually whimpered. He arched and dug his fingers into the sofa cushions.

"Fuck yeah," Jude breathed. "Fuck yourself on my cock!"

Snow could no longer think clearly, his entire mind and body wrapped up in a pleasure so intense, he could only writhe and rock his hips back. His mouth opened in a silent cry as his orgasm slammed into him. He came all over the side of the couch, not giving a shit as sensations roared through him.

Jude let out a cry and went still; then he pumped his hips two more times before he pulled out and groaned and came all over Snow's backside. Panting, he held on to Snow's hip with one hand and rubbed his spunk into Snow's skin.

Snow shuddered and felt another small spurt leave his dick.

"That's it, General. God, so fucking perfect." He staggered back, then pulled Snow to his feet, turning him and taking his mouth in a kiss that ravished. Snow's legs still felt wobbly, so he held on, returning the kiss with fervor. Jude's tongue went deep into his mouth like he was searching for every flavor Snow had. Snow sucked on his tongue, then pulled back to meet those glittering brown eyes. He smirked, happy to see an answering smile on his man's face. They were covered in sweat and semen, the room smelling of sex.

"Feel better?" he asked, kissing the corner of Jude's mouth.

Jude's eyes went half-mast. "Yeah."

"Good. Let's shower and try to sleep now, okay?" He threaded his fingers with Jude's, happy when the man tightened his hand. He led him up the stairs.

CHAPTER 12

"Your timing is perfect!" Andrei exclaimed as they walked through the front door of the penthouse. Snow had barely gotten his winter coat off when Andrei was placing a tiny bundle in his hands.

"Wait!" Snow cried back while already snuggling the little girl against his chest.

"I've got to finish warming her bottle. Just hold her for a minute. Lucas is in the shower and will be down soon," Andrei replied as he jogged off to the kitchen.

Jude looked around Snow to see the largest brown eyes set in a tiny face topped off with thick black hair. Just like her Romanian daddy. Oh yeah, Snow was right. Andrei's genes were strong with her. She was going to be a knockout when she got older, driving both of her daddies absolutely insane.

And seeing her being held so protectively by Snow was melting his heart and brain into a useless puddle deep in his gut. Snow might say that he didn't want kids, but that man had a heart as big as the world. Jude was confident that he'd be a great father. The instincts were there whether he wanted to acknowledge them or not.

But if Snow didn't want kids, then Jude would accept that. He just hated the idea of them both missing out on something that would bring such joy to their lives.

For now, he was content to watch little Daciana Vallois stare up at Snow, her bow lips parted almost in wonder as she reached for him. Snow smiled back at her, whispering a few sweet words in his soothing, baritone voice.

As if realizing what he was doing, Snow looked over at Jude, a sheepish expression crossing his face. "Here. You haven't even held her yet," Snow said. He offered her to Jude, but Jude backed up and started to pull off his coat.

"You're doing just fine there, General. I've got to admit that I'm enjoying watching you with her right now."

Snow rolled his eyes, but he still tucked the baby back against his chest as he walked into the living room. Jude followed him in, chuckling softly.

Almost two days had passed since they'd talked to Rowe. There had been no news so far with regard to his research, and there had been no fresh news on Jordan's progress. He'd not had any more setbacks, which was good, but his healing was proving to be slow. They'd both taken a few days off work under the excuse of a family emergency. Considering that Jordan was in the hospital where they both worked, no one was surprised.

Snow had suggested a trip to the Vallois penthouse for a visit with Daciana. They were both bouncing off the walls at home, waiting for news of any sort. And the little girl was an excellent distraction—at least for an hour or two.

Stepping into the penthouse living room, Jude couldn't help but marvel at the change. When he'd crossed the threshold for the first time roughly three years ago, it had felt like he'd been given access to an exclusive club. Snow, Lucas, Rowe, and Ian were so damn tight, and if he wanted to have a place with them, he'd known he'd have to earn it.

And the penthouse with its large, sweeping windows offering a stunning view of downtown Cincinnati, decorated in high-quality, tasteful furniture, and unique personal touches was their hub. Their headquarters. Their private clubhouse.

Jude had been to this penthouse for so many "family" meetings, emergencies, parties, dinners, and just lounging about for drinks. It had become another home for him almost as much as it was for Snow.

Now he need only take a second to look around and realize that a little girl ruled this roost. Baby paraphernalia covered nearly every surface. There were toys, boxes of diapers, wet wipes, clothes, soft blankets with dinosaurs, and more spread across the large open area. It was like a baby store had exploded across the penthouse.

"Wow," Jude breathed.

"Yeah," Andrei muttered. He came up alongside Jude with a bottle in his hand and a towel tossed over his shoulder. "Mrs. Mason has started bringing along another maid to help clean, and it still devolves into utter chaos within a day. I keep telling myself that it'll get better when we both head back to work and get into a routine with her."

Snow scoffed. "Yeah, and how's that nanny search going?"

"About how you'd expect," Andrei said with his usual smirk. While there were some dark circles under his eyes, there was a happy glow surrounding the former fighter. Andrei seemed to always have a secret happiness about him, but now he was in heaven. Married to the man who captured his heart, dream job, and now his child, Jude could see clearly that he counted himself a very lucky man, even if he was a bit tired.

"It's going just fine," Lucas growled from the staircase.

A second later a squeal came from Daciana that sounded sort of like a laugh.

Andrei chuckled and carefully took the baby from Snow. "She thinks her father's scary serious voice is funny." He then turned his attention to the little girl and cooed. "Don't you, my baby girl? You think your serious dad is funny. He's just a funny, silly man."

Jude and Snow laughed, and Lucas shook his head as he continued to descend the stairs. While not the tallest man in the room, Lucas was easily the most imposing. The self-made billionaire had spent a lifetime pursuing exactly what he wanted, whether it was happiness for his friends or a piece of property upon which to expand his empire. Lucas was used to getting what he wanted and doing whatever it took to get it. Jude smiled at his friend. In the end, what Lucas wanted was a sexy Romanian bodyguard and an adorable little girl.

"I'm not going to let just anyone look after our angel while we're at work," Lucas said a bit primly as he entered the living room.

"Of course not," Andrei said. He'd claimed one of the seats and was currently feeding Daciana her dinner.

Jude could easily imagine the detailed background checks and interviewing process the nanny applicants were going through. The search for a surrogate had been pretty damn intense, so this would certainly be no different.

As he crossed the room, Lucas paused behind Andrei's chair. He pressed a kiss to the top of Andrei's head before he so very gently placed his large hand against the back of Daciana's head, caressing her as if she were the most precious thing in his life. Lucas was normally one to tightly control his emotions, favoring haughty disdain and irritation over anything else. But when he looked at his little girl and husband, love shone from him as bright as a lighthouse beacon. They were his joy.

With one last kiss to his husband and daughter, Lucas continued over to Snow, and he hugged his oldest friend. He then grabbed Jude and pulled him in for a tight hug.

"I'm so sorry about your brother," Lucas murmured. "If you need anything, *anything*, do not hesitate to reach out to us. Andrei and I are always here for you and your family."

And Jude believed him just liked he believed Rowe. This might have been a tough, elite club to join, but once you were considered a part of their family, there was nothing these men wouldn't do to help each other out. Jude felt the same way. They had become his family just like Jordan and Carrick were.

"Thank you," Jude said, forcing those choked two words past the lump in his throat.

"Oh! Lucas! Show them the gift that the security agents sent over," Andrei said as Lucas stepped away.

Lucas walked over to a side table and picked up a box that he held out for both of them to see into. There were a pair of miniature red MMA sparring gloves and a little T-shirt that said, "My Daddy Taught Me How to Use Duct Tape." There was also a tiny Ward Security emblem on it.

Snow snickered. "You are so screwed."

"Not at all," Lucas said with a proud smile. "With all her overprotective uncles, Daciana is going to kick ass and take this world by storm."

"That she is," Jude agreed.

And with a little sigh, Jude let go some of the worry and anger that had been plaguing him. He settled on the couch next to Snow and watched while Daciana drank her dinner and slowly drifted off to sleep in her father's arms. When she was off to dreamland, Andrei carefully placed her into Jude's arms, helping to ease his internal aches just a little bit more.

He'd held his baby cousins and even delivered a few babies while working as a paramedic, but Daciana was different. She was the child of a peer, a reminder of something that he could possibly have in his life one day. Maybe. Well, maybe not.

But he could also be content being the awesome uncle. Daciana was very likely to end up with a brother or sister one day. Ian was undoubtedly going to have a brood with Hollis. Rowe and Noah…er… probably not. They were more likely to run off and raise ostriches or llamas than to have children, but they could still surprise everyone.

And even if he and Snow never had kids, all these little ones could visit Uncle Snow and Uncle Jude. They'd have sleepovers and trips to the zoo. There would be Christmases and birthday parties. And so much laughter.

"Well, I think we've definitely found a babysitter," Andrei said softly.

"Anytime you want," Jude offered. He looked over at Snow to find his lover closely watching. He couldn't read his thoughtful expression, but he was relieved when Snow easily echoed his offer of "Anytime."

With the baby settled in her nearby Pack 'n Play with a full belly and a clean diaper, dinner was ordered and delivered. The new parents were looking more than a little exhausted with dark circles under their eyes. They cleared off the dining room table of random baby items and tucked into some excellent Thai. Apparently, they'd largely been living off whatever Ian was bringing over, but Hollis was keeping him home for a few days to catch up on sleep. The chef had been splitting too much of his time between wedding planning, his restaurant Rialto, and Daciana.

"Of course, she loves Ian. He's the one with the magic touch," Lucas said.

"What?" Snow asked.

Andrei chuckled. "Every time she cries, we hand her to Ian and she instantly stops."

Lucas shook his head as he grabbed some noodles with his chopsticks. "I say it's because he smells like food every time he comes over."

"Ha!" Snow said and then winced when he realized he might have spoken too loud. When he continued, his voice was barely over a whisper. "I'm telling him you said that."

"Asshole," Lucas grumbled.

The rest of the evening passed enjoyably with them talking about lighter topics, though most of it centered around Lucas and Andrei discovering all the interesting little quirks and disasters that came with being new parents. Sleep was currently in short supply. Babies apparently had a magical ability to have more things come out of their bodies than actually went in. Lucas explaining that interesting discovery might have put both Snow and Jude nearly on the floor in tears with laughter.

Unfortunately, it also woke up Daciana.

To Jude's surprise, Snow was the first to his feet, scooping the little girl up. He cradled her close to his chest and proceeded to slowly walk around the open floor plan, rocking her and rubbing her back. Jude's heart pounded painfully in his chest as he watched the two slowly make their progress along the dark windows looking out over the city.

Lucas's hand landed on Jude's shoulder and squeezed. Jude shook his head, smiling at his own surprise. "I would never have expected this," he whispered.

"It looks like he's trying to figure something out for himself," Lucas observed.

"I've told him that I've made peace with us not having kids."

"Maybe he hasn't."

Jude looked at Lucas, who just smiled enigmatically at him. There was no one else in Cincinnati who'd known Ashton Frost longer than Lucas Vallois. And it was enough to give Jude a little hope.

"How have you been, Jude?"

And then the weight was back. He didn't blame Lucas. He knew the man was concerned for him and just wanted to help. Jude had appreciated the couple of hours' relief they'd managed to find with this wonderful little family.

"About as bad as you'd expect." Jude murmured, not wanting to disturb Daciana or her doting uncle. "We...we found some information out about the source of Jordan's injuries. He was...was beaten...and—"

"You know you aren't obligated to tell me anything," Lucas interrupted when Jude struggled to get the words out.

"I know. We found a video of him being..." Jude's voice drifted off as his throat seemed to close up. But Lucas nodded, indicating that he followed Jude's line of thought.

"Do you know who did this?"

Jude shook his head. "We've got Rowe digging into it."

He paused and looked down at his empty hands. When it came to Jordan and this whole situation, he'd never felt so helpless in his life. He'd made a career of helping other people. He'd spent his life helping out his family, working to make ends meet, and just being there for his brothers. How could he be so helpless and useless now?

"I just...I don't understand how Jordan got himself into this situation and why he didn't ask me for help before things got so bad. I feel like I've failed him. I thought he knew that I was always there for him, but he never came to me."

"You see that man in there with my daughter?" Lucas asked.

Jude looked up and a small smile lifted his lips. Andrei had turned on some low bluesy music and Snow was now rocking her in time with the music while nuzzling her little head. Snow looked so utterly content.

"That very happy man in there made me feel the exact same more times than either of us would care to count. I'm sure he's told you about his past."

Jude nodded. "He said that he's told me everything."

"I'm sure he has. And you know how close we are. But he still hated to reach out to me or Rowe. So many times he risked his life, and we had to charge in to save him. There were things he just had to figure out on his own and choices he had to make."

"So we have to sit back and let them fuck up?"

Lucas nodded. "Our job is to be there when they are ready for us and to love them."

Jude rubbed his eyes and took a deep breath. When he released it, he tried to push out some of his stress and worries with it. He didn't want to bring this negativity into Daciana's new life. "It sucks. Never expected it from Jordan."

"If you're lucky, he'll learn something from this or find what he's looking for."

Jude smirked. "How long did you have to tell yourself that when you were protecting that one?" he asked, jerking his head toward Snow.

"So many fucking years," Lucas muttered, then winked at Jude.

It was something to cling to. Jude hoped that this was just a one-off bad decision on Jordan's part that blew up in his face, but they'd be able to work it out only after his little brother woke up. And they didn't know if or when that was going to happen yet.

"If Rowe runs into a roadblock in his research, you do have a potential source at your fingertips," Lucas added.

"What?" Jude followed Lucas's gaze back to Snow.

"Snow's old world could prove to be a resource. He got involved in some dark and violent shit, but I know he was still only scratching the surface. Some of his old contacts might hear whispers or rumors. They might know something useful."

Jude stared at the man still holding the little baby, and the lump was back in his throat for a different reason. It wasn't the first time he looked at Snow and realized how close they'd come to never actually being together. He was grateful for their life with each other.

And he was beginning to wonder if Snow's dark past might actually get them closer to the truth about Jordan.

CHAPTER 13

"How do you feel about driving to Dana's again and seeing if we can get more information out of Anthony?" Jude asked as he started his Jeep.

With Lucas and Andrei keeping new-parent hours, they'd wrapped up the night early. It was only ten o'clock. The car was cold, and he shivered and turned the heat up. It promptly spit out colder air and he turned off the heat to let the vehicle warm up.

Snow rolled his head on the back of the car seat. "You sure you're up to it tonight?"

"Seeing Daciana was just what my doctor ordered, and he was right." Jude winked at him. "I'm feeling more grounded. Ready to try and get some more information out of that guy." And his heart felt so much lighter after watching Snow swaying in that living room with the tiny girl. God, a part of him wanted to cart the man home to bed but unfortunately, the bigger part just needed more answers when it came to his brother.

"Well, at least we have the right shoes for it this time," Snow drawled. They were dressed casually tonight in jeans, sneakers, and short jackets.

He'd known Snow would agree, and he reached out to put his

hand on the man's thigh. "Next vacation, we're heading somewhere out of town. Maybe we'll take up Lucas's offer on that ski chalet. You and me and the whole week in bed like we planned."

"Sounds perfect." Snow flipped on the heat. "Except maybe we'll pick somewhere warmer. Let's go see if we can find Anthony."

Jude drove them to Norwood and parked in the near-empty parking lot. Shivering as he got out of the Jeep, Jude took in the quiet neighborhood, surprised it wasn't hopping more this early in the night. He shoved his hands into his pockets and ducked his head into the wind as they walked to the bar.

Like the other night, only a few people populated the tables and bar. Anthony was nowhere to be seen. Tonight, instead of news, classic rock played faintly in the background. He looked around the bar, noticing that nobody paid them any attention, which was surprising considering they'd run out of here after someone the other night. There were a few patrons loitering around the bar and the same bearded bartender served them. He gave Snow and Jude a few suspicious looks but otherwise ignored them. He wouldn't be getting any more money out of them tonight, that was for sure.

God, this place was depressing. It could definitely use some updating. Paint and a new floor. Bleach.

He bought a couple of beers as Snow got them a table. He sat across from Snow and took in the weariness drawing his features taut. Even exhausted, his classically handsome face and sharp, light eyes drew Jude in. His silvery hair made him stand out in the dingy bar.

But then, the man had always stood out and had from the moment Jude had laid eyes on him in the hospital where they both worked. He'd heard rumors about the grouchy doctor the others called the surgeon general from the moment he'd started working at UC, and though some of those rumors had turned out to be true, the edgy man was also a warm, highly caring person underneath all that bluster. He loved with a loyal ferocity that awed Jude. And most of that love was directed his way.

Snow was his. There wasn't a doubt in his mind about that.

Jude probably shouldn't have dragged him to this dingy bar. Snow was no stranger to dangerous places, but he'd left that part of his life far behind when they'd gotten together. Jude tried to smile, but his heart was aching too much. "Thank you for standing by me through all this."

"I will always be by your side, Jude."

Jude reached across the table and took his hand. He didn't give a shit if anyone in this place had an issue with them. In fact, he was spoiling for a fight and would welcome one. He stared into Snow's eyes and thought again about how lucky he was to have found him. They were building a life that he loved. Together. And though he'd adored seeing his general with that baby tonight, whether that life held kids or not wasn't important. Just being with his lover was all he needed.

"I love you," he whispered. "So much."

"I love you, too." Snow offered him a smile that accented the sexy dip in his upper lip. "What brought that on?"

"Just thinking about how lucky I am."

"I don't know about that." Snow's grin turned wicked. "I come with my own set of challenges."

"I like a good challenge," Jude growled. "You definitely keep me on my toes."

"You're obviously a glutton for punishment."

Jude was able to give him a real smile that time. "I'm not the one who needs punishment most of the time."

Snow's eyes narrowed. "Babe, you can punish me any time you want. In fact, let's blow this joint and go home for the kind of blowing that's a lot more fun."

"Five more minutes," Jude insisted. He had a gut feeling Anthony was going to show up.

Before that five minutes was up, he was proved right. Anthony walked in the door, took one look at them, and darted back out.

"Here we go again," Snow said as he shot to his feet.

Jude jumped up and they ran to the door and pushed it open only to catch Anthony running around the corner.

"Wait," Jude yelled. *Dammit, not again!* He took off after the guy. It had started raining, which made the pavement slick. A flash of headlights blinded him as he faced the street and he lifted his hand to block the light, narrowing his gaze on Anthony, who was now running between a couple of cars.

Anthony didn't listen and started fumbling for his keys. He dropped them as Snow and Jude reached him. "Fuck!" He hit his hands on a red pickup and turned to face them. "Why the fuck are you chasing me again?"

"We just have a few questions," Jude said as he pulled his jacket tighter around his body as wind swept through the tiny parking lot. The rain did nothing to chase away a rancid smell coming from something rotting in a nearby dumpster. "You ran off before we learned anything the other night."

"You have no idea what you're getting involved with," Anthony spit out. He wiped rain off his face and hugged his scrawny arms to his chest. "Look, I feel rotten about what happened to Jordan, but just leave me the fuck alone!"

"Then give us an idea." Jude crossed his arms. "My brother is lying in a damn hospital bed, and we have no idea if he's going to pull through. Just what is he involved in?"

"I told you to check that website."

"We did. Did you hook him up with that?"

"Hell, no!" Anthony's pointy features twisted into a scowl. "I wouldn't have told him to do that. He must have felt he didn't have a choice. Listen, you two are messing with some dangerous people. Trust me, I know. And you should know too. Your brother was fucking shot. Why aren't you letting the police handle it?"

Snow pulled out his phone. "How about we call them right now? And you can tell them all about that website."

The man's face paled in the low alley light. "I have nothing to do with that!"

"Then tell us who does?" Jude demanded, taking a step closer to Anthony.

Anthony held up his hands. "Okay, damn. Tell you what, you give me money and I'll tell you."

Jude scoffed and looked up and down his twitching body. "Like we want to help with your drug habit."

"Drugs?" The guy truly looked insulted. "Who said anything about drugs? I owe money just like your brother did, and I don't want to fucking pay it off the same way. You help me and I'll help you."

"My brother owed money?" Jude narrowed in on that part of the guy's speech. If that was true, then he had been hocking his things. "How much money?"

"I don't know exactly how much he owed, but I need ten grand."

"Right." Jude barked out a laugh. "I'm not giving you ten thousand dollars."

"You want to know who filmed your brother, you help me." Anthony trembled, understandable since he was soaked and only wearing a light jacket when it was thirty-five degrees out. But he honestly did look scared, and he had from the second he'd walked into the bar. Jude had attributed it to him seeing them, but maybe there was more to the story. He did have an air of desperation that pricked at Jude's conscience.

"We'll do it," Snow snapped. "Give us a name."

"We're not giving him any money," Jude insisted, frowning at his partner.

"It's worth it if we can get to the bottom of this," Snow said before looking back at Anthony. "Tell us."

"You think I'm stupid? Money first." Anthony's dark eyes flitted from Jude to Snow.

"We don't have that kind of money in our pockets," Jude said.

Anthony rolled his eyes like he knew that. "Then meet me here tomorrow night at eight with the cash and I'll tell you what I know."

"I think you'll tell me what I want to know now."

"Or what?" Anthony scowled again. "You can't hurt me worse than the people you're after."

Frustration ate at Jude, and he realized this guy wasn't going to back down. He was obviously scared, and if he owed the same people Jordan had, it made sense. "I'll give you five." That was going to make a huge dent in his savings.

"I need ten." Anthony briefly shut his eyes. "Look, I owe this money and he's already coming after me to pay it out with my hide. I wasn't kidding about these people being dangerous. Please, I don't want to end up in the hospital like Jordan. You get him off my back, and I'll tell you all about the poker ring."

Jude perked up. "Poker ring?"

"Shit." The guy scowled. "I guess it don't hurt none to tell you that much. It's why your brother owed so much."

"I thought you said you didn't know how much he owed," Snow said.

The guy snorted. "It was more. I do know that. He got roped into the games same as I did. That's how they get you. They pull you into the smaller-staked games, and then it grows."

"You're saying my brother was gambling?"

"How did you think he came to owe so much money?"

"Why in hell would we trust you?" Jude asked, snarling. "You could just give us the name. You don't have to extort us for money."

"Out of the goodness of my heart?" He snorted.

"You promise to meet us in the bar tomorrow night, and we'll be here with the money," Snow said. "And no more fucking running."

Though Jude didn't agree with giving up ten thousand dollars, he was desperate. It would hack an even larger hole into his savings, but finding out who'd shot Jordan…who'd filmed him being raped…was worth it. "We'll be back here tomorrow night, and you'd better have a name for us."

"I will."

Furious, Jude turned to go to their Jeep. "You think he'll show up? We should have just beaten the name out of him."

"Like you would do that." Snow stopped him with a hand on his arm. "That guy is terrified. Maybe if we help him, he'll be able to get away from these people."

Jude stared at him. He didn't want to help that guy, and it went against everything he usually stood for. But here he was, in front of a man who everyone thought was cold-blooded, and he could see that

Snow meant it. He smirked and pulled Snow in for a kiss, noting his nose was cold. "You're a good man, General."

"Come on. Let's go by the hospital and check on your brother, then go home."

They reached the Jeep just as there were two loud shots. Snow's wild gaze met his, and they both ducked down behind the vehicle as another car peeled past them.

"Fucking gunshots," Snow said. "They came from where Anthony was. Call 9-1-1!"

Cursing under his breath as he ran toward Anthony, Jude pulled out his phone to scroll until he found the number for dispatch. He could see one wound on Anthony's chest right away. Snow kneeled beside the man. "Cara, it's Jude Torres. I'm off duty but need to report a shooting. We've got one man down with two GSWs—one to the chest, so I'm going to need a rig here ASAP. Call the cops, too. The shooter is gone. Is there a supe around?"

He listened for a moment, then gave Cara their location and thanked her. His training kicked in, and he fell to his knees next to Anthony.

Snow had ripped off his jacket and was applying it firmly to the wound on Anthony's chest, trying to stem the bleeding. Blood pooled under his hands, and the rain had it soaking his clothes and turning the concrete underneath him dark. Anthony was gasping, eyes wide and terrified.

Jude did a quick head-to-toe assessment, trying to locate the second wound. After finding a dark patch on Anthony's inner thigh, Jude cursed again. The amount of blood seeping into his jeans meant the bullet had likely hit the femoral artery. He stuck his fingers into the hole in the denim and ripped it wider to expose the area and assess the damage. A steady pulsing of bright red blood gushed out of the wound. He blinked away the cold rain from his eyes as he quickly put his left palm over the bullet hole and applied as much pressure as he could.

Christ, it was bad.

Jude knew his prognosis wasn't good. It would be several minutes before an ambulance could get to them and he'd lost a lot of blood already. There was a good chance he would bleed out before they could get him to a hospital. "Do you see a stick anywhere?" he asked Snow, thinking to use it to help make a tourniquet.

"No, try using the sleeves of your jacket. It's all we got."

"Try to stay calm, Anthony," he murmured, knowing that the panic would only increase his blood pressure and cause the blood to pump out faster. He yanked off his jacket and tied the arms around the top of Anthony's leg, pulling hard to get it as tight as possible.

Anthony didn't seem to hear the words and he started to thrash, coughing up frothy blood the rain washed down his cheeks.

Snow leaned down into his face. "You have to stay still and calm. An ambulance is on its way. Can you hear the sirens?"

Jude had never been more thankful to hear that noise. Anthony's stare began to haze over, and he lost consciousness.

As the paramedics arrived, he and Snow filled them in and the police tried to pull them over for questioning, but Snow, as the highest level of care, hopped into the ambulance. Jude ran to their Jeep and followed. The police could question them at the hospital.

Anthony had lost too much blood, and Jude would be shocked if he survived.

CHAPTER 14

Snow groaned softly and stretched out in the bed as his body sank into the blissfully comfortable mattress and buttery soft sheets. Holy crap, everything hurt. How in the world was he so damn tired? He'd put in eighteen-hour shifts at the hospital and didn't feel this drained.

But the night hadn't gone as they had planned. The visit with Daciana and family had been wonderful, but things had quickly turned to shit after meeting with Anthony. There had been nothing he could do to save the young man. He'd died en route to the hospital. He looked like he couldn't have been more than a few years older than Jordan, and his life was over. Too much of his job was spent trying in vain to save the lives of people who didn't value what they had. Senseless violence and drugs. They were both sucking the life out of this city.

Another couple of hours were spent answering questions for the cops, but they really didn't have any answers. They'd had to come clean about following up on Jordan's activities, but they were honest about the fact that they didn't have a clue as to who shot Anthony.

And why had Anthony been shot? Was it because he'd run out of time to hand over the money he'd owed? Or was it because he'd been spotted talking to him and Jude?

His entire body felt like it had become one giant tense knot of muscles. He'd spent more than a week sitting in uncomfortable waiting room chairs, hours ticking by as they hoped for some shred of positive news on Jordan. The nonactivity was broken up with more stress and trying to track down Anthony so they could identify the fucker who hurt Jordan in the first place. And now the one source of information they did have was dead.

He hated to admit it, but he was starting to look forward to heading back to work. The days were long and exhausting, but there was a predictability to it all that his body liked.

When they finally got home from the hospital, they'd both showered quickly and dropped into bed like lifeless lumps.

Next to him, Jude sighed and rolled over, sliding one of his legs across Snow's. "You okay, General?"

"I have bad news. I'm old."

Jude hummed, nuzzling Snow's shoulder so that the day's growth on his cheeks scraped along his bare skin. "You're not old. Forty isn't old. I thought forty was the new thirty."

"You know that's all bullshit, right?"

He could feel more than hear Jude chuckle against him. "You're my sexy silver fox."

"You're lucky I'm too exhausted to kick your ass." Turning enough in the bed to reach Jude's lips, he brushed a soft kiss across his mouth. "Get some sleep."

"Mmmm...yes. Sleep. Then I'll make you moan for me in the morning."

Snow's dick stirred slightly at the promise, but the rest of his body just laughed. He might live for sex with Jude, but he was content to catch up on some sleep for one night. They had plenty of time to worship each other's bodies.

Jude had barely finished speaking before his breathing evened out. A few seconds later a soft snore slipped from him. He was already out.

Snow nearly sighed with relief. Jude had gone far too many nights recently without getting some decent sleep. He was willing to bet that Jude's body was just finally giving out and overpowering the worry that plagued him on a constant basis. Snow wished his lover would get a full night's sleep this time so he could get on the road to healing himself.

Closing his eyes, Snow focused on the sound of Jude's breathing and the feel of his warm body against his. Images of Anthony's body flashed across his brain, blood soaking into his clothes and sliding across the dark pavement. There was nothing he could have done to save the young man even if he'd been there the second he'd been shot.

The muffled sound of breaking glass had Snow bolting upright in the bed. Jude gasped and jerked upright as well, flailing a bit on the covers.

"What? What was that?" he mumbled.

Snow was already on his feet, grabbing a pair of sweat pants off the nearby dresser. "One of the windows was broken downstairs. Sounded like toward the back in the kitchen."

The darkness of the room was lit up by the screen of both their phones. Without looking, he knew that it was one of the protection agents at Ward Security calling. Before they even moved into the house, Rowe had his people crawling all over it, installing a state-of-the-art home security system free of charge. The only thing they paid for was a highly discounted monthly monitoring fee. Rowe called it a housewarming present, but Snow knew that Rowe did it so that he could be sure his family was safe at all times.

"Where are you going?" Jude threw back the covers and grabbed for his own pants on a chair close to his side of the bed.

"I need you to answer the phone and tell them that someone has broken into the house. Then take the baseball bat from under the bed and go to the guest room. Stay there until I come for you."

"Are you fucking kidding me? You are *not* going downstairs alone and unarmed, General," Jude snarled. The words came out sounding as if he was clenching his teeth.

"I can take care of myself."

"Ashton!" Jude said in an angry whisper. Jude hardly ever used his real name, so this was not a good sign. Some sneaky part of his brain knew that Jude was right. He was being overprotective, but after seeing Anthony shot and Jordan hanging on by a threat, Snow needed Jude to stay safe.

"We can't go down together. The staircase is too narrow. Wait up here with the bat. Go to the spare bathroom or the guest room. If someone gets past me to attack you up here, he will come to the master bedroom first. You can strike from behind."

He could have sworn he heard Jude growl at him before he finally nodded. "I'm giving you two minutes, and then I'm coming down behind you."

A part of him wanted to cross the room and kiss him one last time before descending the stairs, but they'd already wasted too much time arguing about their options. Besides, there wasn't a last time. He was going to survive this. Jude was going to survive this. They had so many more kisses in their future.

Opening the bedroom door a crack, Snow peered out through the slender opening. A night-light was burning in the hallway, casting a pale, yellow glow. They'd added it over a year ago for a member of Jude's family who'd stayed the night so he could find his way to the bathroom in the darkness. They'd just never bothered to take it down again. The hallway was empty, and he heard no additional noises from the first floor.

He imagined that the intruders had broken the glass in the back door in the kitchen that led to the patio. By now, they should have managed to unlock the door and were likely in the kitchen. He had to keep them from reaching the stairs and the second floor.

His heart thudded painfully in his chest as he crept out of the room and across the short distance to the stairs. Pausing at the edge of the wall, he peered down into the thick darkness of the lower level. There was no movement within the shadows. He started forward again, but immediately stopped. Ears straining. There was a distant scrape and a crackle of fracturing glass. Someone was crossing the kitchen. Possibly stepping on the broken glass from the window or door. He needed to hurry.

Balancing on the balls of his feet, Snow quickly and silently descended the stairs, expertly skipping over the third stair from the bottom. A poorly hammered nail when the stairs were built now creaked under any pressure. Snow had lain awake far too many nights, waiting to hear Jude hit that step after a long shift, announcing that he was finally home safe and about to crawl into bed.

Jude knew that creak too. He'd listen for it while he waited for his chance to join in the fight. It was one of the few little early warnings they had in this very new home.

As he reached the ground floor, Snow grabbed a large jar candle Rebecca had given them as part of a housewarming gift. The candle and glass had a nice weight, and he could comfortably wrap his hand around it. Not a great weapon, but it was the best he could do on short notice. He'd been tempted to grab the gun he kept in a lockbox in the bedroom closet, but the truth was that the damn thing had gotten buried under random shit over the past years, thanks to a quieter life. He wasn't even sure if he had ammunition for the thing anymore.

Snow paused in the hall as he heard footsteps crossing the living room toward the front door and the staircase leading to the second floor. Silently, he drew in a deep breath and waited. There was just enough light from the front windows and a nearby streetlight that he caught a glimpse of the man's harsh features before he brought the candle down hard on the man's head. The glass broke, and Snow was vaguely aware of it slicing into the palm of his hand, but his main focus was on the intruder collapsing to the floor in a motionless heap.

Another man swore, but Snow didn't catch what he said. He swung out with his right, knocking away the gun the man was raising. A wild shot brought a flash of light before it clattered to the hardwood floor. The sound was deafening in the enclosed space, leaving a ringing in Snow's ears.

The man recovered quickly. A fist slammed into Snow's jaw, snapping his head to the right and causing him to stumble backward a step. Pain exploded across his face. He managed to dodge a second blow and backhand his attacker with his left. A new jolt of pain lanced along his palm from the cut. He could feel his hand growing wetter as blood coated it and ran down his wrist.

With a grunt, the man came at him again, but Snow was ready. Adrenaline coursed through his system and dulled the pain in his body. He landed two more punches, sending the man backpedaling. The bastard tripped backward over a low ottoman. He reached out with both hands, trying to save himself from falling, and snagged Snow's arm, jerking him off balance. The larger man's weight pulled them both down into a heap on the floor.

"General!" Jude shouted as Snow tried to untangle himself from the other man. There was another loud cry, and then Snow caught a blur of motion as it looked like Jude launched himself off the stairs onto the man who had just picked himself up off the hallway floor. There was a loud thud as they both hit the floor and possibly the front door.

Snow didn't have the chance to join Jude and lend him a hand. The man he was struggling with had broken free and kicked him hard in the stomach. Air rushed out of his lungs and Snow instinctively curled into a ball to protect himself. The attacker tried to kick him a second time, but Snow caught his foot and gave it a good jerk, twisting it until the man screamed. He kicked out with his free foot, clipping Snow's chin. Everything went bright white for a second and he released the man's foot.

"Fucker," the attacker snarled. "Keep your fucking nose out of our business, or you're both dead."

Jude shouted and Snow fought to sit upright while trying to get his damn head to clear. Where the hell was Jude?

The other intruder said something that sounded like a curse, and then their footsteps thundered back the way he came. Snow scrambled around the overturned furniture and through the house in time to see the two intruders exit through the rear door with the broken window pane.

"Snow!" Jude shouted. He sounded closer as if he was coming through the living room.

"I'm here. I'm fine," Snow shouted back. "Be careful. There's broken glass."

A moment later, a light in the living room popped on and Snow blinked against the brightness, trying to get his eyes to adjust. When he could see, he found the living room in shambles. They'd fallen over the ottoman and knocked over the coffee table in their struggle. The chair had gotten shoved at one point, tipping over an end table. More glass glittered across the floor from either a glass they'd left out or a picture frame.

Jude was standing in the middle of the chaos with a baseball bat still in hand. "I heard a fucking gunshot," Jude snapped. His nose was bloody, and it looked like his left eye was starting to swell from his fight with the man Snow had initially managed to knock out. Jude carefully stepped over the ottoman to get in Snow's face. "You came down here unarmed. I was not about to leave you alone."

A smirk pulled up one corner of his mouth. As much as he wanted to be mad at Jude for putting himself in danger, he knew he couldn't without being a massive douchebag hypocrite. He would have done the same if their roles were reversed.

"Thanks," Snow murmured

Jude groaned before he reached up and grabbed a handful of Snow's hair, pulling him forward for a brutal kiss. "You make me insane."

"This was not my fault."

"Not this time, at least." Jude released him and stepped back. "What did that asshole say to you?"

"Threatened me...us, really," Snow said. He paused and rubbed his sore chin. "Told us to keep our noses out of their business."

"That's annoyingly vague," Jude muttered. He tossed his bat onto the nearby couch and sighed. "But considering that this happened the same night as Anthony getting shot—"

"And we're not involved in any other kind of shady investigation at the moment," Snow quickly added.

"I guess this is about Jordan and that gambling ring. Someone is afraid of us getting too close to the truth."

Snow nodded and winced. His head was starting to fucking ache. "That's usually a good sign."

"I could have done without it," Jude muttered. Snow had to agree. "The police are on their way and so are Rowe and Noah."

"Are we going to tell them the real reason for the break-in?"

Jude stared at the mess around them for several seconds, his lips pressed together in a hard, thin line before he finally shook his head.

Snow frowned down at the chaos around them as well. He had to agree with Jude on this. He didn't want to involve the police now. Those men had invaded his home, threatened the well-being of his lover. Snow was all too happy to handle this personally.

It was probably for the best that the Masters of Mayhem were on their way. He wasn't fond of ruining their sleep, but Rowe and Noah could offer some insight and valuable advice on what to do next.

"What the fuck happened to your hand?" Jude said, reaching for it.

"Cut it on the glass when I broke that candle over his head," Snow answered while Jude carefully inspected it.

Jude snorted. "And Rebecca thought we'd never use it. This doesn't look too deep. Might need stitches."

"Luckily, I'm a doctor." Jude just rolled his eyes at him. "What about you?"

Jude smirked. "Nothing a bag of frozen peas won't help. It's a shame the one guy woke up. We could have finally used the kitten duct tape Rowe gave us as a housewarming present."

"Fucking Rowe," Snow muttered under his breath. The man had the most twisted sense of humor. He had no idea where Rowe got his strange supply of duct tape, but he made sure that all his friends had several rolls on hand for occasions just such as this.

He might as well put on a pot of coffee. Between the report they'd have to file with the cops and the upcoming conversation with Rowe and Noah, they wouldn't be getting any sleep for a few hours.

CHAPTER 15

"Are you sure you're cool with Sergeant being here, too?" Snow asked as he settled on a barstool in Ian's kitchen. Sergeant was busy inspecting his surroundings, running from room to room. Their cat was strictly indoors and had long exhausted his exploration of their home, so he seemed to be in heaven.

Snow loved the open floor plan of Ian's condominium—the kitchen being separated by a breakfast bar and everything exposed to the living and dining area. Morning sunlight streamed in through the windows. They'd arrived in the middle of the night after the cops had left, and Rowe had insisted they not stay at home until the place was secure again. Just a night or two. Rowe had walked out, muttering about new tech and motion-sensor cameras. For now, the cops were left to work off the belief that Snow and Jude had thwarted a burglary attempt. "We would have stayed at Rowe's, but his dogs and our cat refuse to be buddies."

Ian got down coffee beans and scooped them into a grinder. The blond streaks in the shorter, slender man's brown hair shone in the bright kitchen. "Are you kidding? I'm thrilled you came here. For once I get to be of help. I'm assuming you didn't go to the penthouse because of little Daci."

"Of course. I wish we hadn't gone there last night now. I had no idea I would be putting her in danger." Snow frowned. "But I shouldn't be putting you in danger either. If you're really okay with our cat being here, Jude and I are getting a hotel if we need to be out another night."

"You sure as hell aren't!" Ian put his hands on his hips, a scowl on his cute face. "You guys are always trying to protect me and for once, you came to me for help. Don't take that away from me now." Ian turned to transfer the coffee grounds to the pot. "I'm thrilled you're here and I'm not afraid of whatever it is you've gotten yourselves into. You always went to the others for help in the past, so let me have this."

It wasn't long before the scent of fresh brewing coffee filled the bright kitchen. Ian bustled about as he got out the ingredients for French toast. Snow sighed, feeling a bit of warmth in his chest for the first time since holding Daciana. And he'd never admit what that did to him and the thoughts that tiny baby had him rethinking.

But here, in the warmth of Ian's kitchen, Snow felt at peace. Ian had that effect on him and had from the moment he'd first met him many years before. Ian had been in a rough situation against his will and Snow, Lucas, and Rowe had yanked him out of it, then took him in as their own. He didn't feel fatherly toward the younger man, but his affection went beyond that of a mere friend.

Jude had gone to the hospital to see his brother after catching a couple of hours' sleep, and Snow hadn't only because Ian talked him into staying for breakfast. Jude had also promised to make it a short visit before he returned.

It didn't sit right with him being separated from Jude, though. Not with them obviously now in the sights of whoever had shot Jude's brother. And now Anthony.

Snow felt bad about that—they truly hadn't meant to put that guy in danger with their questions, though they had no way of knowing if that had anything to do with them. Far as they knew, Anthony's time to pay up had run out.

"What's going on exactly?" Ian drenched a thick piece of bread in his egg mixture and set it on the griddle. The scent of cinnamon, bourbon, and vanilla joined the coffee as he dredged another piece.

Snow's stomach growled. "You know about Jude's brother, Jordan?"

Ian nodded. "Rowe and Lucas have kept me filled in. I know he's in the hospital and that he was beaten."

"And shot."

"And let me guess, you and Jude are trying to figure out who did it instead of letting the police handle it."

"The police are taking care of their side of things, but Jude is determined to figure out what was going on with his brother." He didn't plan to tell Ian about the video, not with the young man's difficult past. But mostly because this was Jude's story to share should he decide to. "We've stumbled into some bad stuff, but we aren't really any closer to figuring things out than we were the first night. Well, not much anyway. Someone we were questioning got killed last night."

"So, the bad guys are on to you two?" Ian took the golden toast off the griddle and added another piece.

Hollis came into the kitchen and walked up to Ian to wrap his arms around him and nuzzle his neck. The big guy made Ian look small because he towered over Ian's five-foot-nine-inch height. Ian turned to lean up into a kiss. "Good morning," he murmured. "Got time for bourbon French toast?"

"I can grab one on the way out. Smells fantastic." Hollis turned toward Snow and gave him a pointed frown. "What fresh hell have you brought to my home, Frost?"

"Don't you dare make him feel unwelcome," Ian growled as he turned back to his batter. "I want him to feel safe here."

"And I want *you* to be safe, so sue me." Hollis smacked a kiss on top of Ian's head and grabbed a piece of toast.

"Don't you want that with the maple syrup?" Ian asked. "I brought home the good stuff from the restaurant."

"No time. This is good by itself. Nice and crispy."

Snow watched them interact, remembering a time when he hadn't wanted the gruff ex-cop anywhere near Ian. He'd been wrong. So wrong. The man was perfect for his friend. Still, he wanted to reassure him that he wouldn't deliberately bring danger to Ian's door.

"I'm pretty sure whoever came after us last night was just sending a warning. They didn't seem to be trying to kill us, just frighten us. Rowe's people are looking into it for us. We just needed a place to stay while our house gets put to rights, then we'll be out of your hair." Snow frowned. "But I do think a hotel would be a better idea."

Ian shot him a warning look that made him smother a grin. He did not pull off fierce nearly as well as he obviously thought he did. Not with that silly apron on. This one didn't have a funny saying on it like the others Snow had seen him wear, but it was bright yellow with a happy face on it.

While Ian finished the French toast, Snow got up to pour himself a cup of coffee. Ian was a bit of a coffee snob, so he knew the first sip would be wonderful. And it was. He sighed and took another before resettling on the barstool.

"I have to go in for a few hours, but I'll be back around noon." Hollis grabbed another piece of toast and grinned at the frowning Ian. "It's good like this, too. Promise."

Ian was a bit of a stickler about how his food was served, but all he did was shake his head as he plated a couple of thick pieces of toast on a plate and drizzled them with syrup before placing them in front of Snow. Snow planned to indulge while he was here. He could hit the gym later.

His first bite of the sweet breakfast made him moan. "You're missing out," he warned Hollis, who just smirked, kissed Ian one more time, and headed for the door. On his way out, he let in Jude. Snow turned to watch him as he came into the kitchen, noting the tense shoulders.

"No change, huh?"

Jude shook his head. "He's fighting though, so there's hope."

"There is always hope," Ian said, moving to hug Jude.

His big boyfriend wrapped his arms around Ian, and Snow

couldn't help but appreciate how much his man adored one of his best friends.

"Sit," Ian ordered. "I have fresh toast coming up here in a sec."

"You don't have to tell me twice," Jude said as he settled on the stool next to Snow. When Ian slid a plate in front of Jude, he picked up a fork. "Any word from Rowe?"

Snow shook his head. "He called a few minutes ago, and I told him we were about to have breakfast."

Ian laughed. "Then he'll be here any moment."

Jude took a bite of the toast and groaned. "Oh, yeah." He looked at Snow. "Did you fill Ian in?"

"Not on everything. I wasn't sure how much you wanted to share."

"Go ahead. More heads are better when it comes to this."

Ian took his own plate and stood on the other side of the island to eat his breakfast, but he was all ears.

"What we've been able to discern so far is that Jordan owed money to some pretty bad people because of a poker game or maybe a bunch of poker games." Snow took another bite of his toast.

"They beat him and shot him?" Ian asked. "Not the best way to get their money back."

"Oh, he paid, trust me." Jude made a noise in his throat and set his fork down.

Ian, concerned, stared at him before he turned and got Jude a cup of coffee. He set it down in front of him, then laid a hand on his wrist. "You think the beating was the payback?"

Jude looked at Snow and nodded.

"The beating came from a video. We found a website where they post videos of non-consent. Jordan was in one."

Ian put his shaking hand over his mouth, his face going pale.

"Yeah," Snow said. "It was bad. But we found all this after tracking down the guy who got killed last night. He owed the same people money, it seemed."

"You guys are really caught up in something bad." There was a knock on the front door and sure enough, Rowe came striding into the house.

"I heard breakfast and came as fast as I could." He grinned at Ian.

Ian, still shaky and pale, seemed thankful for the interruption as he went back to his bread and batter.

Rowe frowned and lifted an eyebrow at Snow.

"We just caught him up to speed."

"So, I can talk freely?" Rowe asked.

"Go ahead," Jude said, turning toward him. "You have information?"

"I do." Rowe walked into the kitchen and poured himself a cup of coffee. He went to the refrigerator, completely at home, and pulled out the half-and-half creamer. After he doctored his coffee, he leaned against the counter and stared at Snow. "You're not going to like this, but we found the tattooed man from the video. His name is Donald Banks."

"That doesn't ring any bells for me," Snow admitted, confused.

"He has ties to a guy named Phoenix Phillips. That ring any bells?"

Snow shut his eyes as his past swarmed up to blacken his vision.

"Who is that?" Jude asked.

"Someone I used to know," Snow answered in a low voice filled with shame. "And he's not someone you want to know. Remember that sex club I took you to? He was one of the organizers."

"Terrific," Jude muttered, pushing his plate away. "So, what now?"

Ian, who'd been quiet as he prepared a meal for Rowe, set the plate down in front of him and walked around the island to Jude. "Either Snow or I contact him."

"Oh, hell no," Snow said, getting to his feet. "You aren't going anywhere near that fucker."

"But I know him, too," Ian admitted, his voice low. "He used to run in Jagger's circles."

"Ian," Rowe said. "I'm with Snow. You're staying out of this. Jagger is dead and this part of your past is closed permanently."

"But I can help this time."

"And so can Snow," Jude said. "I have to agree with them."

"You guys are always protecting me! When are you going to realize I'm a grown fucking man now?" He took off his apron and threw it over a chair. Underneath, he was dressed in fashionable torn jeans and a maroon sweater. He swiped a hand through his short, streaked hair.

"I don't know why we're arguing about this." Snow snapped. "All I have to do is contact him and see if he can give me a location on this Donald."

Jude buried his head in his hands. "Fuck. Why didn't Jordan just come to me? I can't believe this." He lifted his face to Snow, his expression bleak. "I don't want you involved in any of that either. Not again."

"You want to find this guy or not?" Snow knew his tone was harsh, but he didn't like this any more than the rest of them did. He'd moved past all that crap and wanted it to stay in his past as much as Jude did.

Rowe cleared his throat, bringing their attention back to him. "This isn't going to be as simple as a phone call. Plus, you don't have to. I have the location of the next club gathering."

"How the hell did you get that?" Snow asked. "It's not like they have an online calendar."

Rowe shrugged. "Cole is good at what he does. I only hire the best."

"So I go." Snow shrugged. "I can still move in those circles easier than any of the rest of us."

"I need some air," Jude announced before he walked out the door to the deck. A cold wind slipped through the opening, chilling the warmth that had flooded the room just minutes ago.

"Let him go," Rowe said when Snow moved to follow. "There's more."

Snow sat back down, the knot in his stomach tightening.

"This Donald guy is a wanted man. Assault and rape. He's done this before, it seems. You find his location, drop a tip to the authorities, and he's snapped up. I'd rather you did that than whatever that angry man"—he pointed toward the deck—"has planned in his upset mind right now."

"Then why not just tip them off to the next club meeting?" Ian asked.

"Because it would be better if Snow went and made sure he was there."

"I hate the thought of you going to one of those places again." Ian crossed his arms. "I'm serious. I don't like this plan at all."

"Neither do I, Ian," Snow murmured. "I turned my life around, thanks to you and especially thanks to that man outside. I wouldn't do anything to jeopardize what I have with him, and reintroducing him to my past isn't going to do us any favors."

"Then just call the fucking police!" Ian yelled.

"Whoa." Rowe came around the bar to put his hands on Ian's shoulders. "You know how we do these things. Noah and I'll be there as backup. Snow won't be in any danger—not really."

"Jordan is really caught up in that world?" Ian's voice was small.

"He really is."

"God, he's such a kid."

"And you know more than most, that's what some like. The young ones." Rowe snarled. "That may be blunt, but it's the truth."

"Then we have to help him. He's a sweet guy, and I hate knowing he's caught up in all that." He looked at their half-finished plates. "In fact, I'm calling in today and taking Anna some food in the hospital. But for the record, I say again, I hate this plan."

"It wouldn't be a Snow and Rowe plan if you loved it." Rowe smirked.

Ian's shoulders slumped as he looked from Rowe to Snow. "Should we call Lucas? It feels weird not having him involved."

"No!" Rowe and Snow said in unison. Rowe grinned at Snow, and he shook his head.

"Let Lucas and Andrei focus on Daci for now," Snow said.

"Lucas would just try to plan the hell out of this little mission, sucking all the fun out of it," Rowe added.

Snow shook his head. His friend had the strangest idea of what constituted fun. "Lucas knows enough of what's happening. We'll loop him in later."

"The next club meet is in two days. But remember, no going after this Donald yourself. He's wanted for fucking rape, so he's going down when he's caught."

"Got it."

Rowe looked outside. "He going to be okay?"

Snow followed his gaze to find Jude leaning on the railing, the wind ruffling his hair. "He's one of the strongest people I know."

"You sure attract a type." Rowe rinsed out his coffee mug and hugged Ian. "I gotta make tracks. I'll call you later. Thanks for breakfast. It rocked."

"You're the only one who finished."

"It's good," Snow insisted. "I just got a little nauseous at the reminder of the video."

Ian, who knew Jordan through family gatherings, went pale again. "Rowe said that guy is wanted for rape…"

Snow nodded, lips tight. "The video was bad."

"Oh, God." He shut his eyes. "And Jude watched it?" His eyes flew open. "Anna didn't, right?"

"Anna doesn't know about it and never will, if we're lucky."

"Good." He hugged himself and Rowe wrapped his arms around the thinner man. They were the same height, but Rowe was built like a tank while Ian was slender. Ian had thankfully never been caught up in any videos, but the life he'd led before Snow and his friends had found him had been horrifying. He'd been basically sold by his parents to pay off a debt as a teen and had lived with a horrible man for years. So, videos no, but Ian was well aware of what the people in those circles did and last Snow heard, he still had nightmares.

He wondered if those had eased at all.

Rowe left and Snow got up to help clean the kitchen. He could see Jude through the window over the sink and his heart ached for his partner.

"I'm so sorry about his brother, Snow. I really like Jordan and I'm pulling for him. Do you think Anna would appreciate some company today?"

"She loves you, so of course she would."

"Are you really up to going to that club?"

He turned and leaned against the counter. "Honestly? No. I said good-bye to all that and did so happily."

"I know." Ian smiled. "Jude is so good for you."

"He's incredible. I couldn't be happier."

"You know what's incredible? All of us finding the perfect mates. Just a few years ago we only had each other, and now we have these extended families—especially you. I got such a kick out of the last family gathering Anna invited me to. So many people!"

"Jude's family is daunting, but for the most part, they're lovely, accepting people. We haven't had any issues with them."

Ian looked outside. "You can't let Jude do anything he'll regret. He's a good man, Snow. One of the best I've ever met."

"I know." Snow stared at Jude, his love for the man swelling in his chest. "I won't."

CHAPTER 16

This was nothing like the sex club that Snow had taken him to years ago. This one was in someone's home. A sprawling monstrosity set back in a treed neighborhood. Rowe was there for backup, and he gave them a wave from his truck as they parked down the street. They weren't wearing earpieces this time—he was only in place for an emergency since they planned on calling the cops.

Thankfully, it wasn't raining tonight, but the cold wind was a bitch. Jude was glad for the thick Tom Ford coat he'd borrowed from Snow. He looked at the man, admiring the fit of his brown Brioni cashmere topcoat. It suited his long, lean frame perfectly and he remembered when Ian had talked him into the purchase. Ian sure knew his stuff. Snow looked so sharp in it. They both wore suits under the fancy coats, but Jude still half expected them to be turned away at the door.

The man who greeted them recognized Snow instantly.

"Ah, haven't seen you in years, Ashton. Last I heard you'd hooked up permanently."

"Still have, Bill." Snow nodded toward Jude. "We were interested in observing only tonight."

"Spicing things up, eh? Well, tonight's show is a little bondage session that starts in about fifteen minutes, so you're just in time. And this one is extra special tonight. Wait until you see."

Jude's gut churned. He didn't have a problem with BDSM, and in fact liked things a little rough here and there, but he had a gut feeling this wasn't going to be like any show he'd seen before. Not that he'd ever frequented these kinds of parties...

They walked inside to find the place packed with people. It never failed to surprise him how many were involved in this underground scene. But tonight wasn't about men who looked underage like the last place Snow had taken him.

In fact, this was more...tame. Felt like a cocktail party. Almost. People were in various stages of dress from suits down to a few who were completely naked. Those were mostly being led around by leashes. None of this bothered him, and there were a few guys in leather who looked pretty damn good.

But his mind was on finding the one tattooed guy who'd hurt Jordan.

He wouldn't be able to stay neutral then.

"Remember," Snow murmured into his ear, his breath warm on Jude's neck. "This Donald guy has a warrant out for him. We see him, we leave, and we call the cops. It's that simple."

But it wasn't that simple.

Jude wanted a piece of the guy. He wanted to wail on him with his own fists, hear him plead and beg the same way Jordan had. Wanted the man to feel pain and fear the same as his brother.

Unfortunately, Jude hadn't realized how hard it would be to spot him in this crowd. There were lots of tattoos. Lots of big, muscular men. And he'd worn a mask in the video. Jude focused in on arms. The man from the video had a decorative skull with an owl on his right bicep. Jude was sure he'd recognize it.

The one nice thing was that he didn't stand out at all looking over the bodies because everyone was looking. And a lot of people were on display. There were dancers in every corner—slim, sinuous-looking men who thankfully looked old enough to be here. He couldn't have stomached seeing anyone underage. And there were couples with leashes who had their subs on display—one had his sub on some kind of wooden pedestal. One Dom in particular wore nothing more than a leather jockstrap. He caught Snow eyeing his ass and couldn't help but grin at him.

"Can't say the scenery is bad," Snow said.

"I'd have to agree," Jude murmured back as he took in a couple in the corner making out. While this wasn't his usual scene, he could appreciate the aesthetics of a room full of mostly attractive men.

Soft music with a heavy, thumping beat played behind the conversation noise, and the few pieces of black leather furniture in the room had people in various states of dress on them. One couch held a couple who obviously didn't need any privacy as they provided live porn to the room. The shorter man was all top and he fucked into his bigger partner with force. Jude watched them for a few moments, because it was damn hot, until Snow tugged him toward the bar in the corner and asked for bourbon. Jude didn't much care what he held in his hand—he didn't plan on drinking a thing.

Glancing over at his companion, there was no missing that Snow was struggling. He stood with his back to the room and his eyes locked on the glass tightly clenched in his hand. His face seemed paler than normal, and a bead of sweat gathered at his temple even though the house wasn't particularly hot.

While he'd told Jude that he'd never been into participating in *scenes*, he'd frequented parties worse than this one in the past. But he hadn't missed how Snow's sharp eyes went over everyone in the room as they passed through or how he looked faintly uncomfortable. Did anyone else recognize Snow?

Had any of these men slept with Snow?

Jude wasn't the type to be jealous, not when he knew he had the doctor's complete heart, but the thought was a little disconcerting.

"Are you okay?" Jude asked, his voice barely reaching over a whisper.

Snow gave a jerky nod and when he finally spoke, his voice sounded as if it had been rubbed raw with sandpaper. "Never thought I'd be back here."

Jude watched him for a moment. Snow had been up-front about his past, but they'd never really discussed it. He'd just laid out the information and then worked to distract Jude from the information by any means necessary. And Jude had let him because it eased Snow's pain as much as his own.

"Was it all bad?"

Snow looked over at him, surprise widening his blue eyes and helping to remove some of the lines of strain. "No," he admitted. One corner of his mouth tilted up in a tentative smile. "It wasn't all bad. And it definitely didn't start that way. But it got darker as time passed and the deeper I went into…this." He finished, slowly turning back to face the room, his drink in hand like a lifeline. "It was like I got sucked down into the mire and couldn't get out." He softly sighed. "I don't think I really wanted to get out. Didn't have a good enough reason."

Jude reached up and placed his hand against Snow's cheek. "Until now."

"I never wanted you to see this," Snow murmured. Shame and pain blazed in his eyes. "It's one thing to tell you, but for it to be right here in your face is worse."

Jude pulled him close and slowly kissed him, again and again, until he felt Snow relax against him. "You have nothing to be ashamed of. I love you. All of you. Past, present, and the future we have together."

"I love you too."

When Jude stepped back and looked around the room again, he definitely noticed a few men giving Snow welcome looks. And yeah, some were very familiar.

Jude couldn't help but smile as he threaded the fingers of their free hands together. Snow lifted an eyebrow, then smirked and fuck, if that wasn't the sexiest fucking look. For a moment, he forgot why they were there and thought about taking Snow home for their own live porn show. But only for a moment, because the air in the room changed.

A hush fell over the crowd as a man strolled into the area. He was the right height and build as the one they were looking for, but he wore a shirt with the sleeves rolled up to his elbows so Jude couldn't see if he had any tattoos. A mask covered half his face, and Jude's heart kicked over with adrenaline when he realized this could be the same man. He tried to remember the shape of his mouth, but all he could remember was the toothy grin and his brother's cries.

It was all he could do not to stomp forward and rip off the man's sleeves to see if the owl tattoo was on his upper arm.

Another man was led into the room. He was blindfolded, his head whipping right and left as if he tried to see through the black mask. Jude's back went instantly up because that didn't look like a willing expression on the part of his face they could see. There was no way in hell he could stand by and watch something if both parties weren't here voluntarily. This guy was breathing fast and whimpering—obviously terrified.

Nobody said a word, but a few of the expressions around Jude gave him hope. Some looked uncertain about the situation they'd found themselves in. He knew enough about BDSM clubs to know that everyone had to be completely willing. There was a strict code of honor. Seeing others uncomfortable reassured him.

Because when he caused a scene, he'd need backup. He looked at Snow, and from the tight expression on his face, his usual backup was standing strong and ready. Snow's narrowed eyes had zoomed in on the whimpering guy, and he looked a little green around the gills.

Jude knew that Snow liked things rough, but he also knew Snow's partners had always been willing. They may have been the noisy sort, because Snow had professed to liking the screamers, but always one hundred percent consensual.

He looked back at the guy now being strapped onto a Saint Andrew's cross. His thin body quivered in a way that screamed the opposite.

The first guy started unbuttoning his shirt, and Jude held his breath as familiar tattoos hit his vision. His hands curled into tight fists as rage roared through him. He took a step toward the guy only to have Snow grab his arm to halt him. It took everything he had not to run forward and beat the living shit out of that guy.

Before he could figure out his next move, a man next to him spoke up.

"Is that a willing sub?"

Jordan's rapist turned and snarled at the man. "Does it matter?"

"Fuck yeah, it matters. What kind of shit show are you putting on here if he's not?" This came from another of the Doms who had his own sub on a leash. Even the sub looked pissed.

The man who'd let them into the house, Bill, stepped forward. "Everyone here is willing." He stepped up to the shaking man who was strapped into the cross and stroked his head. "You agreed to this of your own free will. Tell them."

The guy didn't say anything, and Bill grabbed the back of his hair.

"Tell them," he ordered.

"Okay, okay. I agreed."

That didn't sound like consent to Jude and apparently, he wasn't the only person here with a damn conscience, because the first Dom who spoke up stepped forward. "He is obviously here under duress, and I can't agree to this scene."

Voices broke out in the room as people started arguing. Jude tuned them out, his attention on the man who had hurt his brother—the man now putting his shirt back on just as a someone threw a punch. Within seconds, a fight had broken out.

"Come on," Snow said into his ear. "We need to get out of here and call the police."

The fighting grew worse as someone crashed into a mirror and shattered it. Bill started yelling, but nobody was listening as fists started flying.

"Hell no," Jude muttered. "I got a chance here."

He surged forward through the crowd to get to the one who'd hurt his brother. Donald. His name was Donald. *Fucker*. Jude pushed past two men who had pulled a third off another and hauled back and punched Donald in the face. The eyes behind the mask flew open wide, then shut as his nose made a crunching noise. He brought his fist up into Jude's gut, but rage and adrenaline dulled any pain. Jude let another punch fly, relishing the sound of flesh hitting flesh. The guy's head flew back as he stumbled a couple of steps.

Jude lunged after him, bringing him down next to the cross. The guy hit the floor with a grunt and Jude sat on his chest and punched him in the face again. This time, he caught his knuckles on the guy's teeth, leaving a long scrape.

Before he could get in any more hits, hands pulled him off. He fought, so blind with rage, he wanted to pummel the man to death.

While he was still being held, Donald had enough time to get to his feet and slam another fist into Jude's face.

Snow let out a roar of fury and laid into the man so hard, he flew back into a group of spectators. Snow just kept going, his fists flying one after the other. Donald threw his hands up as his mask flew off.

Shit, Snow was losing his fucking mind. Blood splattered the people around Donald as he tried to block Snow's blows. Someone finally grabbed Snow, who stood breathing hard and glaring at Donald like he planned to kill him.

When Donald lurched to the side and took off through the crowd, Jude fought free of the hands holding him and scrambled to his feet to follow. The fighting was still going on around him, and he had to dodge blows from all sides. Donald shot through the front door, Jude on his heels. Jude tackled him on the front lawn.

"What the hell, man?" Donald yelled.

Jude had no intention of talking to him with anything but his fists, and he got in two more blows before Snow yanked him off the guy.

Rowe ran up with duct tape in hand and had the guy hogtied within seconds.

"Who are you fuckers?" Donald struggled but the tape was too secure for him to do more than roll on the ground.

"I called in the tip as soon as I saw you two come outside. We have to book it." Rowe ran toward his truck and Snow and Jude took off down the street to Jude's Jeep. Snow peeled out like the hounds of hell were after him.

"Dammit, Jude, we had a plan! And now you got blood all over your face. How's your nose?"

Jude pulled down the mirror, gratified to hear sirens in the background as they left the neighborhood. He looked in the mirror and touched his nose, wincing. "I don't think it's broken, but he got me good, eh?"

"Not as good as you got him. Guy's face was starting to look like ground beef."

"That was partly due to you, too. I thought I was pissed at him."

"He hit you, Jude," Snow growled.

"Well, to be fair, I laid into him first. Not that I give a shit about fair when it comes to that fucker. I just wish you hadn't pulled me off him."

"Last thing we need is cops right now. I'm sure they got him. Rowe strung him up well." Snow snorted. "He could be a champion cow roper with that duct tape."

"Never met anyone who loved the stuff that much before." Jude wiped a smear of blood off his lip and saw that it was split and puffing up. Damn, there went his plans for kissing the shit out of Snow. He felt good. Fantastic even. He'd beat that asshole, and he had no doubt the cops would snatch him up. One piece of this crazy puzzle was taken care of. "You were hot jumping to my defense in there."

"Oh, yeah? Care to show me how much?"

"Find a place to pull over." Jude grinned.

"Hell, no. Let's go home."

Snow drove them home and they managed to wash the blood off their hands and Jude's face before they were on each other. Jude winced with the first kiss, and Snow pulled back to touch his lip. "Shit, he got you good."

"I don't care." Jude reached down and unbuttoned Snow's slacks. He reached inside and wrapped his hands around Snow's cock, but Snow had other plans and dropped to his knees. He had Jude's pants open and his dick out fast. He swirled his tongue around the head once before he sucked Jude down his throat. Jude's head hit the bathroom door as he grabbed on to Snow's head and moaned. "Fuck, your mouth," he breathed. "I love your fucking mouth."

Snow pulled back, then sucked him in deep again, his gorgeous lips wrapped around Jude's cock. He enfolded strong fingers around the base and tightened his suction. He let spit build in his mouth and swirled it around before he came down, then up, feeling like he was trying to suck Jude's brain through his dick. Jude cried out and thrust into that hot cavern, sending himself deep into Snow's throat.

Snow groaned around him, pulling away enough to whisper, "Fuck my throat."

This time, Jude's moan was long and ended on a whimper as he pressed his cock as deep as he dared. Fuck, Snow could take this and loved it. He fucked into his mouth, loving the hot, wet suction, the tight clasp of his throat. He pulled back so Snow could breathe before pressing in just as deep as before. He reached under Snow's jaw to feel his dick in his throat. "So. Hot." He bit down on his lip and winced; then his head hit the door again when Snow deepened his suction.

He started bobbing his head, each time letting Jude go deep into that tight throat. The repeated slides had his vision going black around the edges. A hoarse cry escaped his throat as Snow pressed his tongue hard against him. Jude bent over him as pleasure coursed through him hard and fast.

"Such a hot, fucking mouth," he growled. "Get yourself out for me."

Snow complied, freeing his beautiful dick.

"Stroke yourself but keep sucking me. Don't stop."

Snow groaned and wrapped a hand around himself. He was so gorgeous like this and he loved so fiercely, Jude felt it in every fiber of his being. Snow sucked harder as he stroked himself, and the dual visual made Jude's balls draw up. But he wasn't ready to come. He wanted this to last longer. But Snow was moaning and sucking him so well, and his long surgeon's fingers were stroking his own cock. Jude's orgasm swelled and crashed over him, and he yelled and spilled deep in Snow's throat.

Snow swallowed around him and started jacking his dick faster and faster until he cried out around Jude's cock and spilled all over the floor.

Jude's legs gave out and he slid down the door. Snow leaned forward and pressed their foreheads together, both panting.

"Shit, look at your hands."

Jude barely had the energy to raise them and he grimaced when he saw his knuckles. "Worth it," he said. He'd beat the guy all over again if he had the chance. "Think the cops got him?"

"I doubt anyone took the time to cut him loose with the cops showing up so fast, but yeah. Rowe will be able to find out tomorrow."

"Good. I wanted to kill him, General."

"I know you did." Snow leaned back on his heels to stare at him. "But I'm glad you didn't. It's not something you want to live with and not something I want you to live with either."

"We still don't know who runs that website. Who forced my brother into doing that video."

"No, but the man who raped him will be behind bars, so it's a start." Snow groaned and got to his feet. "That floor is fucking hard." He smirked that wicked grin that was always a punch to Jude's gut. "Come on. Let's shower and go for round two."

CHAPTER 17

*J*ude leaned against the wall outside of Snow's office, scrubbing his hand across his face. They'd both started back to work that day for the first time since Jordan's attack, ending what had become their extended vacation. Both he and Snow had lucked out with the morning shift, so they'd carpooled to the hospital.

A part of him had felt good about sliding behind the wheel of the ambulance again. He was more at peace and settled than he had been in nearly two weeks. Rebecca had been kind enough not to ask about Jordan but then, he was sure she was getting regular updates from Carrick. Jude had managed to put Jordan from his immediate thoughts for several hours as he focused on the people he was called to help.

The day had been a brisk one. There were at least three heart attacks, two women in labor, a possible broken hip from a fall down the stairs, and kidney stones that had left one man curled up on the floor in pain. Unfortunately, they were also called to a shooting near the end of their shift. The young man couldn't have been more than nineteen or twenty, briefly reminding Jude of his brother. They hadn't been able to save him.

After a quick shower and changing into street clothes, Jude trekked up to ICU and sat with his brother for a while. His *mana* was absent, but his aunt Shelley was sitting in the waiting room working on some knitting while watching the evening news. His uncle Gary had apparently stopped by, dropped off Shelley, and taken Anna home for a few hours to eat, sleep, and shower. His entire family was taking turns sitting with Jordan and making sure that Anna went home regularly.

Jordan was starting to show some small improvements. The doctor was talking about taking him off the ventilator the next day, and the neurologist was hopeful that he hadn't sustained any permanent spinal damage. It was likely that Jordan would walk again, but he was going to need a lot of physical therapy. Jude just wished his brother would wake up. He knew it was better that Jordan stay unconscious, that he rest and let his body heal from the trauma it had suffered, but Jude needed to look in his brother's dark brown eyes and see that he was going to be okay.

He also needed to look in his brother's eyes and tell him that it was all going to be okay. That Jude was going to get his hands on the men who had hurt his brother. That he was going to be there for Jordan in every step of his recovery. He needed to apologize for failing him. Somehow, some way, he'd slipped up, and his brother didn't feel he could come to Jude for help and it was killing him.

After nearly an hour with his brother, he wandered over to Snow's office and waited outside for him to finish his work.

The sound of a door opening had Jude's head popping up. Snow stood in the open doorway, his coat in his hand and a confused expression on his face.

"How long have you been waiting out here?" Snow asked.

Jude shrugged. "Not long. Maybe five minutes."

"You know you could have come in."

Shaking his head, Jude pushed off the wall and gave his general a weary smile. "You were finishing up your charts for the day. I know you. If I'd stopped in, you'd have procrastinated and bitched, taking twice as long."

"I hate the fucking paperwork," Snow grumbled. He stepped closer and brushed a quick kiss across Jude's lips. When they were out in the open at work, they kept the PDA to an absolute minimum, but Jude was not going to turn away a "Hello, I missed you" kiss from Snow.

As they turned toward the elevator, Jude bumped his shoulder against Snow's. "You make voice recordings of all your notes, and your assistant puts everything into the charts. You're not actually filling out any paperwork," he teased.

"Close enough. When I was going through medical school, I was worried about memorizing the names and functions of everything. I was learning life-saving techniques. I didn't know I was going to spend so much damn time behind a computer keeping insurance companies happy."

"You saved lives today, General. That's the important thing." Jude stopped at the elevator and smiled at his companion. "Besides, you didn't spend the day in an ambulance with a broken heater."

"Fuck! I thought they were getting that fixed."

Jude shrugged. "Apparently it didn't take. Rebecca kept stealing blankets from the back of the rig to keep warm." He started to hit the button and stopped. "Do you want to go up and see Jordan before we leave?"

Snow shook his head. "I saw him at the end of my shift before I started my paperwork. His stats are looking a little better. Let's go home. I need food, sleep, and you…not necessarily in that order."

They remained silent the rest of the long walk out of the hospital and to the parking lot where Jude had left his Jeep early that morning. The sun hadn't yet peeked over the horizon when they arrived and was now sinking low as they cut across the cold lot. He doubted Snow had even seen the sun that day as he rushed from one patient to the next. Jude might have been able to soak in a little sunlight, but he'd spent the majority of the day fighting the bitter cold. He was done with winter.

"Did you hear from Rowe today?" Jude asked while they were sitting at a red light.

"He texted me this afternoon. The bastard hasn't coughed up a name yet," Snow replied.

It had been two long days since that night at the sex party where Jude had beaten the shit out of Donald Banks and they'd run from the cops. The man was originally charged with three counts of rape and assault.

It was after a long discussion with Carrick that they handed over the copy of the video they had of Jordan's attack. It had meant another round of questions and a long, painful talk with their *mana*. They didn't allow her to see the video, but the details were enough that Snow had felt compelled to give her a mild sedative.

Jude felt like he was betraying Jordan's privacy by telling both their mother and the cops, but he was more concerned with getting justice for his brother. Donald Banks needed to go to jail for what he did. Fuck, Jude was ready to send the man straight to the chair. For now, he had to be content with the fact that Banks wasn't running around hurting anyone else.

But it wasn't enough. Not by a long shot.

The fucker was already claiming that the scene with Jordan was consensual. That Jordan had fucking asked for it, *begged for it*. He said that all Jordan's denials and pleading were an act for the camera, but Jude knew better. He knew his brother. Jordan had been terrified and in pain. But until Jordan woke up, they couldn't get the full story. And there was a good chance that he wouldn't remember most of what happened to him. While a small blessing for his own recovery, it could mean that Banks would get away with the attack.

They also had zero evidence that Banks had been the one to shoot Jordan. Not that Jude really thought that Donald shot Jordan. No, he was just there to beat and rape his brother. He had a feeling that the person who shot Jordan was the one behind the poker games and the porn site. He wanted to take down that fucker, and he honestly wasn't sure if simply handing this man over to the cops was going to be enough.

Whoever this asshole was, he was responsible for hurting his brother and damaging his family.

"Jude..." Snow said in a low voice, drawing him from his darker thoughts. "I need you to move into the right lane like you're planning to take this exit."

"What?" he asked, but he still checked his mirrors and flipped on his signal before doing as Snow requested. They'd just gotten on southbound I-71 heading back toward the bridge that would take them across the Ohio River and to their home in Northern Kentucky. As they settled in the new lane, Jude glanced over at Snow to find him staring into the rearview mirror with a deepening frown.

"Someone is following us."

Jude jerked a little in his seat, eyes snapping up to the mirror as well just as another car moved into the same lane two cars back. It was a large, dark-colored SUV—a menacing-looking vehicle—but Jude had to wonder if he'd think that if Snow hadn't said it was following them.

"Are you sure? It could be just a coincidence. It's almost rush hour. Traffic is picking up."

"The SUV has changed lanes at the same time as you two other times."

"Where do you learn this shit?"

Snow flashed him a weak grin. "Rowe has taught us all kinds of stuff that I was sure I would never use. And yet here I am, being followed by an SUV." He reached into the interior pocket of his coat and pulled out his cell phone. Jude was sure that he was calling the man in question at that moment.

"Did he also teach you what to do if you found yourself being followed?"

"We never got to that lesson. He just said don't wreck."

"Wonderful. Just fucking wonderful," Jude muttered under his breath. He remained in the far right lane while trying to sort through his various options. He had a feeling that it didn't make much sense to try to go to the cops since the people following them would just drive off. They couldn't see a license plate and there wasn't much description they could give other than a dark SUV.

And maybe he didn't want the people following them to completely disappear. He had no doubt that these assholes were linked to the person who killed Anthony and the attack on his brother. If they could just get their hands on one or more of the persons in the SUV, then maybe they could finally get the name of the person who hurt his brother.

Unfortunately, that meant putting Snow's life in danger. Not that Snow would choose to walk away at that moment. No, the man would never leave his side, especially when he was in danger.

"Rowe said to take the first Newport exit after we cross the I-471 bridge and then cut across Covington to the northbound branch of I-75," Snow said as he put his phone back into his coat pocket.

Jude's frown deepened as he mentally mapped out that route. It would take them through some extremely busy streets and a ton of traffic lights. "What the hell is he thinking? There are going to be a ton of people and cars along that route."

"A lot of witnesses. He also has his people tapped into all the traffic cameras throughout Covington. They'll be able to get a good look at the SUV following us and possibly the people inside."

"And heading north along I-75?"

"He and Noah are jumping into a Ward SUV now and speeding down 75 toward us. They're hoping to intercept and accompany us back to Ward Security."

Jude sighed and nodded. "It's not a great plan."

"Not even remotely close," Snow conceded.

As they got closer to downtown Cincinnati, Jude's hands tightened around the steering wheel. The forest of skyscrapers rising up in front of them was starting to glow in the early evening light. The trees blurring past the car windows were just brown sticks, desperately waiting for winter to finally be over. They hadn't gotten a lot of snow or ice this year, but the bitter cold had seemed endless.

They remained in the far right lane and took the exit to switch from I-71 to I-471, which would take them over the yellow bridge that locals referred to as the Big Mac Bridge. He glanced in the rearview mirror to find the SUV still behind them, but this time there was only one car separating them instead of two.

Jude glanced over at Snow who was watching the car in the side mirror. "You know, this is the second time you've had someone following you in a car in roughly a year."

"Huh?" Snow said, his head snapping up so he could look over at Jude.

"You think I forgot about your little escapade with Lucas in Oklahoma?" Snow rolled his eyes and Jude continued. "I should think twice about getting in a car with you if this your kind of luck."

"Whatever. After this, I just might decide to never get in another car."

Jude started to say something, but he noticed as they crossed the bridge, the car between them and the SUV changed lanes. The SUV sped up, closing the distance between them. Jude's heart raced and his palms grew sweaty. They were on a fucking bridge. Just a couple hundred more yards until they were safely across. They could make it.

Images of them crashing through the concrete barrier and plunging down into the icy river flooded his brain. He sucked in a deep breath. Jude stepped on the accelerator, speeding up as much as he could without ramming the car in front of him. He started to hit the turn signal for the exit ramp out of habit but stopped himself.

Before they could reach the exit, the SUV surged forward, sneaking the nose of the vehicle beside the back passenger-side tire. There was a crunch of metal, and the Jeep lurched forward. Jude wrestled with the wheel as his car tried to jump across lanes to the left. Other cars jerked away from him and several horns sounded, but he ignored them. The SUV driver was keeping them from taking their normal exit.

It was far too late to slow down as Jude regained control of the Jeep but sped past the exit that Rowe had wanted them to take.

"Fuck!" Snow snarled.

"Now what?"

"We need to get off the road and away from these assholes. I don't want to play bumper cars in rush hour traffic."

Jude couldn't agree more. He stomped on the gas again and the Jeep jumped forward. They wove through the cars, climbing the hill away from the Ohio River and heading deeper into Northern

Kentucky. Around him, he saw glimpses of cars filled with people heading home from a long day at work or school. Mothers and fathers were driving kids home from after-school activities and the only things they all had on their mind was home, dinner, homework, and maybe what was on the TV that night. Their lives could all be torn apart in a second by these ruthless assholes determined to get their hands on them.

"What about the next exit?" Snow suggested.

Jude shook his head. "It's too busy. Too many cars. Someone will get killed if they ram us again and I lose control of the Jeep."

"Then where?" Panic and frustration were starting to harden the edges of Snow's voice. Jude wanted to reach across and grab Snow's hand, but he was afraid to take one of his off the wheel.

"The Fort Thomas-Southgate exit. It's not as busy and there's a shopping plaza right there. Call 9-1-1 now. Tell them that's where we're headed. They can dispatch cops there to meet us."

"You know, one of these days I'd really like to be on the other end of this," Snow muttered as he reached back into his pocket.

"I'd really like to never be in this position again. Period."

Jude looked over to see Snow pulling out his phone when the SUV hit them from behind again. Their bodies jerked slightly forward before their seat belts tightened against their chests. Jude's back and neck ached, but the pain was almost immediately swept away by another rush of adrenaline.

He thought he heard more cars honking, and he hoped that someone driving near them was now calling the police. Yeah, he'd like to get his hands on these fuckers, but at that moment, he was more concerned with getting Snow out of this alive and unharmed.

Beside him, Snow barked instructions at the poor 9-1-1 dispatcher. He sounded like he was in full surgeon-general mode, expecting anyone within his reach to immediately jump to his commands. His instructions were succinct and clear as he demanded that at least two squad cars be dispatched to the shopping plaza off the exit. The one thing that did lack details was the description of the SUV, but there wasn't much they could tell at this point.

Changing lanes, Jude rushed them past the exit Snow had mentioned and up the winding hill. The cars grew a little more spaced out as the steep grade sapped the power of some of the older cars. Jude gripped the wheel so tightly that his knuckles were white, and his fingers were slick with sweat despite the cold air.

The SUV had drifted back a couple of car lengths as it climbed the hill behind them. Dark tinting on the windows made it impossible to see the face of the driver or how many people were even in the vehicle.

At the top of the hill, a new lane branched off on the right to form the exit ramp for the Fort Thomas-Southgate exit. Gritting his teeth, Jude waited as long as possible before jumping over into the new lane. Not surprisingly, the SUV changed lanes with them.

Jude glanced into the rearview mirror just in time to see an arm extend from the front passenger side of the SUV with what appeared to be a gun gripped by the gloved hand.

"Get down!" Jude shouted. He released the wheel with this right hand and grabbed the collar of Snow's coat, yanking him forward. A second later there were two muted shots filling the silence of the early evening. The back window of the Jeep shattered followed by a loud popping sound. It had just registered that the shooter had hit the rear right wheel of the Jeep when the SUV rammed them yet again. This time, the driver crashed into them from the left side.

Everything seemed to happen in the blink of an eye. Jude could only react as quickly as possible. The Jeep fishtailed. He fought to keep it on the road, but the combined weight of the SUV and the blown tire threw the Jeep off balance. They plowed through the metal guardrail on the passenger side of the lane, and then the world turned upside down.

Metal screamed and crashed around them. Pain exploded in the top and the side of Jude's head, leaving him disoriented. He couldn't tell if only a few seconds or minutes passed before he was finally able to blink and find…nothing made sense. Everything was upside down.

"Jude! Jude!" Snow shouted beside him.

"Here," he croaked. Even making that small noise made his head ache and throb.

"Are you okay?" Snow demanded.

"No." He wasn't going to lie. Everything seemed to hurt. A cold wind rushed into the Jeep from a broken window and chilled something wet on his face. "I think I hit my head."

"Stay there. I'm going to help you out."

Jude slowly turned his head to watch Snow struggle with his seat belt. It took him several seconds to get free, and then he landed in a heap on the ceiling of the Jeep. That was when Jude noticed the tight pressure on his chest and across his waist from where the seat belt was holding him while still hanging upside down.

More noise filled the Jeep as Snow fought his way out of his door and disappeared into the cold. Jude lifted his hand to the damp side of his face and pulled his fingers back to see blood.

"The cops are already on their way!" Snow's voice drew Jude from his fragmented thoughts and back to the present. They'd been run off the road by an SUV. Someone had shot at them. Snow was out there with the people who were trying to kill them. He was alone and unarmed.

Jude's heart rate ramped up and all his pains were forgotten in an instant. The only thing that mattered was getting to Snow. Jude grabbed at the belt buckle, but it refused to release. He couldn't get free.

"Snow!" he shouted, but there was no answer.

A second later he could make out the faint sounds of flesh hitting flesh and a sharp cry of pain from Snow. They were attacking him, beating him. Fear and rage pumped like poison through Jude's veins and he increased his struggles to be free. He had to get to Snow.

"Here...help me load him in the truck." The words were low and from a voice Jude didn't recognize.

"Snow! Snow!" he screamed over and over again, but there was no answer. Just the sound of rubber tires pealing out on asphalt and then a few seconds later, the growing wail of an approaching police siren. But they were already too late. They'd taken Snow, and Jude had no idea how to find him.

CHAPTER 18

The smell of piss, sex, and sweat filled his nostrils as Snow slowly became aware of his surroundings. It didn't make sense, but the foul odor was unmistakable. He tried to open his eyes to see where the smells were coming from, but he was blind. Panic pumped in his veins, making him more aware of the throbbing headache that started at the back of his skull and splintered out toward his temples and into his eyes.

What the fuck had happened? Where was he?

The last thing he remembered was leaving the hospital with Jude. They were still waiting to see if Rowe could get any more information on the man behind the porn website and likely Jordan's assault. Jude had driven. They'd carpooled that morning. Snow didn't want Jude out of his sight any more than necessary.

They were followed.

The crash...

Jude!

Snow tried to lurch forward from where he was sitting to find that his hands were actually bound above him. He was...he was chained to a wall, he guessed by the sounds of the clinking links filling the silent room. He'd been grabbed and beaten by three men when he'd rushed to Jude's side of the Jeep to help him get free. Had Jude gotten out safely?

Gritting his teeth, Snow grabbed on to the chains running from the manacles and used them to pull himself up to his feet. His body ached and throbbed in time to the pounding of his head. He couldn't tell what pains were from the car wreck and which ones were from the beating. It was all just one big ball of pain now.

There were no memories after they got him into the SUV. Someone must have clocked him over the head or drugged him to knock him out.

Snow leaned heavily against the wall, panting once he gained his feet. Tilting his head as close as he could to his right hand, he ran his fingertips along his temple until he finally felt the rough cloth that had been used as a blindfold. It took three tries, but he got the damn thing ripped off his face.

He blinked several times against the bright overhead light. His vision was blurry, but when his eyes finally focused on the room in front of him, he almost wished he hadn't removed the blindfold.

Not more than a few feet away was a bare, queen-sized mattress and box spring on what looked to be a sturdy wooden frame. The cinder block walls were mostly bare except for the occasional splatter of blood or the dried remnants of some other bodily fluid. At the foot of the bed were two apparatuses he'd seen used in photography and video lighting. And an empty tripod that likely held a smartphone or camera for filming.

Oh, fuck…he was in the same room where Jordan was beaten and raped.

He jerked at the manacles and chains, trying to pull free, but the chain was bolted into the wall and there was no give in the iron manacles. Pain lanced through his body from his thwarted escape, leaving him panting and leaning back against the wall. Bile boiled up from his stomach and Snow swallowed hard, fighting to keep the contents of his stomach down. The video had been hard enough to watch, but to know that he was now standing in the room where Jordan's desperate screams had beaten against the walls left his knees trembling and threatening to buckle.

Dropping his head back, Snow forced himself to take several slow, deep breaths, and he found himself mentally rolling his eyes as a wayward memory skipped across his brain. At Christmas, Rowe had joked about wanting to chip all of his family so that they could be found at all times. They'd all laughed and said that dangerous adventures were finally done for all of them. Snow had thought they wouldn't see anything more exciting than whatever shenanigans would ensue at Ian's wedding and just the insanity that would inevitably follow when it came to Lucas attempting to raise a little girl.

But no. He was chained to a wall by some homicidal lunatic, and he had no idea what had happened to Jude. The wail of police sirens had sounded close. He didn't think the men who grabbed him had a chance to grab Jude, but he also didn't know whether they'd simply shot his trapped lover before they made their escape.

Jude is alive. He has to be alive.

Snow repeated those words over and over again in his brain. He was not going to lose Jude. They needed more time together. It had taken Snow a lifetime to find Jude, and they'd had only three short years with each other so far. He needed to see his Jude, hold him tight against his chest until he could feel Jude's heartbeat pounding against his own. He needed to get married and hold their child, not just because those things would make happiness glow in Jude's dark eyes. But because he needed to experience these things with Jude. He wanted that life with Jude because with Jude, he finally felt like he deserved all the things that "normal" families had.

Fuck...how the hell was he going to get out of here?

He doubted that Jude nor Rowe nor anyone knew where to find him. He was completely unarmed and chained to the wall. He wanted to believe that he'd been in worse scenarios, but even when he found himself in over his head during his darker years, it seemed like Lucas or Rowe always knew where to find him, knew exactly when to swoop in and pull him out. That wasn't the case this time. He believed that Rowe and his team of genius hackers would find him, but they would need him to buy a little time and help where he could.

With renewed determination, Snow forced himself to study the room around him. Eventually, someone was going to come in and unchain him. He needed to be ready to fight back. After getting over the shock of being in the same room as Jordan's beating, Snow was disappointed to find that there wasn't much available that might help his escape. The bed had no blankets or sheets and appeared to be bolted to the floor and wall. There was a metal hook above the bed next to the light fixture that also turned his stomach.

Snow might have been into more violent and rough forms of sex, but there had been little to no bondage involved. The only person he trusted enough to tie him up was Jude, and they'd played around with it only a little bit in the past. Everything about the room screamed pain and torture and nothing about pleasure. At least not for one of the participants.

The only other things in the room were the lighting stands and the tripod. There looked to be a couple of extension cords that could come in handy if he could get to them, but there were no heavy objects for bludgeoning and no sharp objects for stabbing. Getting out was not going to be easy.

Metal scraping across metal drew Snow's gaze to the only door in the room as someone turned the deadbolt, unlocking it. The door swung soundlessly open and the first thing to enter was a black nine-millimeter handgun at the end of a long, muscular arm. The arm was attached to a large man that had to be nearly seven feet tall and all fucking muscle. He easily stepped around the video equipment as if he'd been in the room dozens of times before. With the gun pointed directly at Snow's face, he stood in front of the doctor, glaring at him.

"Stay silent and you stay conscious," the man threatened.

Snow clenched his teeth together to fight the urge to launch a series of snarky remarks. He needed to stay conscious. It was the only way he was going to figure out where the fuck he was and who the hell had him. The man standing in front of him had all the earmarks of being security. The muscle and hard attitude made Snow think that the man was there to protect someone else and to potentially make sure that Snow behaved himself.

As if to prove Snow correct, another man stepped into the room with a cell phone pressed to his ear. The two men couldn't have looked more mismatched. While the security guard wore jeans and a cotton long-sleeved shirt that was molded to his powerful shoulders and arms, the other man looked like he was fresh from the office in his dress slacks and white button-down shirt. His dark navy tie had been pulled loose and the top couple of buttons had been unfastened.

"Okay, Pumpkin. You help Mommy fold the towels and pick up your toys before I get home," the man said in a sweet, gentle voice. He turned to look at Snow and smirked before he continued speaking in the same tone. "No, I'll be home soon. Don't worry. I'll be there to read you a story before bed. I promise. I love you too."

As Snow stared at the man, he thought was going to be sick. The man standing just past the bodyguard looked like the average middle-class husband, father, and corporate drone. And Snow was willing to bet that the vast majority of the world had no idea that this...this monster...when he slipped away from his wife and kid each night, was coming to this secret place to film the rape, beating, and torture of so many poor, innocent people.

"Sorry about that," his captor said with an easy smile as he slipped his cell phone into his trouser pocket. "Kids, you know. Well..." he paused and his smile turned a little more evil, "I guess you don't know. You and your paramedic don't have kids."

To Snow's surprise, the man stepped around the hired muscle and sat on the edge of the bed closest to him. "I asked around about you, Dr. Frost, when I found out that you were concerned with poor Jordan."

"Poor Jordan?" Snow demanded in horror. "You're the one who put Jordan in that state. He's lucky to be alive."

"Lucky is the appropriate word here. He is *very* lucky to be alive right now." The man leaned forward, his watery blue eyes narrowing on Snow. "But I'm sure you're aware of how easy it is for a patient of

Jordan's fragility to take a sudden and unforeseen turn for the worse. It would be a shame if he were to suddenly die."

Snow shoved off the wall, lunging toward the man until his chains jerked and clanged, holding him half-suspended in the air, unable to reach his target. "You stay the fuck away from Jordan and all of Jude's family!"

The bodyguard stepped forward and backhanded Snow, slamming him against the wall. Pain radiated through Snow's face and the back of his skull from his previous injury. Nausea rose again with the pain, and he fought the swell back.

"Why?" he croaked.

"Why? Why did Jordan end up in the hospital? Why did he end up in one of my little videos?" Snow blinked, focusing on the man in front of him. He was sitting with his hands on his knees and a smug look on his face. "Because he owed me."

"What could he have possibly owed you that warranted rape and being beaten?"

"Money, of course. But the amount really doesn't matter," he said with a shrug. "He knew what he was getting into, and he couldn't cover his promises. There have to be consequences for things like that. And the consequences are sometimes severe."

"This is bullshit. Jordan and Anthony played poker with you and got in over their heads, so you tortured Jordan and killed Anthony."

The man pushed back to his feet and stepped closer to Snow. He tensed his muscles, ready to strike when the asshole got just close enough, but before he could move, the bodyguard also stepped close. The cold steel muzzle of the gun pressed painfully into his temple, warning him not to move while the other man spoke.

"You know, not everyone has a billionaire in their pocket like you. We have to scrape and struggle to make something of ourselves," the bastard started.

It was on the tip of his tongue to point out that neither he nor Lucas had a dime to their names growing up. They'd worked all their lives for everything they had, but he really doubted the man had any interest in the truth.

"I just so happen to be good at poker. Good enough to make a steady stream of income from it by playing friends. But the problem is that friends get tired of losing to you night after night, so you have to keep bringing in fresh blood. And sometimes the stakes start to get high and sometimes…I'll extend a player a loan or two."

"You fucking conned Jordan and all the others. You tricked them—"

"I have never fucking lied to one of them!" he snarled, getting right in Snow's face. "They all made promises to me. 'No worries, Gene. I've got it.' And 'I can get the money in just a couple of days. You know I'm good for it.' " Gene stepped back, his fat upper lip curling in disgust. "They were the liars. Not me." Gene stomped over to the bed and plopped down on the edge, glaring at Snow as if he were the one telling all those poker players to lie to Gene.

Seconds ticked by before Gene shook his head and looked down at the floor. "I don't know who's raising kids these days, but it's a fucking disgrace. A man's word is his bond. It's the only way to judge his worth. And if he doesn't fucking keep his word, then he has to pay a price."

"How much is a person's life worth to you?" Snow snarled, ignoring the gun still pressed to his head. "How much did all the dead men owe you? Ten thousand? A hundred thousand each? Is that what a life is worth to you?"

"Those dead men aren't worth shit to me. They had a choice. Pay me what they owed…" he paused and stood. Stepping away from the bed, he waved his arm toward the stained and sagging mattress. "Or they could shoot a video for me. I had to get my money back somehow, and you'd be amazed at what people will pay for when it comes to sex and getting off."

"Fuck you! Jordan didn't agree to that. He wasn't willing!" He tried to push away from the wall again, but the man with the gun grabbed him by the throat with his free hand and shoved him back.

"No, Jordan wasn't willing. But he also couldn't pay the forty-five thousand dollars he owed me. The longer I waited on him, the more money I lost. That's why he was in the video. He had to understand that his childish, irresponsible behavior had a price."

"And you shot him…?"

"Because I knew he'd never be able to keep his mouth shut. No matter his humiliation or the threats, he'd eventually open his mouth. Couldn't allow that." Gene shook his head again. "I've got two kids to feed and clothe. Customer service rep is shit pay, but this…*this*…keeps my kids in private school and clothes and with a roof over their heads."

"You're feeding your kids on ruined lives."

Gene just chuckled at Snow. "I never held a gun to their heads to get them to sit down at the poker table. I didn't force them to bet, let alone bet more than they could afford. They all chose to do that themselves. I just made sure they paid for their mistakes."

Snow leaned back against the wall, pulling his throat free of the other man's hold. There was no point in arguing with this fucker. He had his excuses and his carefully planned rationales for the horrible things he'd done. There was no convincing him that he was making an enormous mistake and that he should just hand himself over to the cops. Never going to happen.

No, his main concern was what Gene planned to do with him and how the fuck he was going to escape before Gene could go forward with his plan.

"But here we are. You couldn't leave this to the cops to bumble around and foul up." Gene sighed, frowning at Snow.

He pushed to his feet with a little grunt. The belly that protruded over his belt spoke of a man not used to regular exercise. No, Snow was sure he was happy to just sit back with his poker and his porn, raking in his illegal gains, while the rest of the world thought he was just some middle-class schmuck.

"What am I going to do with you and your boyfriend? Killing Jordan and Anthony. That's easy. Punk-ass kids die all the time. The world almost expects it. Jordan's brother? Well, we can argue that grief drove him to do stupid things. But you?" Gene made a tsking noise. "Respected surgeon. Friends with that billionaire and that hoity-toity chef. Too many people will start asking questions if you just turn up dead."

Some of the fear tightly gripping Snow's chest eased a bit, and he made the mistake of finally taking a deep breath.

"Of course, Donald mentioned knowing of you," Gene added slyly. "Seems you liked darker things in your past. Does your boyfriend know about the bad things you used to do?"

"Jude knows everything about my past. I've got nothing to hide from him!" Snow snapped. He jerked his arms, rattling the chains above his head. His arms and shoulders ached from being held at an unnatural angle above his head. Gene would not be able to blackmail Snow over his past. He wasn't proud of it, but the people who knew him, loved him, were well aware of the dark places he traveled before meeting Jude.

Gene just snickered. "True, but how many of those people would be surprised if your body was one day found in one of those places from your past? Fallen back on old habits. The police might not dig too deep when looking into your death."

"Fuck you! Jude would know. Jude would never stop. Neither would Lucas and the rest of my family."

The expression hardened on Gene's face. "Exactly. But I'm sure with the right leverage, you could convince them all to stop and walk the fuck away." As he stepped closer, the bodyguard made sure to have his gun ready and in Snow's face so he wouldn't contemplate attempting to attack Gene. "My little enterprise might not earn me Lucas Vallois money, but it's enough to allow me to hire some ruthless people. We got to you on your drive home from work and we got to you in your home. How hard do you think it would be for us to get to that chef friend of yours? Or Jordan's momma? Or how about Lucas Vallois's new little baby? Rumor has it she's a sweet little thing."

"Fuck you!" Snow roared as rage consumed him. He tried to lunge at Gene, but the hulking mass of muscle was right there to slam him back against the wall. The butt of the gun came down on his temple, creating a bright white flash before his eyes. Snow blinked and found himself on his knees, his arms stretched uncomfortably above his head.

Gene had stepped away and was smiling smugly down at him. "Just some food for thought while I work out the right button to push to get you and your family to back the fuck off."

Gene left the room with his bodyguard following on his heels. The door slammed shut behind them, and then the lock clicked into place.

Snow remained on the floor, his body aching and his head throbbing in pain. But they were nothing compared to the knot of fear and anger growing in his chest. They were not going back to a life of looking over their shoulders in fear, waiting for someone to rip their happiness away. They'd lived that for too many years when Boris Jagger had been a shadow over everything they'd built. He and Jude didn't want that life. Little Daci didn't deserve to grow up like that. Nor did any of the kids that Ian and Hollis inevitably had.

The only bright spot was that in all Gene's ranting and taunting, he never mentioned Rowe. If he knew about Lucas and Ian, how could he have possibly missed Rowe freaking Ward? He was a devious SOB and just as dangerous as Lucas. Well, probably more so since Rowe worried a whole lot less about doing things legally.

Snow allowed himself a small chuckle in the silent room. It didn't sound like Gene had his hands on Jude, which was good. That meant Jude and Rowe were already working on an evil plan to free him and unleash hell on Gene's head. He was just sorry he was going to miss out on a round of new code names.

CHAPTER 19

Jude pressed the medical tape against his skin with his free hand while looking back over his shoulder. It was holding down the gauze he'd snatched up after pulling out the IV needle. Rebecca was doing a good job of distracting the cop and nurse who had been headed toward his room, but he knew she could keep it up for only so long. She'd rushed over after getting his text that he'd been in an accident and needed her there for help. His partner had not been thrilled about his desire to escape, but she didn't argue much.

He needed to get the fuck out of the hospital. He'd been there too damn long already, and he needed to get to Snow.

Cursing himself and the pain that spread through his skull from where he'd hit his head, Jude hurried down the corridor. He didn't know this Northern Kentucky hospital. All his runs took him to the various hospitals around Cincinnati. He paused in an intersection, looking for signs that would point him toward an exit when a strong hand grabbed his elbow and jerked him toward the right. A little yelp escaped him as he stumbled sideways, falling against a strong chest. He looked up to find himself leaning against Noah Keegan. Rowe's boyfriend was a welcome sight.

"If you're looking to escape, you're going the wrong way," Noah said with a wicked grin. "Let me give you a hand."

"Thank God," Jude sighed. He got his feet under him again and jogged behind Noah as he wove down a few more corridors with beige walls until they reached a staircase. An ambulance had arrived ten minutes after the cops did, and Jude had been bundled off to the hospital for a handful of stitches and a scan of his head. He'd been tucked into a room while they waited for another doctor to read the scan and make a decision about what to do next.

There was no question that he had a mild concussion and really needed to be resting, but nothing was going to keep him from finding Snow. Nothing.

Nearly two hours had already been wasted at the hospital with the cops peppering him with questions he either didn't know the answers to or wasn't comfortable responding to. He'd told the cops the truth. He'd had no idea who had followed him or why they'd run him off the road or what the fuck happened to Snow. However, he might have held back on the why, suspecting that it was all tied to Jordan's attack and Anthony's shooting.

The only good thing to come out of this was that he hadn't been taken to UC hospital. His mother didn't yet know about the accident or Snow's kidnapping. He couldn't worry about her health. She needed to focus her energy on Jordan and leave him to finding Snow.

On the empty landing, Noah turned and pushed Jude against the closed door. He narrowed his eyes and stared into Jude's. "I'm stealing you out of here on the belief that you're not gonna keel over due to internal bleeding or some other injury from the car wreck."

"No, I'm fine," Jude said sharply, but Noah didn't even budge. "Yeah, yeah. I'm not in danger of dying. Mild concussion, few stitches on my left arm and neck from broken glass, and bruised ribs. Nothing rest and painkillers won't help."

Noah grunted and released Jude. Lifting his right hand, he handed Jude a heavy black parka with the Ward Security logo on the front. "Here. Put this on and try to look less like a patient. Rowe's got a car waiting out front."

Jude happily accepted the coat. His had disappeared at some point, and he felt lucky they'd left him with his T-shirt. He managed to find only his keys, wallet, and cell phone before he escaped his room.

"Have you found him? Do you know anything yet?" Jude demanded as he followed Noah down the flight of stairs while fighting to pull on the coat. It was blissfully warm, and Jude was grateful Noah had the forethought to bring it along for him.

"The triplets are working on it. They managed to hack the traffic cameras around the area and are tracking the SUV that hit you. Rowe was checking in on them when I came in to get you," Noah said.

"The triplets?"

Noah paused in front of the door on the first floor and smirked at him. "Quinn, Cole, and Gidget. Rowe's IT specialists. They're all working on tracking down Snow."

Sticking his head out the door, Noah briefly looked around before leading the way. Jude joined him, acting as casual as possible. It was likely that they'd only just now discovered his disappearance, and the word hadn't yet spread to the rest of the hospital. They quickly crossed the lobby and out the double automatic doors.

Bitter cold night air greeted them as they stepped forward. It had gotten even colder since they left work, and his breath fogged in front of his face. Stuffing his hands into his pockets, he pulled the coat tighter around his body and walked alongside Noah. He was about to ask where Rowe was when a low roar echoed across the parking lot. A large black SUV surged up the rounded drive and stopped right in front of them. Jude's heart nearly leaped out of his chest at the sight of the black monster. It looked too much like the same one that ran them off the road.

Noah stepped forward and pulled the back door open for Jude, motioning for him to climb in, before he grabbed the front passenger door. Taking a deep breath, Jude got into the seat and pulled the door closed. Warmth wrapped around him, battling back the winter cold.

"Look, I...of course, I've thought of that! I...no, I've already assigned two bodyguards, and—" Rowe said brokenly into the cell phone pressed to his left ear while he drove with his right hand. "I've got it covered. Just get here safely. I'll keep you updated." Rowe ended the call with a groan and tossed it over to Noah, who was chuckling beside him.

"Was that Lucas?" Jude asked as he buckled himself in. After flipping in his Jeep already that night, he was never ever going to sit in a vehicle without a seat belt of some kind. The damn thing had saved his life.

Rowe chortled and gunned the SUV, racing down the drive and onto the main road, turning toward the nearest expressway ramp. "I so can't wait to tell him you said that. It was Andrei."

"Is he coming to help?"

"Not this time," Rowe said with a sigh. "He headed down to see his parents early this morning. Needed to help with something. I don't know. Their heater maybe. When the news of Snow hit, he started north, but he's down in the fucking wilds of Kentucky. He's still at least another three hours away, and that's assuming the weather holds."

"Fuck," Jude muttered, slouching in his chair. The former MMA fighter was great in a fight, and if they were lucky enough to locate Snow, Jude would have liked to have Andrei at his side. The man had become a close friend over the past couple of years, helping him learn the ins and outs of Snow's unique family.

"No worries. We've got plenty of hands on deck for this little mission."

Jude looked up to meet Rowe's hard gaze in the rearview mirror. No, Jude wasn't worried about the prowess of the men who would rally to Snow's side. Rowe was scary all on his own as a former Ranger and just a general devious bastard, but throw in his boyfriend Noah, who'd spent several more years in the Army as a Ranger and had the same twisted sense of humor, and the pair were positively lethal.

"Does this mean you know where Snow is? Or who's holding him?"

"We've got a good lead. The triplets are pulling together all the details they can on the location. We'll lay everything out when we meet with the rest of the team."

"But they can confirm that he's still alive?" Jude pressed.

Rowe frowned and dropped his eyes to the road. His hands tightened around the steering wheel until something creaked. Noah reached across the seat and put his hand on Rowe's bicep, squeezing.

"We don't know for sure," Noah answered.

"But we're not going to fucking wait around until we can confirm it. We're going in tonight."

※

The drive to Ward Security had felt like the longest of Jude's life. He sat back, listening as Noah made a series of phone calls either to the IT specialists working to track down Snow or the other bodyguards. It sounded like Noah and Rowe were rounding up people to join in the rescue mission, but he was catching only snippets of it.

Most of the time, Jude just stared out the window at the lights of the city as they passed in a glittering blur. He wondered if Snow was in pain or if he was being tortured. Guilt ate at him. His family had pulled Snow into this danger. Of course, he could hear Snow's growly voice that Jude's family was his family too. Snow would do anything for the Torres family, even if it meant risking his life.

But he didn't want this for Snow. Their entire relationship started while Snow and his friends were being hunted by a lunatic. Mel had been killed and Ian was very nearly killed. A lot of their first year together had been spent dodging one disaster after the next. But after the insanity of Oklahoma a year ago, Jude had started to think that life was settling into a kind of quiet normalcy. No more car chases or people wanting to kill them. There was work and home. Saving lives and building a life with his general.

Sighing softly, Jude rubbed his eyes. If this was life with the general, then he'd happily take it. He'd embrace the insanity, explosions, and danger if it meant that at the end of it all, he was able to crawl into bed with Snow and wrap his body around his lover's.

"We'll get him back," Rowe said firmly. Jude nodded. The sooner they got him back, the better.

Despite being after eight in the evening, Ward Security was a beehive of activity. Most evenings there were self-defense classes, but tonight the various employees were running around, preparing equipment and discussing tactics. Jude and Snow had attended a few parties that included the majority of the Ward Security employees. They'd started to feel like an extended family, and it was quite touching to see that they were all rallying around their boss and Snow.

It was even more touching when Jude thought about the fact that what they were planning to do was highly illegal. From hacking into the traffic cameras to going into a private building heavily armed, it was all illegal. Jude's brain said that they should be going to the cops with their information, but Jude's heart said fuck it. He wanted to march in there and pull Snow out. He couldn't trust the cops to care about Snow's health and safety the same way these men did. They would give everything to get Snow back alive.

"We're meeting up in Rowe's office," Noah said, pointing toward the metal stairs leading to the second floor. Jude followed the two other men up the stairs, taking two at a time to keep pace with them.

"I'll poke my head into the Torture Chamber and tell them we've got Jude," Noah announced before jogging down the hall away from Rowe's office.

"When did you get a torture chamber?" Jude asked, stopping Rowe before he stepped into his office.

"It's what I call the IT room. Every time I step in there, Quinn or Gidget starts throwing all this techie geek jargon at me, and it's torture to listen to."

"I don't know how your employees put up with you," Jude teased.

"I pay very well and offer discounts to Ian's restaurant."

Jude smiled. Yeah, that would do it. Ian's cooking was amazing, and Rialto was the perfect date spot in the city.

He stepped into Rowe's office behind the owner but stopped over the threshold to see Lucas sitting behind Rowe's desk.

Rowe gave a sharp whistle and motioned upward with his right hand. "Up, you ass. That isn't your desk."

"Definitely not. My desk is cleaner," Lucas said crisply as he rose. As he stepped past Rowe, he added in a low voice, "I also have a better selection of lube in my bottom drawer than you."

Rowe flipped his friend off as he flopped into his chair.

Jude looked the other man over and his stomach knotted. The billionaire was dressed in a black turtleneck that looked like it was made from a material designed to guard against the colder weather. His black cargo pants and boots were a little worn, and Jude could only assume that it was from other moments just like this one. Lucas wasn't there just for support from the office. He was planning to go into the field with them.

"You can't do this," Jude said in a strangled voice as he met Lucas's dark gaze. "You have a baby daughter. She needs you."

"And Snow is my brother. He needs me too. The rest of my family isn't going to take a back seat to my daughter."

"But—"

"Daciana is safe," Lucas said calmly, placing a hand on Jude's shoulder. "She's spending the night with her adoring Uncle Ian and Uncle Hollis."

"Who are also playing host to two of my bodyguards, Jackson and Garrett," Rowe added with a smirk.

"Before tonight is over, I'll have seen Snow in your arms, and I'll have Daci in mine."

"When do we get to see the lil lady?"

Jude turned to find Dominic Walsh sitting on the couch opposite Rowe's desk. The redheaded bodyguard stared up at Lucas with bright eyes and a wide smile. Royce Karras, another bodyguard, was leaning against the wall with his arms folded over his chest.

"After she's had her first round of vaccinations. It's too dangerous to have her visiting with everyone right now."

"Fine," Dom grumbled. He lounged against the back of the sofa and stretched his long legs out in front of him. "But she needs to come in for visits. She's gonna be a fighter like her Daddy Andrei."

Noah stepped into the office followed by a tall, broad-shouldered man with dark brown hair and a closely trimmed beard. The man was built like one of Rowe's bodyguards, but he was actually one of the IT specialists. Jude had met Cole McCord only once before and he came off as a quiet, serious man who was very focused on his job.

"What's the plan?" Royce asked as soon as Cole shut the door behind him.

Yes! Jude was ready to get down to business.

Cole stepped through the crowd and turned on the TV hanging on Rowe's wall. He tapped a couple of times on the small tablet in his hands before the image on the screen changed to reveal a darkly tinted SUV. The same one that had run Jude and Snow off the road.

"We tapped into the local traffic cams for Northern Kentucky," Cole explained. "Jude and Snow were fortunately run off the road right in front of one. We caught the rear license plate as well as images of the three men that hopped out of the SUV."

He paused and tapped on the tablet again. The static image of the SUV turned into a grainy video. At the bottom of the screen, he could see two tires and part of the undercarriage for his Jeep. At the top of the screen was the SUV. Snow stumbled around the Jeep, unsteady on his feet as he tried to move from the passenger side to the driver's side in hopes of pulling out Jude. But he never reached Jude.

Three men swarmed out of the SUV and descended on Snow. His lover tried to fight them off, but he was still dazed and sore from the accident. Snow hadn't stood a chance against three men. Jude's heart cried out to see Snow hit several times by the men before one finally hit Snow on the back of the head with the butt of his gun. Snow went down in a heap, unconscious. They quickly grabbed him and shoved him into the SUV before surging onto the expressway in a spray of gravel and smoke.

The video stopped, but Jude could see it all replaying in his brain. It was like a part of his soul had been ripped in half. His general had been hurt trying to protect him, trying to save him.

"I'm sorry, Jude," Cole said softly.

Jude sucked in a harsh breath and shook his head. "It's okay. We at least know he was taken alive. If they wanted us dead, it would have been easier to shoot us both after the accident and then leave."

"He's alive," Rowe said.

"Do we know where he was taken or by whom?" Lucas prodded.

"It took a bit to piece it all together, but he was taken north to a newer office building development near Blue Ash."

"Blue Ash?" Dom said. He shifted on the couch, moving to sit perched on the edge. "That's all financial companies. Who the hell stages a kidnapping out of freaking Blue Ash?"

Cole tapped his tablet again, and the screen shifted to the picture of a man in a navy blazer, white shirt, and plain blue tie. He had thinning brown hair and pale blue eyes. He looked like some middle-class, middle-management drone in a bad suit to Jude.

"By our research, the man behind the kidnapping, break-in…and Jordan's assault is Gene Schaefer. He's a customer service representative for a large financial advisory company that's based in Blue Ash. He actually has a house in Forest Park. He's married and has two kids. A five-year-old daughter and a one-year-old son."

Jude stepped closer to the TV screen, eyes narrowing on the face of the man. After a second, he shook his head and stepped away. "You've got to be wrong. That can't be the person behind it all."

"I don't believe I'm wrong, Jude," Cole said.

"No," he said sharply. He turned and faced Cole. "That man"—he stopped and pointed to the TV—"has a family and a good job. He has kids! How could he run that hideous porn site? How could he be behind the attack and violation of my brother?" His voice rose and cracked at the end. The man in the picture didn't match what he'd imagined.

"Just before you arrived with Rowe and Noah, he was spotted arriving at the office building with one of the men from the SUV," Cole added.

"But…" Jude turned back to look at the picture of Gene Schaefer.

"It's just a mask," Royce murmured. "I've known some truly evil people in my life, and if you passed them on the street, you would have thought them to be the souls of kindness. But it's just an act. And this fucker is going to pay for hurting people. Doesn't matter if he's crafted this lie for his wife and kids."

"It took some digging, but Gidget also managed to trace the LLC that owns the website back to Schaefer." Cole paused and frowned. "If we had another month, I think we could get all the missing pieces of proof, but I feel confident that this is the man we're looking for."

Jude nodded woodenly. He believed Cole, but after facing Dwight Gratton with Snow, he had expected to be once again tracking down someone of the same kind of evil. "How do we do this?"

Cole changed the TV screen over to a blueprint of the building. "Right now, we don't know which floor Snow is being kept on. None of the rental records can be tied back to Schaefer, but we're still digging."

Rowe stepped up to the TV and folded his arms over his chest as he looked around the room. "Since we don't know exactly where Snow is being held, we're breaking up into teams. Lucas and Jude, you are entering from the rear and going directly to the top floor. Noah and I are going to enter through the front and start with the first floor. The place is five floors. Each team gets three minutes to sweep the entire floor, and then you move to the next level. That means we should be in and out in roughly ten minutes. Dom and Royce are watching the perimeter. No one but us is allowed in or out during that ten minutes. Any questions?"

"You're letting me go with you?" Jude asked in surprise.

Lucas snorted from where he was sitting on the edge of Rowe's desk. "We didn't think you'd let us leave without you."

"I wasn't, but I thought I'd have to fight you more."

"We don't have time to waste on this. You're going," Rowe announced. "Any other questions?"

"How do we know the cops aren't going to be there at the same time?" Jude asked. "They have all the same information, right?"

"Very unlikely," Noah said.

Cole cleared his throat. "We've got at least a several hours if not a day's head start on the police. All this happened across multiple cities and states. It takes time and red tape to share all the info."

"We're ahead of the cops, but we still need to move fast," Rowe said. "Any other questions?"

Dom's hand shot up. "Have you picked the code names yet?"

"No, not yet," Noah said with a chuckle.

"I'm picking the code names," Jude asserted before anyone could even draw a breath. He looked smugly around the room at his gathered friends and family. "My boyfriend, my mission, my code names."

Rowe groaned loudly. "Fine. Everyone, go get outfitted. We leave in fifteen." Jude started to follow the rest out of the room, but Rowe stopped him. He stared at the man for a moment before shutting the door behind Noah as he left last.

"We've already had the talk, Rowe," Jude started when they were alone.

Rubbing one hand through his hair, Rowe watched him, green eyes wary and sharp. "We have. You were resolute in being hands-on and fuck the law when it was just your brother. I can't imagine that you're less determined now that Snow is being held."

Rowe walked over to his desk and sat down. Pulling open the top drawer, he reached in and pulled out a black handgun. He set it down in the center of his desk with a heavy thud. Jude's heart actually sped up at the sight of the weapon. Some part of his brain had known that taking part in Snow's rescue would require guns and more. Jude wouldn't call himself a pacifist, but he definitely wasn't a fan of guns simply because he dealt with their aftermath nearly every day while on the job.

"Have you ever used a gun?"

Jude nodded, his gaze never straying from the weapon. "After Snow and I moved in together, he took me to a firing range. He's still got his, and he wanted to make sure I knew how to use it safely if we were going to be living together." He took a shaky breath and looked up at Rowe. "I wasn't great."

"I'm not looking for great," Rowe admitted, but he didn't smile. "I need to know that you'll pull the trigger to protect Snow or Lucas or Noah if things go south tonight."

Jude stared at Rowe, running the question through his head, but he knew the answer in an instant. "I'll pull the trigger," Jude said firmly. "All my friends and family are coming home in one piece tonight."

CHAPTER 20

The five-story office building rose up against the black sky, its large windows reflecting the lights from the barren parking lot. Standing there with a gun in his hand, Jude couldn't shake a feeling of surrealness. Dom was right about Blue Ash. It was an older, established township north of Cincinnati, and it was known for being the home of several large financial companies and brokerage firms. They'd passed numerous signs glowing in the night, boasting their offices amid stands of old maple and oak trees.

Even in the middle of winter, everything remained nicely manicured and maintained, as if nothing could disturb the façade of peace and order of the city.

But there was something rotten within its core. Jude could only assume that this bastard Gene Schaefer had chosen the location as a way of thumbing his nose at the entire group. Or maybe it was just a great cover. Who would look for a secret place for the rape and torture of people in such a quiet, suburban town? No one. That kind of activity was reserved for the darker parts of the city where the cops turned a blind eye to things in hopes of keeping the rest of the city intact and safe.

Jude shivered against the wind that raced across the open parking lot. Rowe had parked the SUV Jude had ridden in, along with Noah and Lucas, down the road in a sleepy little neighborhood with older, ranch-style homes. There were only a handful of lights on in the windows facing the street. It was nearly ten o'clock in the evening. Jude was sure it was far too early to be conducting a raid of this building, risking other people seeing them, but he kept his fears to himself. He was more worried about waiting and leaving Snow in the hands of this bastard.

Dom and Royce had left ahead of them and parked in another area. They then crept over to the building where they scouted the immediate area for signs of security. The second team had walked over minutes later, their boots crunching through the dead undergrowth. Jude was grateful for the black cargo pants and sweater Rowe had loaned him. He was stuck in his tennis shoes from earlier, but they meant he could easily run if he needed to. Anything to get him more quickly to his general.

As they reached the edge of the woods, Rowe motioned with his hand for the team to split. Lucas gave a sharp nod, and he was off with Jude following quickly on his tail. A thin strip of woods surrounded the building on three sides, offering them some much-appreciated cover, while the entrance to the parking lot opened to a somewhat private street that was home to only a few other office buildings.

"Roll call, family," Rowe said through Jude's earpiece. "Everyone check in."

Lucas looked over his shoulder at Jude and gave a little roll of his eyes before he nodded once.

"Cousin Itt and Lurch are in position in the rear," Jude said softly. The small microphone was pressed to his throat with the use of a narrow strap wrapped around his neck. It allowed him to be completely hands-free while talking to his other teammates.

"Pugsley in position on the street," Royce came back. "We're all quiet here."

"Wednesday in the crow's nest," Dom said. He'd had instructions to climb a tree with a sniper rifle to give them coverage if they needed a fast escape. "We're clear."

"Uncle Fester has control of the security system," Cole chimed in from his office back at Ward Security. "The cameras are set on a loop for the next fifteen minutes. We're good to go."

"Gomez and Morticia are moving for the front doors."

"My favorite childhood TV show has been forever ruined, Cousin Itt. Thanks," Dom grumbled in his ear.

"Go to hell! I'm fucking gorgeous as Morticia," Rowe swore.

Jude shuddered again, but it wasn't for the cold. When he'd announced that they were doing *The Addams Family* for code names, he'd never have guessed that Rowe would immediately claim Morticia, but apparently the stout redhead had a thing for the pale, willowy woman. That or he and Noah were planning some twisted roleplaying later that night. Either way, he was going to need some mental bleach when this was all over.

"Enough chatter. Let's get Thing and get out of here," Lucas snapped. Jude couldn't agree more.

Lucas had barely finished speaking when the red light on the security panel next to the gray metal door flashed to green.

"Outer security is down," Cole announced.

Lucas didn't hesitate to grab the door and pull it open. There was a loud whine of metal rubbing against metal as if the door was too heavy for the hinges. They both cringed and moved inside the dimly lit hallway. Jude caught the door and carefully made sure it didn't bang shut. Off to their right was another metal door marked for the stairs. Lucas entered first and held it open for Jude.

"Do you want me to take the lead?" Jude offered as they approached the first set of stairs.

"Afraid I'm not in shape enough to climb to the top floor?" Lucas asked.

Jude smile at him. "I'm thinking you might have been preoccupied with your new bundle rather than keeping up with your workout routine."

"Let the man lead, Lurch," Rowe grumbled, instantly reminding Jude that anything he said would be heard by the rest of the group. Jude winced. He hadn't meant to embarrass Lucas, but he was sure the billionaire hadn't been making it to the gym, and five flights of stairs could be a lot to run at once. He didn't want the man to be vulnerable if he was still trying to catch his breath.

Lucas stepped aside and waved Jude toward the stairs. "Lead the way, Cousin Itt."

Jude moved quickly, taking the steps two at a time, stretching his long legs. Not surprisingly, Lucas kept pace with him, not making a sound except for the occasional squeak of rubber against linoleum. They had barely made it past the second floor when Noah swore softly.

"We found the first-floor guards. Two of them." There was a soft grunt and the sounds of a struggle. An unknown voice cried out in pain followed by more painful thuds of flesh hitting flesh.

Jude's heart picked up more than from just a little running up the stairs. The silly hope that Snow would be found alone died in his chest. He didn't want to put the lives of his friends and family at risk. He didn't want anyone he loved and cared for hurt trying to rescue Snow.

"They're fine. Don't slow down," Lucas said. His voice was softer, and Jude knew that he was speaking to him and not the rest of the team.

Jude picked up his pace, clinging to Lucas's reassurance. The man knew what he was talking about. He'd participated in plenty of missions with Snow and Rowe while they were in the Army and then more than a few after they left the Army but continued with their own personal shenanigans outside the law. If anyone could handle themselves in a dangerous situation, it was Rowe and Noah.

By the time they reached the landing for the fourth floor, Jude was starting to get a little winded. He and Snow regularly went jogging, but apparently he needed to spend a little more time climbing stairs. A burning sensation was starting in his thighs and calves. He glanced over his shoulder to see Lucas grinning at him. Lovely. He was never going to let Jude live it down if he didn't finish strong. Digging deep into his reservoir of energy, Jude ran up the last flight of stairs while trying to make it seem like he wasn't panting.

Lucas placed a hand on his shoulder as he stepped around Jude. "Don't beat yourself up. You were in a car wreck earlier today."

Today?

Jude could only shake his head. That already seemed so far away. He'd rolled out of bed at five a.m. that day and put in a full shift with Rebecca before the car accident. And now he was on an insane rescue mission with Snow's family to save him from a madman. No wonder he was so damn tired. He was running on pure adrenaline.

Lucas grabbed the door handle but didn't open the door. "Gomez and Morticia? What's the good word?"

"That Morticia forgot to bring my rainbow duct tape," Noah complained.

"Next time," Rowe said, his voice serious. "First floor is quiet, but I'm not sure if they got off a warning. Be careful."

"Security is down on the other floors. You're in the clear."

"Cousin Itt and Lurch hitting the fifth floor. Start your timer now."

Lucas had barely finished speaking when he pulled open the door and flowed smoothly into the hallway. Jude had caught his breath and followed directly behind him, once again making sure the door didn't bang. But there wasn't much reason for it.

Snow wasn't on the fifth floor. There wasn't much at all on the fifth floor. The builder hadn't completed construction yet. The walls were a mix of bare two-by-fours and drywall. The mud hadn't even been applied to the seams yet. There were spools of wire, white buckets of mud, and other supplies strewn a bit haphazardly around the place. They were still building out the various offices that would fill the space before the new occupants claimed it.

"Search everything. We've got two minutes," Lucas said as he rushed over to the left.

Jude moved in the opposite direction, eyes skimming over random notes and other pieces of paperwork that had been left behind. A small radio was balanced at the end of a makeshift table and a crumpled bag from someone's lunch was nearby. There was no sign of anything happening on that floor other than construction work.

If Snow was being held in the building and other nefarious things were happening there, Jude was willing to bet that the construction workers on that floor had no clue it was occurring below them.

Less than two minutes later, Jude met Lucas back in the center of the massive open space and shook his head. "I got nothing."

"Me too. We're heading for the fourth floor," Lucas agreed.

"Gomez and Morticia are on the second," Rowe answered.

Two floors down and three to go, Jude counted down in his head. In a matter of minutes, he'd have his general back. That was all that mattered.

He and Lucas moved quickly down the stairs to the fourth floor, repeating their silent entrance into the hallway. Except this floor looked finished.

"Fester," Lucas growled. "I'm seeing lights that look like security."

"I see you, Lurch," Cole came back without an ounce of amusement in his voice. Jude was surprised by his tone. It seemed like all the men that Rowe hired had a strong sense of humor, but he'd seen very little evidence of a lighter side when it came to Cole. The man was all business, but then, at that moment, he held the lives of seven men in his hands. The seriousness made sense. "I'm the only one viewing the live feed. Nothing is being recorded."

"The doors?" Lucas prodded.

"Unlocked."

Lucas grunted and started down the hall. He had his gun drawn, but down at his side. Jude had his own in his hand, the weight of it making his palm sweat inside the leather gloves Rowe had given him. A few sessions at a shooting range didn't make him comfortable carrying the weapon. At least, not while knowing that if he did have to use the gun, he wouldn't be shooting at a paper target.

They stopped halfway down the hallway. There were glass doors on either side separated by two elevators. On the left was a long string of names that sounded like a law firm. On the right, there was no sign to indicate what the company did. The office beyond the door was bland and plain as if they didn't expect to have visitors.

"We're starting on the left," Lucas announced. "We go together."

"But if we split up, we can cover the floor that much quicker," Jude argued, already taking a step toward the right office.

"And if either one of us gets into trouble, it will take twice as long for the other to find them in that damn office maze."

Jude frowned but nodded in agreement as he followed behind Lucas. The man was right, and he understood why he was following Lucas's lead. He'd come to plenty of offices while working as a paramedic, and he'd gotten turned around in more than one cube farm trying to get to a suffering patient. They were there to rescue Snow, but Jude's job was to also watch Lucas's back. He couldn't do that if he couldn't even find the man.

The door to the law firm opened easily. The marble floor shone in the low ambient light from the receptionist's little desk lamp. There was a pretty Persian rug in the center of the lobby and several vases overflowing with flowers. The furniture was all dark leather, while the receptionist's desk was an imposing dark mahogany. The owners of the law firm were definitely looking to make an impression.

The rest of the office looked much the same. Things looked a little more spartan and bland in the few offices that were probably not expected to entertain clients, but the rest of the place was filled with heavy law tomes, leather, and dark woods. The rooms smelled of old coffee and books and dust. Not a horrible odor, but something about it left Jude longing to take a nap.

They covered the law firm in roughly two minutes, but there was nothing to see. There was no time to skim over the copious amounts of papers on the desks, but Jude felt confident that Gene Schaefer had no dealings with the law firm. They were just unlucky enough to share the same space as the evil man.

As they left the law firm and crossed the hallway to the second unnamed office, something crawled along Jude's skin. He fought the urge to shiver while a weight sank down on his chest. Something felt off about this place before they even stepped foot into it.

Lucas pulled open the glass door, and they were immediately hit with the sharp scent of bleach and an overly sweet flowery scent like someone had used too much of an air freshener to cover up the smell of something else. Jude's stomach turned and he lifted his empty hand to his nose to try to block some of the horrific odor accosting him.

"That's never a good sign," Lucas muttered.

"What do you got?" Rowe demanded.

"Lot of bleach."

"Fuck," Dom muttered softly, reminding Jude that they still had protection waiting outside for them in the cold.

"You want Morticia and Gomez on four?"

Lucas stopped, hesitating. It sent a chill down Jude's back. Lucas didn't hesitate and Jude definitely didn't like the way that Lucas looked back at him, as if he were secretly weighing some heavy decision. "No, continue on to three when you're done," he replied to Rowe at last.

"Lurch, there are no cameras in this office. I'm blind," Cole admitted, which didn't exactly help Jude's mounting anxiety.

Lucas grunted and slowly started across the reception area. They stopped at the desk, which held just a phone, a brand-new pad of paper, and a pencil. There were no magazines or even chairs for guests to sit in as they waited for their meeting. No flowers or art on the walls. It was possible that the business owners just moved into the space, but Jude figured there would at least be some business cards or something.

Judging by Lucas's grim expression, Jude was certain that his companion wasn't feeling any better about the office. He reached the one door leading out of the reception area but was stopped. It was locked. They both frowned at the door, noticing that it wasn't the typical swipe card lock. A silver deadbolt was just above the doorknob.

Lucas shoved his gun into a holster in the middle of his lower back and reached into his pocket for a small black packet. "Go watch the door."

"What?"

"I've got to pick this lock, and it will go better if I know you're not watching over my shoulder."

"Seriously?" Jude asked, unable to hide the amusement in his voice.

Lucas glared at him as he dropped to his knees to give him a better view of the lock. "If you can believe it, this isn't a skill I get to practice all that often. I might be a little rusty. Now go watch over there."

With a smirk, Jude walked back toward the glass door and stared out at the empty hallway while listening to the soft sounds of metal on metal as Lucas worked on the lockpick in the deadbolt. He couldn't help but wonder: if Lucas Vallois knew how to fight, use a gun, and pick a lock, what unique skills did Snow have that he had yet to discover? God, he needed to find Snow so they could work on uncovering all those hidden skills that Jude had yet to experience.

Lucas grumbled under his breath as he continued to struggle with the lock. "Do I need to send Wednesday up to help you?" Noah teased.

"I can fucking do it," Lucas snarled.

Jude had heard about Dominic's rather shady childhood and was glad the man had managed to not only find a new life in Cincinnati at Ward Security, but also find love.

"There," Lucas said with a sigh. Jude turned to see Lucas pushing back to his feet while shoving the picks into his pocket. With his gun in his hand again and Jude at his side, Lucas slowly pushed open the door. The smell of bleach and air freshener was stronger, but there was an underlying scent that couldn't be masked. The smell of urine, old blood, and sex. There was no question…they were in the right place.

The hallway seemed narrower than the one in the law firm and the walls were no longer drywall but painted cinderblocks. There were just three metal doors. One on the left, one on the right, and one facing them at the end of the hallway.

Jude held his breath as Lucas turned the knob for the door on the left and it easily opened. The room was empty of furniture except in the center of the room was looked to be a spanking bench. A number of leather whips, floggers, and paddles hanging from hooks lining the wall. Facing the bench were a pair of tripods as if the room was prepared for filming.

Normally, there was nothing about the setup that would put Jude ill at ease. He'd played safely in this scene in the past and there was nothing wrong it with when it was done with care and consent. But the streaks of blood on the plain white walls whispered of something much darker happening in that room in the past.

Jude backed up and stepped across the hall, opening the door before Lucas was at his side. The second room was completely empty of both furniture and sexual instruments, but there was a stain on the floor that couldn't quite be cleaned away with bleach. The smell of blood was stronger in the room.

"We've got to find him," Jude choked out, backpedaling into Lucas. He didn't want to think about Snow or his brother in a place like this. Neither man deserved to be somewhere so evil. This place wasn't about pleasure and enjoyment. This was about torture and hurting another person.

He needed to get Snow out of there. To hold him and know that he was safe. He needed to get back to the hospital and hold his brother's hand, just to reassure himself that Jordan was safe and alive. That he was going to recover and be safe again.

"One room," Lucas said, leading the way out of the second room and down to the end of the hall. Lucas reached out for the doorknob, and Jude noticed that his hand shook slightly before his fingers wrapped around the silver handle. He turned it, but the door didn't budge. Another deadbolt. "Fuck. Locked," Lucas muttered.

"You've got this." Jude backed up a couple of steps to give him some room to work.

"We've got company," Royce suddenly announced.

"How many?" Rowe demanded.

"One SUV, and it's approaching fast."

"Lurch? What do you have?"

"He's working on the last door on four. I think we may have him," Jude answered quickly so Lucas didn't have to take his attention away from the deadbolt. "This office is just a façade. It's…it's a fucking sex torture chamber of horrors."

"Three is almost cleared," Noah chimed in.

"Let the SUV come," Rowe growled. "If the team on four confirms they have Thing, then let it park. After the occupants enter the building, take out the tires and be ready to take out any runners. Gomez and I will head back to the first floor to stop them there."

"Got it!" Lucas said in an excited whisper. He pulled the picks free and stood. Both he and Jude got their guns ready. There had been no sounds from the room as Lucas worked, but that didn't mean it was empty.

Lucas entered the room first, but Jude was following as quickly as possible. His heart skipped at the sight of the bed. He knew that damn bed and it made him sick. But before he could empty the contents of his stomach, his eyes caught on Snow chained to the far wall. His lover was kneeling on the ground, his arms pulled above his head.

There was no stopping the pained cry that leaped from Jude's lips. Snow's head popped up at the sound and he blinked weary eyes several times as if he couldn't believe what he was seeing.

"Jude!" he cried out, his voice rough.

Stepping around Lucas, Jude rushed across the room as Snow slowly rose to his feet. He winced and moaned in pain, but there was still a look of intense relief on his face as his eyes never left Jude's face. Cupping Snow's face carefully with both hands, Jude kissed him again and again between desperate gasps for air. He'd never felt such relief as that moment. Each ragged breath he could draw in was nearly choked by the lump in his throat. He didn't want to live without his general, didn't want to face another day without this man right beside him.

"Shhh...baby, I'm okay. I'm okay, I promise," Snow repeated over and over again as they kissed. It was only when those words finally permeated his brain that Jude even realized that he was crying.

"Sorry," Jude mumbled against Snow's lips. "Just so relieved."

"We both are," Lucas said. Jude looked up, a little surprised to find Lucas standing on the other side of Snow, his arm wrapped around the back of Snow's waist. A streak of tears ran down Lucas's cheeks as well, and the man did nothing to wipe them away. He just bent his head and pressed a long kiss to Snow's temple.

Stepping back, Lucas cleared his throat and quickly swiped at his cheeks. "We've got Thing," Lucas announced in a slightly louder voice before turning his attention to the iron manacles around Snow's wrists.

"Thing?" Snow repeated, looking from Lucas to Jude.

"Your code name. I'm Cousin Itt, and that's Lurch," he explained, nodding at Lucas.

Snow threw his head back and laughed. Probably the first pure and genuine sound of amusement that room had ever heard. Jude smiled, but his attention was on the one eye that was nearly swollen shut and the crust of dried blood he could see on the back of Snow's neck. He desperately needed to get Snow to the hospital so he could be thoroughly checked over. And then, he was thinking that maybe he wouldn't let him out of their bed for at least a week. Yes, he needed a week alone with Snow to at least start the progress of purging this room and Snow's disappearance from his brain.

"Our company has parked in the rear," Dominic suddenly announced. "There's…fuck…there are five of them. Repeat. Five."

"Take out the tires and guard the exit," Rowe barked. "We're heading down to the first floor."

"We've got company," Jude said. He looked over at Lucas. "Can you pick the lock?"

"No." Lucas shoved a hand through his hair in frustration as he glared at the manacle. "Doesn't look like it takes a normal key." He then looked over at Snow. "You wouldn't happen to know where the key is, would you?"

"I haven't even seen a key yet. I woke up like this."

"We need a fucking bolt cutter," Lucas muttered.

"The fifth floor!" Jude said. "There were a bunch of tools up on the fifth floor in all the construction. I think there might have been a bolt cutter with all the tools."

Lucas frowned for several seconds at Jude in indecision before he finally sighed. "I'll go. Watch your fucking back, and don't shoot me when I return." Before Jude could say anything, Lucas darted out of the room, his heavy footsteps echoing down the hall as he ran.

"I'm so sorry, Jude," Snow murmured.

Jude turned to his lover. "What are you talking about?"

"I should have been more careful. If I'd just been able to hold those fuckers off for another minute, the cops would have been there."

Jude carefully pressed his lips against Snow's, silencing his apology. There was nothing for Snow to apologize for. He'd tried to save Jude, pull him free of the overturned Jeep, and then protected him from the men who'd run them off the road in the first place.

"No apologies. But I think we're both going to be fired from our jobs."

"Really?"

"Oh, yeah. I'm not letting you out of my sight or out of my bed for a long, long time."

Snow flashed him a crooked smile. "I can live with that."

"I—" Jude broke off as the sound of fighting and gunfire filled his ear. It sounded like Rowe and Noah had managed to locate the men entering the building, but they weren't able to take them by surprise. There was shouting and cursing, but Jude couldn't make much sense of it all. He prayed that Lucas was would return soon. Maybe they could go up to the fifth floor and barricade themselves in until Rowe and Noah announced that it was safe. He wanted to help them, but Jude knew his limitations. He was more likely to get in their way than to save their lives.

"I talked to the man who was behind Jordan's attack," Snow said, jerking Jude's attention from the action he'd been listening to.

"What? You saw Gene Schaefer?"

"He's a bastard. He runs the poker ring."

Jude shook his head. "How did Jordan get involved in a poker ring? He just plays a little here and there for fun. I've heard him making jokes at dinner about people who don't know when to stop." But even as he spoke the denial, he knew he was wrong. He saw the evidence with his own eyes. Jordan in that video. Jordan fighting for his life in the hospital bed.

"That's probably how it starts," Snow continued, his voice becoming gentler. "Jordan probably was playing for fun, but this snake draws people in, gets them to bet more than they can afford.

Probably makes it sound like the debt is no big deal. But when they can't pay off their debt…"

"Go ahead, Frost. Tell him," said a cold, hard voice from the hallway.

Jude lifted the gun he'd almost forgotten he was still holding in his hand and pointed it at the open doorway. He'd forgotten that he was supposed to be listening for anyone approaching or even listening to the chaos that was still happening on the first floor. Even now, he could hear Rowe and Noah demanding to know where the fifth man had gone.

"He's here," Jude whispered.

A middle-aged man walked in with a gun held out in front of him. He glared at Snow and then Jude, pointing the gun at both of them. "The doctor and I had a long discussion about people being irresponsible. People like your brother, Mr. Torres. When they can't pay me the money they promised, they play out a little scene for the camera."

"You sick fuck!" Jude shouted. "Jordan didn't play at anything. You forced him! You had him beaten and raped for your camera. And then you sold it!"

Gene grinned at Jude. "You paid for it."

Jude was nearly sick at those words. He did pay for it, but it had been the only way to get to the truth of what happened to Jordan.

"But you're going to pay now," Jude forced out.

An ugly laugh shook Gene's shoulders and made his eyes glitter in the harsh overhead light. "I really don't think so."

"We've got you outnumbered. There's no way you're getting out of here."

Gene continued to grin, his amusement unwavering. Jude's own confidence started to waver. The bastard really was outnumbered, his own men taken down by Rowe and Noah. He couldn't see how Gene was planning to get out of there unless Royce and Dominic had missed something. Were there other men hidden somewhere?

"I don't have to outnumber you to win. I just need you," Gene continued.

"What?"

"Frost's friends all rushed to his side to save him when he went missing. And I bet they would let me walk right out of here with you if it meant keeping him alive."

Jude shook his head, incredulous. "I've got a gun on you."

"But are you going to pull the trigger? A paramedic? A person who has dedicated his entire life to protecting and saving the lives of others. Are you really going to shoot me?" Gene mocked. He was practically laughing in Jude's face, and there was a part of Jude that was terrified that he was right.

He hated the man standing opposite him with a passion that he knew would never fade. Gene deserved to die. Not rot in a jail cell. No, he deserved to die. The world would be a better, safer place if he was dead. But he couldn't pull the trigger to deliver that fatal blow. Protecting and saving lives was his entire existence.

"Go ahead, Torres. Pull the trigger. Get your revenge. It wasn't your brother's fault for getting in over his head, right? Your saintly brother didn't do anything wrong. Go ahead, kill me for your brother," Gene mocked.

"Don't listen to him, Jude," Snow said calmly. "The others will be here soon. They will take care of him. We'll hand him over to the cops, and we can go home."

Gene laughed again. "I don't think so. Drop the gun, Torres."

Jude shook his head. "No."

"I'm not going to jail for this. Those people deserved what they got!" Gene argued, his voice taking on a more frantic desperate edge. "I was doing the world a service. Teaching them an important lesson."

"No," Jude repeated. He couldn't get himself to pull the trigger, but he kept it pointed at Gene's chest. His brain scrambled to calculate how long Lucas had been gone or how much time had passed since he'd told Rowe and Noah that Schaefer was with him. It had to have been more than a minute or two. That was plenty of time for any of them to run to his position. They had to be close, had to be getting into position to save them.

No one made a sound over the earpiece. He knew they were all listening to at least his half of the conversation while help raced to his position. Soon. They would be there soon.

"If you don't drop your gun, I'm killing Frost." As he spoke, Gene shifted the gun to point at Snow's head.

Everything seemed to drop into slow motion. The muzzle moved as if lifting through a thick marsh, but despite Jude's scream, it pointed at Snow's forehead. It was too clear, too horrific. A terrible movie played before his eyes. Gene was going to pull the trigger. He was going to kill Snow. His lover knew too much about his illegal activities. Even if Jude dropped his gun, Gene would kill Snow, possibly kill the others to protect his secret, all while using Jude as a shield to safely escape the building.

A pained roar ripped from Jude's lips as he squeezed the trigger again and again, all while taking a step to the side, putting his body as much in front of Snow's as he possibly could. Gene's body jerked and twisted. His hand convulsed and two shots were fired from his gun, but Jude wasn't sure where the bullets hit. He just kept firing. He couldn't stop squeezing the trigger even after the magazine was empty. There was only the desperate need to protect Snow, to protect his family.

Snow's ragged cry finally rose above the loud beating of his heart in his ears. Jude blinked and looked over at Snow.

"It's okay, baby. It's okay. He's dead. I'm safe. It's okay," Snow said over and over again, but there was no stopping the shaking.

Jude looked back at where Gene had been to see Lucas hurrying into the room with his own gun pointed at Gene's lifeless body. He gave Jude a weak little smirk. "We got him."

"We?" Jude asked, his voice broken and raw.

"When you started shooting, I started shooting from the hall." Holstering his gun, Lucas stepped over Gene and carefully extracted the gun from Jude's clenched fingers. He then turned Jude toward Snow. "I think Snow needs you right now."

Jude knew he was holding it all together by a single frayed thread and that Lucas was just using Snow to distract him, but he didn't give a shit. He'd killed a man. A horrible man. But still, he'd taken a life. He wrapped his arms around Snow and buried his face in his lover's neck. He wasn't sure how he was going to live with this.

"Thank you, Jude. Thank you for saving my life."

And just like that, Snow provided him with that first step forward.

"I love you, Ashton Frost," Jude whispered. "Love you so much."

"I love you too, Jude Torres. Let's go home."

CHAPTER 21

*J*ude walked into his brother's hospital room and firmly shut the door behind him. Jordan was in a private room now and someone had opened the curtains, letting in the bright afternoon light. For once, he was alone. This room was a huge improvement over the one in the ICU. It had a warmer feel, which was helped by all the flowers and balloons filling every free surface.

Jordan looked up and must have seen the determination on Jude's face, because he flushed and looked back out the window. It had been a month since he was found brutalized, and it had been touch-and-go for a long time. Add in the fact that he was always surrounded by family, and Jude hadn't had a chance to sit down and have the heart-to-heart they both desperately needed.

Jude was still trying to live with what he'd done, but whenever the horror rose in his throat, he remembered that gun pointed at Snow's head.

"I know what you're going to say," Jordan said, his voice quiet.

A weak smile jumped to Jude's lips for a heartbeat. "How could you when I'm not sure myself where to begin?"

Jude pulled a chair up to the side of the bed and sat down. He eyed Jordan, who looked a hell of a lot better than he had a month ago, though his hair was a mess and he was still so thin, he looked like a fierce wind could blow him over. The bruises were fading, but the dark circles under his brown eyes spoke of sleepless nights. It was hard to sleep in the hospital, but Jude knew some of his insomnia probably came from what he'd gone through.

Jude had experienced a couple of nightmares so he could only imagine what Jordan felt. To have gone through something like that... it fucking broke Jude's heart. And some of Jude's nightmares involved that room with Snow in the bed. He knew Snow would have fought like hell, but in his dreams, all sorts of horrific scenes played out. And he wasn't the only one. Snow was waking at night again.

He ran his hand through his hair and stared at his brother. "Why didn't you come to me for help?" he finally asked as he leaned forward, his elbows on his knees.

Jordan hadn't met his eyes, and he still didn't then. He stared down at his hands on the white, hospital blanket as he remained silent for several long moments. He finally took a deep, shaky breath. "I'm supposed to be an adult. I told myself that I needed to take care of it myself." Jordan paused and heaved a heavy sigh. "It started out as just getting together with a few people. We'd sit around, tell stories, joke, and play some hands of poker. I was winning a lot. Thought I was pretty good at it."

"You probably were, but I have a feeling you fell in with some people who were cheating. What happened with your friends? Brian? Emily?"

Jordan balled his hands into fists but winced in pain and instantly relaxed his fingers again. "You don't get it. Growing up around you and Carrick. No matter what I did, how old I was, I felt like a little kid. I thought after I got out of high school, got my own place and a job, that feeling would go away. But it didn't. I'd sit around playing video games with Brian or hang out with Emily, and I felt like I was still in freaking high school. Because I was doing the same things I did during high school."

"And then somewhere along the way, you met Anthony."

Jordan's eyes jumped up to Jude's face in surprise. "Yeah. We hung out and played poker. He had older friends that also got together and played on weekends. When I was with them, I didn't feel like a little kid pretending anymore. They treated me like an adult. Respected me like an adult."

"Was Anthony the one to introduce you to Gene?"

"No, it was someone else we played cards with. It didn't start out bad. I was winning kind of regularly, and Gene just seemed like this nice guy."

Jude's stomach turned at the mention of Gene and his fake façade. Of course he'd seemed like this nice, normal family guy in the beginning. It was all about getting Jordan to trust him, luring him in. "What happened?"

"After a few months, I started losing. It wasn't a lot, but I got in a hole and I couldn't cover it. I was going to stop playing, but Gene told me about this big tournament they had right after Christmas. The pot would get me out of the hole and give me a nice little nest egg, but I didn't have the buy-in money, so Gene said he'd cover me."

"I'm guessing you lost," Jude said softly.

"Bad."

"Why didn't you come to me then?" Jude pressed.

"Because I'm an adult!" he said raising his voice. He broke off in a fit of coughing. Jude jumped up to get him a drink, but Jordan waved him away, back to the chair beside his bed. "Because it was my mess. I owed the money and wanted to take care of it myself."

"Like that?"

His lips tightened. "I didn't know it was going to be like that. I thought…I thought it would be getting slapped around and…fucking. I had no idea—" his voice broke and he cleared his throat and was silent a few moments before he swallowed and said, "I had no idea what I'd gotten myself into. I still don't know why Gene tried to kill me. I wouldn't have talked. Why would I want anyone in the world to know about that?"

Jude stared hard at his brother, hating that he seemed so ashamed with him. "He killed your friend, Anthony, too. Did you know that?"

Jordan's head snapped up and he finally met Jude's gaze. "No, I didn't. Why didn't you tell me before now?"

"I didn't think you were strong enough for this conversation until now. Plus, with our family, there's hardly ever a quiet moment."

His skin washed pale. "Fuck. Poor Anthony. He wasn't really that bad of a guy. Just stupid when it came to gambling. Like me. But I didn't think he'd owed as much. How did you find out?"

"I was there when he got shot. Snow and I tried to save him, but the damage was too bad."

"Why the hell did Gene do that? What possible reason did he have for coming after us like that?"

Jude shifted in his chair. "The guy was a lunatic, and he was only roping you guys into the games to get unwilling actors for his videos."

"How do you know that?"

"Who do you think got him out of the picture?"

Jordan stared at him, his mouth opening and closing. "What did you do?"

This time Jude couldn't meet his eyes. "Nothing you need to worry about." As it was, he'd be worrying about it the rest of his life. There was no need for Jordan to know the entirety of what had transpired. Even Jude didn't know what Rowe had done to cover up everything, and it was probably better that way.

They were both silent for a few moments, and the heavy weight of it all felt like a thick fog around Jude.

"Jude?" Jordan asked quietly.

He looked up.

"Did you…did you see the video?"

Jude nodded, his stomach churning.

Jordan closed his eyes. "Oh, God. I'm so sorry. *Mana* didn't see it, did she?"

Just the thought of that made Jude more nauseous. "No, but she knows about it, because we had to turn it over to the authorities to get the other man in the video behind bars. You really didn't think I'd just let something like this go, did you?"

"I didn't think you'd ever know about the video!" Jordan bit out.

His cheeks had flushed with anger and he was gripping the blanket in two fists. "I didn't think it would be a site you'd ever visit. The odds of you happening upon it were astronomical."

"Well, we only found out about it after tracking Anthony down. He's the one who told us about the site."

"I wish he hadn't done that." Jordan shivered and pulled his blanket up higher. "I hate that you saw it," he whispered, his gaze flitting back and forth from Jude to his lap.

"So do I. But I hate that you were the one who suffered through it more. We're both going to need therapy over this, and you will go if I have to take you myself."

"No, I'll go." He looked out the window and his throat moved in a hard swallow. "That messed me up. In my head. I may have been stupid getting myself involved in that, but I'm smart enough to know I need help now."

"Good." Jude leaned forward and reached out to lay his hand on the edge of the bed, palm up. He felt a little of his tension ease when Jordan took it. "I don't want you to ever think you can't come to me. For anything. Please."

"God, Jude, you have this perfect life, and I didn't want to mess with that."

"Nothing you could do could ever mess with my life. I love you so much, Jordan. Brothers are supposed to be there for each other. If not me, you could have gone to Carrick."

"He didn't have the kind of money to help me and as far as I know, you don't either. Your doctor maybe, but this was my problem to fix. I just went about it the wrong way." He tightened his fingers.

"When you have a problem, you ask for help. It doesn't make you less of an adult. Just a smart one." Jordan looked at him a bit dubiously and Jude gave him a small smile. "If you had any idea of the kind of shit Snow and his friends got into." Jude paused and just shook his head.

"What? Really? What kind of stuff?" Jordan asked, showing the first little spark of his old self.

"No, not now. That's Snow's to tell, and it's not the point. The point is that they ask for help all the time. They rely on each other, and that's what we should do, always."

"I know. I'm sorry, Jude. I should have reached out. Said something."

"We will always be there for each other."

Jordan sighed, closing his eyes for a moment as if he was running out of energy. Almost as quickly, his eyes popped open again and he frantically looked around the room as if to reassure himself of where he was. When he met Jude's gaze again, he frowned. "I didn't know that would affect me as much as it did."

"Bad dreams?"

Jordan nodded and his bottom lip quivered briefly. "The worst. It's like I relive it in my mind every night."

"Oh, Jordan." Jude put his other hand on top of their joined ones. "Promise me right now that if you ever get into trouble again, you'll come to me first. Promise."

"I promise." Jordan cleared his throat again. "But I'd like you to tell me what happened. How did you track Gene down?"

"Through a series of trial and error. Once we started poking into what happened, he came after us. Kidnapped Snow."

"What?"

He hadn't thought Jordan could go any paler, but he did.

"They didn't…he didn't…please tell me that what happened to me did not happen to him."

Jude shook his head. "No, but he was hurt. It's why you didn't see him for a while. He was worried about upsetting *Mana*. These people you were dealing with were the worst kinds of bottom feeders, Jordan. You can't let yourself get involved in that kind of situation again. Is the gambling a problem?"

Jordan shook his head. "No. But I don't plan to play poker again. Ever."

"You can still enjoy the game for fun, you know."

This time when he met Jude's gaze, the bleak expression in his eyes cut into Jude like a knife. "I don't think I'll ever enjoy that game again, Jude."

Jude nodded because he understood. He understood that Jordan would be recovering mentally and emotionally so much longer than he would from the coma and that would take time as well. He'd already started physical therapy and would be continuing that for some time.

"I'm going to move back in with *Mana* until I'm on my feet, physically and financially."

Jude nodded. "That would be best. Unless you'd like to stay with Snow and me."

"No, thanks for the offer, but I feel like going home for a while. Letting *Mana* spoil me a little." He finally smiled. It was wobbly and barely visible, but it was a smile nonetheless. It gave Jude hope. His brother was still there. Battered and a lot worse for wear, but there.

There was a knock on the door and before Jude could take another breath, family members were pouring into the room. His mother, Carrick, and his Uncle Gary. They rallied around Jordan, and Jude hoped that his brother realized the incredible support system he had, that he'd never try to take care of a problem of that magnitude on his own again.

All he could do was hope.

Anna eyed him for a moment, then pointed to the door. Jude sighed. He knew that look. He stood and followed her into the hall. She continued walking until they were out of earshot of Jordan's room, turned and plopped her hands on her hips. His mother was a small woman who dressed in bright, primary colors and more often than not—like today—had her hair in a ponytail. Today's yellow sweater had blue and pink stripes.

"You've been keeping me out of the loop, and I don't appreciate it," she announced, her dark eyes narrowed as she stepped out of the way of a nurse hurrying through the hall. "What was in that video you turned over to the police?"

"*Mana*, you know what was in it. I told you that Jordan had been beaten on camera."

"Is that all?" she demanded.

It was all as far as she was concerned. He would never expose her to the entire truth. None of it.

"You think I'm stupid, eh? Or just not strong enough to handle the truth? The police told me they cracked down on an adult site that had actual violence in it. That the man responsible has taken off. What do you know about that?"

"Nothing more than you do. Jordan got mixed up in a gambling scheme, and he paid for it by ending up in the hospital. You know what I know."

She stared hard at him and her expression suddenly caved in. "Oh *yie mou*, what did you do?"

It took everything Jude had to keep his expression innocent. He was so far from innocent and as far as he was concerned, his *mana* would never ever know just how far he'd taken things. As it was, he had to live with what he'd done, and he didn't know how he was going to do that.

"And why have I not seen Snow in weeks?" she asked.

Fuck. Nothing got by her.

More people rushed through the hallway, and he pulled her aside out of the way. "He was hurt in the car accident, remember? He's stayed away to let his bruises heal. He loves you and didn't want to worry you."

She scowled. "He was hurt worse than I knew?"

He nodded, actually thankful he had an excuse for the wounds on his man's face.

"I want to see him, and I don't want any more excuses."

"He's here in the hospital today. You can track him down." He couldn't help but grin a little at the thought of his little mother barreling through the place searching for Snow.

"I have no intention of chasing him." She pulled out her phone and called. Of course, Snow wouldn't answer if he was in surgery, so Jude had to smother a laugh at the message she left. "If you don't get your butt down to my son's room sometime in the next two hours, I'm coming after you and…I'll be very hurt."

She disconnected the call and the naughty smile on her lips warmed his heart.

"No qualms about guilting him at all, eh?" Jude teased.

"None whatsoever. He's been avoiding me just as you have, and I'm done with it. Our family has gone through a hard time and we pull together through it, not avoid each other. If I'd known how badly he'd been hurt, I could have helped. I love that man you've chosen to spend your life with as if he's my own son. He is my son as far as I'm concerned, so no more lies."

He started to tell her he hadn't lied, but he had in fact lied to her, so he kept silent.

She abruptly grabbed him into a tight bear hug. "I know there's more to this story. I raised stubborn boys on my own. I'm no one's fool, Jude Torres. I also know you aren't going to tell me everything. I can see that something is tearing into our Jordan. If there is anything I should know, please tell me."

He hugged her back. "*Mana*, I..." Jude started to give her more reassurances to smooth over his lies and omissions, but instead he nodded against her shoulder. "I promise we will."

She sighed and tightened her arms.

All he could do was hold her. She would never know the entire truth. It wasn't his truth to tell. If Jordan decided to tell her about the rape, that was another thing. But she'd never know what Jude had done. He wouldn't want her to live with that knowledge, too.

CHAPTER 22

A nightmare woke Snow. He lay still, staring at the ceiling, his heart beating fast. Although a month had passed, the stress of everything that had happened had brought up some old tendencies—mostly in the form of bad dreams.

As usual now, though, he quickly remembered where he was. He was safe and happy, and the reason why was next to him.

He turned and found Jude asleep facing him, moonlight lighting up his beautiful face. His black hair was in disarray, his chiseled jaw shadowed by scruff that grew faster than he could shave it, so he mostly kept it trimmed close. His full lips were pursed in a sleep kiss. Snow stared for the longest time, calming in one way while his body woke to another more pleasurable reason for being awake. His heart ached with the love he felt for this man. Even though Jude also had trouble sleeping, he still leaned close and kissed him, smiling when those brown eyes opened.

"Is it morning?" Jude rasped.

"No. Almost," Snow whispered, kissing him again, licking along his bottom lip. He scooted closer and pressed his hard dick to Jude's thigh, loving the rasp of hair there.

Jude smiled against his lips. "Your cock thinks it's morning."

Snow rolled him onto his back and came over him, straddling his waist. Jude's hands came up to rest on his hips. Snow propped his hands on either side of Jude's head and stared down at him, his chest feeling full and hot. The moonlight streamed bright through the open curtains of their bedroom, giving Snow a clear look at his expression.

He couldn't help but worry about Jude. The man was too good to have been forced into taking a life, and Snow fucking hated that he'd been brought to that. He'd never forget facing down that gun, but what had come right after was the reason for a lot of his nightmares. He hated that Jude would have to live with it.

His man stared back, silent, waiting to see what Snow wanted. He was always there for Snow no matter what, and he knew with every fiber of his being that he always would be. Jude stroked his thumbs over his hipbones.

"Marry me," Snow whispered. He pressed his mouth down on Jude's, opening his lips and sliding his tongue inside his mouth. Their tongues rubbed together as he took the kiss deeper. He kissed down Jude's neck, nipping and licking. "Marry me," he said softly against Jude's collarbone. He kept kissing his way down. He licked his nipple, then opened his lips over it to suck it into his mouth. Jude writhed against him, his nipples always extra sensitive. He moved to the other, giving it the same attention. "Marry me," he breathed as he got off Jude and kissed down his stomach. He nuzzled the wet tip of Jude's cock, licking at the drops of pre-cum there, then took it into his mouth. He swirled his tongue around the head, sucking him down deep.

"Yes, yes, yes." Jude thrust up into his throat, pulled back, then pushed up deep again. He let out a soft, humming moan.

The swell of emotion in Snow's chest made tears burn the back of his eyes. He made love to Jude's dick, sucking and licking, taking it as deep as he could, loving the slide of smooth, silky, warm skin. Jude smelled so good here, musky and warm. He pulled off and ran his hand over his wet length, dipping down to lick his sac. He took one ball into his mouth, then the other. He licked underneath, nuzzling Jude's pubic hair, pulling his scent deep into his lungs. "Marry me," he said, his voice raspy and low from emotion.

"Any day, any time." Jude spread his legs wider, reaching down to haul him up his body.

Snow settled on top of him and Jude cradled his body, thrusting his cock alongside Snow's. Sweat had started to build on his skin, so they slipped beside each other, the glide mind-meltingly hot. He cupped the sides of Snow's face, staring hard at him. "You mean it? You really want to get married? What happened to my general who doesn't believe in it?"

"He wants you permanently tied to him."

"I already am," Jude whispered. "My heart and my soul are yours." He came up to softly kiss his lips. "So, we're doing this?"

"I'll tell Ian tomorrow."

Jude laughed. "Now I know for sure you're serious."

Snow sobered, staring down at Jude. "I really am. We'll do this thing up right. But now, I'd like to seal the deal." He slanted his lips over Jude's, the man opening up to let him inside. They kissed and kissed, Snow thrusting against him, enjoying the rasp of chest and belly hair against his smoother skin. He rolled off Jude to get the lube from the nightstand, dropping it on the bed. Jude watched him a moment, then turned over, and Snow ran his hands down that muscular back to cup his ass. God, he loved Jude's round, full ass. Jude clenched his cheeks and spread his legs.

"So fucking hot." Snow's voice broke. He stroked his fingers between, then spread Jude's cheeks for his tongue. He licked over that warm pucker, and Jude cried out and pushed against him. He kissed and nipped before pushing his tongue inside.

"Want you, Snow." Jude's voice broke.

He came over Jude, picked up the lube, and coated his fingers before bringing them to Jude's hole. Jude gasped and spread his legs more. Snow leaned over to run his lips down Jude's back while he prepped him. The tight clasp on his fingers made him groan. Jude writhed beneath him, bringing his ass up, moaning into the pillow. And when Snow slid inside his body, the long rumbling moan made him smile into Jude's shoulder. Jude loved being taken like this from behind. Loved the angle and the intimacy of being plastered together, his back to Snow's front. He often took Snow just this way and Snow loved it.

Pleasure pooled in Snow's balls and up his spine as passion coursed through him. Fuck, he loved this, too.

Snow sucked on his neck, rubbing his nose in Jude's soft hair. He rolled his hips slowly, pressing in and out, deep and deeper. Jude's ass cradled him and sweat slicked between their bodies. Jude's hand came up over his shoulder and Snow took it in his, holding tight as he fucked into the man's body. Jude turned his head, his mouth opening on a gasp. Brown eyes met his and locked. Snow pressed far inside him, watching his mouth opening and closing as pleasure glazed over his eyes. His own pleasure built but he held back, wanting this to last. Jude felt so fucking good. He always did. Nothing in Snow's life had prepared him for the unbridled joy he felt with this man. He'd never expected to find something like this for himself, and he was so goddamned thankful.

"I love you," he breathed into Jude's neck. "So much."

Jude panted the words "Love you" back, lifting his ass and groaning. He clenched around Snow's dick, and Snow let out a hoarse cry.

"Do that again."

Jude did, a slight grin starting and falling on his face as Snow thrust in deep and made him gasp again. "Right there."

Snow began nailing that spot, his gaze glued to his lover's face, watching his pleasure just as much a delight as feeling the snug heat of his body. Jude's hand came up to grasp his hip, his fingers tight on Snow's flesh.

"That's it," Jude whispered. "Take what you need."

"Need you. Always need you." Snow opened his mouth over the smooth skin of Jude's shoulder. Sweat slicked his front to Jude's back and he bit down, relishing Jude's shout as the man shuddered beneath him. Jude began clenching his ass and pushing back, fucking himself on Snow's cock. Snow's eyes rolled at the scorching pleasure roaring through him. He fucked Jude faster.

"Yeah, baby, yeah," Jude yelled, his fingers tightening to the point of pain. Then he let go and wedged his hand underneath his body, letting out a grunt of frustration.

Snow came up off him and pulled him to his knees so he could reach his cock. Jude shouted at the deeper angle when he thrust into him.

"Oh shit, oh fuck," Jude snarled, jacking himself in time to Snow's thrusts.

Snow wasn't sure how much longer he could hold on. "Gripping me so good," he moaned, which made Jude clench again. Hard.

Snow roared as his orgasm slammed through him. He managed a few more pumps, gratified when he felt Jude shuddering beneath him, this time as he came. He slumped over Jude, kissing his back over and over. "How did I get so lucky?"

"I'm the lucky one," Jude murmured. "Come here." He rolled over and pulled Snow down on top of him. "I'm so happy you want to get married."

"That's not all I want," Snow whispered, nuzzling into Jude's neck.

"You just fucked my brains out of my head, so you can pretty much ask for anything right now."

Snow was quiet for a few moments as he caught his breath and his thoughts. "I've changed my mind about us having a family."

Jude went still, his mouth hanging open before he snapped it shut. "First the sexiest marriage proposal ever, then this. Who are you and what have you done with my general?"

Snow pushed up, his expression serious. "I was manacled in that horrible room and all I could do was think about whether you were okay. I didn't know if they'd shot you or what, but I just knew I was terrified. The thought of losing you felt like I was losing the whole world. It hit me then that I want this with you. While the idea of a little Jude running around is appealing as hell, I think I'd like to adopt, though. There are so many kids out there who need homes, and I feel we could give them a good one."

"I'd love to do that."

"I don't know what kind of father I'll be, and I have to admit to being terrified of trying."

"But you truly want this? You're not just saying it because you know it's what I want?"

Snow softly kissed his lips. "I know how much you long for a family, and I love you more than I ever thought it possible to love anyone. So yes, I want it for you. But I also want it for me. We can adopt and then maybe discuss the surrogate idea."

"Oh, you're talking more than one child." It seemed Jude was holding his breath.

God, he'd known, of course he'd known, how much Jude wanted this, and he wanted to kick his own selfish ass for holding out so long, but he also knew he hadn't been ready before. Seeing the look of hope and wonder on Jude's face brought that heavy swell of emotion back up his chest. "You and I make a beautiful family and I would be happy if we stayed that way, but I truly feel we'll be even happier with children. I'm ready."

Jude blinked and Snow realized he was fighting tears. He smiled, touched as always by how big and beautiful this man's heart was. He had lots of love to give, and he'd make the best father in the world. Snow wanted to give him that.

❄

Snow looked around his living room, taking in his friends gathered for dinner. Rowe, Noah, and Andrei talked with Jude quietly on the couch, Rowe probably making sure Jude was still feeling okay. Snow had no idea what Rowe had done to cover up their rescue of him, and he could only be thankful that whatever it was, it had kept Jude from being in the law's crosshairs. As far as the police knew, Gene Schaefer had run off, leaving his business and family. That was all they ever would know.

Since Jude had told the police at the hospital that Snow had been kidnapped, they'd stopped at a lonely gas station north of Cincinnati and had Snow call Jude's cell phone from the pay phone. The story was that Snow had been beaten and dumped at the gas station after his wallet was stolen. Snow doubted the police were at all satisfied with that story, but since there was no other information forthcoming, they closed the case.

Ian and Hollis had yet to arrive for the evening, but they were on their way. A fire crackled in the fireplace, and the smell of Anna's mac and cheese had his mouth filling with saliva. He was completely addicted to the stuff, and Jude now made it for the group often. Ian was bringing a lasagna. Tonight was carb city, apparently.

Snow didn't care. He was just happy to have everyone together and in one piece. He touched his eye, which was mostly healed, and smiled when Lucas walked up to him, little Daci cradled in his arms. Her tiny fist came up and Lucas brought it to his mouth for a kiss. The man was pure putty in that baby's hands, but Snow got it. She made him feel things he'd never expected himself. He looked down at her beautiful, brown eyes.

"That is one gorgeous child," he murmured.

"She gets that from her daddy," Lucas replied, kissing her fist again. He wore casual clothes tonight, a sweatshirt and jeans, and he had a small blanket over his shoulder. He still managed to look perfectly put-together, even with a small bit of spit up on his shirt.

"Admit it, you knew she'd look like this when you insisted on a surrogate, didn't you?" Snow touched the top of her head gently. She had pitch-black hair and it was so soft, he couldn't help but stroke it.

"I had my hopes, but I knew I wanted our first child to come from him. I was hoping she'd get his eyes."

"First one? You plan to do this again?"

"Of course. Just look at what we made. And I'm next." He ran his finger down Daci's cheek, the corners of his mouth going up when she tried to suck on his finger. She cooed and waved her fists in the air. The child might not biologically belong to Lucas, but he considered himself her father just as much as Andrei. Love did that.

He looked forward to having that himself.

"Jude and I are going to adopt," Snow said softly, knowing that news would get Lucas's attention.

Lucas's head came up and he regarded Snow closely. "It's what you want?"

Snow nodded. "I do. I really do."

"Then that will be the luckiest child. To be brought into your home. Adopting a child out there in need is a beautiful thing, Ash." He smirked. "What happened to the man who never wanted children?"

"I could ask the same."

"But you were always more adamant."

Snow looked at Jude to find him watching Snow, his affection plain for anyone looking at him. They'd stayed awake the rest of the night before, both too excited about their plans. His entire life was about to change, and he couldn't be more thrilled. "We go through hard things in life and we change. Then grow. And I understand now that we make our own happiness, and I can't think of anything in this world that will make me happier than seeing that man as a father. He has a lot of love to give."

"So do you."

Snow managed to tear his gaze from Jude's to look at his best friend. "I do. And that's partly thanks to you."

"I was just there for you, that's all."

"That's not just all. It was everything. I wouldn't be who I am and living this life if I hadn't had you. Would never have met Jude."

Lucas lifted Daciana to his shoulder, kissing her head. "And I wouldn't have met Andrei, so I say we're both blessed."

At one time, Snow would have scoffed and made some smart remark then, but Lucas was right. He looked around the room at his friends, at his family. Noah had his head back, laughing at something Rowe must have said if his smirk was anything to go by. Andrei watched Lucas and Daciana, his heart in his eyes. And Jude watched Snow. Their eyes locked as that infinitely strong connection moved between them, pulling him toward the man.

But the doorbell rang and he smiled, that warm feeling returned to his chest. He rubbed it as he walked to let the rest of his family in, and he thought about all the years he'd searched for something to give his life meaning. He'd always had Lucas, then Rowe and Ian, and now he had Jude and Jude's family. He had Noah, Andrei, Daci, and even the annoying Hollis. He was going to have children.

He was no longer searching.

Blessed felt too small a word for how truly fortunate he was.

WHAT'S NEXT?

Coming This May...

Killer Bond
Ward Security #5

Daniel Hendricks wants a vacation. Ward Security's accountant and resident code breaker just needs a little R&R from the chaos and usual shenanigans of the office.

But what was supposed to be a sexy vacation hook-up explodes in his face when he's mistaken for a rogue secret agent.

Now he's on the run with CIA agent Edward Raines from Bermuda to Barcelona to Paris as they try to find the secrets the real rogue was trying to sell before another foreign spy does.

The chemistry between them is just as explosive, but how is Daniel supposed to trust a man who had originally set out to kill him?

The next Ward Security book will be out in late May. Be sure to sign up for our newsletter at drakeandelliott.com/newsletter so you don't miss it!

If you haven't started the Ward Security series yet, now is a great

WHAT'S NEXT?

time to get in on all the action.

Check out book 1:

Psycho Romeo — The Ward Security Series — Jocelynn Drake, Rinda Elliott

Geoffrey Ralse is known for being the life of the party. He loves the club scene, hanging with his friends, and flirting with whomever catches his eye. He certainly isn't going to stop living his life just because some would-be stalker starts sending him threats.

But it all changes when Geoffrey is drugged and wakes up half naked in his own home with a new message from his stalker.

He needs help and there's only one person he trusts…

Protective Agent Sven Larsen has been fighting Geoffrey's flirtatious advances for months, even though he's impossibly drawn to the man. There's no way he can be around him twenty-four/seven and not Finally crack. But one look at Geoffrey's haunted eyes, and he knows there's no way he's letting Geoffrey walk out of Ward Security without him.

Even if it means breaking his own rules, he will keep Geoffrey safe.

Get your copy now on Amazon.

ABOUT THE AUTHORS

Jocelynn Drake is the author of the *New York Times* bestselling Dark Days series and the Asylum Tales. When she's not working on a new novel or arguing with her characters, she can be found shouting at the TV while playing video games, lost in a warm embrace of a good book, or just concocting ways to torment her fellow D&D gamers. (She's an evil DM.) Jocelynn loves Bruce Wayne, Ezio Auditore, travel, tattoos, explosions, fast cars, and Anthony Bourdain. For more information about Jocelynn's world, check out www.JocelynnDrake.com.

Rinda Elliott is an author who loves unusual stories and credits growing up in a family of curious life-lovers who moved all over the country. Books and movies full of fantasy, science fiction, and romance kept them amused, especially in some of the stranger places. For years, she tried to separate her darker side with her humorous and romantic one. She published short fiction, but things really started happening when she gave in and mixed it up. When not lost in fiction, she loves making wine, collecting music, gaming, and spending time with her husband and two children.

She is the author of the Beri O'Dell urban fantasy series, the YA Sister of Fate Trilogy, and the paranormal romance Brothers Bernaux Trilogy. She also writes erotic fiction as Dani Worth. She can be found at RindaElliott.com.

Jocelynn and Rinda can be found at: www.DrakeandElliott.com

Or you can sign up for their newsletter at drakeandelliott.com/newsletter to stay up to date on all upcoming books and news.

They are found on Facebook as Drake and Elliott and on Twitter as @drakeandelliott.

And don't miss out on all the sneak peeks and speculation at the Facebook Group, Unbreakable Readers.

Made in the USA
San Bernardino, CA
30 November 2019